ABANDON
the
DARK

MARTA PERRY

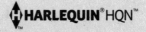

Recycling programs
for this product may
not exist in your area.

ISBN-13: 978-0-373-77884-3

ABANDON THE DARK

Printed in U.S.A.

HARLEQUIN®
www.Harlequin.com

Dear Reader,

I hope you'll enjoy the third book in my latest Amish suspense series. If you happen to come to my area of north-central Pennsylvania, you'll find many small towns that look very much like Deer Run, nestled in the valleys with the wooded ridges rising above them. In fact, our farmhouse is at the narrowest point of a creek valley, which makes life interesting when the creek rises!

I enjoyed revisiting Deer Run for this conclusion to my story. The characters became very real to me, and I wanted to show them finding their happy endings after all the trials they went through. If you guessed who the killer was all along, congratulations!

Please let me know how you felt about my story. I'd be happy to send you a signed bookmark and my brochure of Pennsylvania Dutch recipes. You can e-mail me at marta@martaperry.com, visit me on Facebook or at www.martaperry.com, or write to me at Harlequin HQN, 233 Broadway, Suite 1001, New York, NY 10279.

Blessings,

Marta Perry

This story is dedicated to my granddaughter, Ameline Grace.

And, as always, to Brian, with much love.

No winter lasts forever. No spring skips its turn.
—Amish proverb

CHAPTER ONE

LAINEY COLTON JOLTED AWAKE, her heart pounding in her ears. She stared into darkness so intense she couldn't make out anything beyond the outlines of the strange bed. She sat upright, turning. A pale rectangle marked the window, and her panic waned.

How stupid. She was in Great-aunt Rebecca's house, in tiny Deer Run, Pennsylvania. She'd fallen asleep, exhausted after the flight and drive and the stress of the past few weeks, in the bed that had been hers the summer she was ten.

That had been twenty years ago, but the room felt intimately familiar now that she was awake. She rubbed the gooseflesh on her bare arms. The dream that woke her must have been something out of a horror movie. Odd, that she couldn't remember anything about it.

But maybe just as well, since she had no desire to slip back into nightmares. Lainey plumped the pillows, straightened the hand-stitched quilt, and settled herself to sleep.

Sleep seemed to have fled. As her eyes grew accustomed to the dark, she made out the shapes of the chest of drawers, the rocking chair, and the book-

shelf that still held the complete set of Laura Ingalls
Wilder books she'd devoured as a ten-year-old. Her
Amish great-aunt probably wouldn't have approved
of most of Lainey's reading choices, but she'd been
happy to see her *Englisch* great-niece reading the
Little House books.

Twenty years. Lainey moved restlessly on the pillow. She hadn't been back in all that time, at first
because of her mother's habit of jumping from husband to husband, and later because of her own gypsy
tendencies.

Guilt flickered. Aunt Rebecca had been kind to
her during one of the most difficult parts of a troubled childhood. Lainey should have managed to come
back, instead of being content with the weekly letters
they exchanged. Being Amish, Aunt Rebecca didn't
have a phone. Or electricity, a fact brought home to
Lainey earlier when she'd fumbled for nonexistent
light switches in the dark kitchen.

But now she was here, summoned by an abrupt
phone call from her great-aunt's lawyer. Rebecca
had had a fall and suffered a stroke. She'd asked
for Lainey. The attorney, one Jacob Evans, hadn't
sounded particularly approving. Well, Lainey would
deal with him in the morning.

She'd planned to get a motel near the airport in
Pittsburgh and drive up tomorrow morning, but once
she'd picked up a rental car, worry and tension had
impelled her onto the road to Deer Run. What difference did it make if she arrived after midnight? She
knew where the house key was kept, though if she'd

thought about the absence of electricity, she might have opted for a motel.

Aunt Rebecca would laugh at Lainey, coming to visit an Amish home equipped with her smartphone, her computer, her hair dryer, and all the other devices she thought she couldn't do without.

But the laughter would be gentle. Aunt Rebecca never judged, never made a person feel stupid or guilty or unwanted. Her love had been a balm to a lost child whose familiar world had slipped from her grasp one too many times. Even when the details of that summer visit had slipped away, Lainey had still been aware of that solid sense of being loved without condition.

Now it was Lainey's chance to repay that kindness. In the morning she'd touch base with the attorney and then head for the hospital to find out how bad Aunt Rebecca's condition was and what needed to be done. Lainey's mind ran up against a blank wall of ignorance when it came to helping someone who'd had a stroke, but she'd figure it out. She owed Aunt Rebecca far more than that.

If this trip had happened to coincide with an excellent time for her to leave St. Louis—well, no one here need ever know that, although if the task of helping her great-aunt was as difficult as the attorney's tone had suggested, she might have jumped from the proverbial frying pan into the fire.

In any event, she was clearly not going to drift back to sleep. Lainey swung her legs out from under the covers. She'd go downstairs and brew a cup of

Aunt Rebecca's herbal tea. But first she'd pull on some sweats. The house had grown cold, and she hadn't the faintest idea how the furnace worked.

Thanks to her aunt's habit of leaving a flashlight on the nightstand, Lainey was able to light her way to the stairs. She started down, her heavy socks making no sound on the treads. The beam of the flashlight picked up the hooked rug in the living room, the rocker that had always been her aunt's favorite chair, the—

She stopped, gripping the banister. A noise, faint and indefinable, came from the kitchen. Maybe the gas refrigerator made noises.

Another step, and Lainey froze again. This time there had been a soft but definite thud. Someone… or something…was in the kitchen.

She held her breath, afraid the intruder would hear the slightest sound. The whole town probably knew that the homeowner was hospitalized, making the house an easy target for a break-in. Could she get back to the bedroom and her cell phone without being heard?

She eased back a step. And heard a loud meow. Lainey's tension dissolved into a shaky laugh. Not someone. A cat. She hadn't known Aunt Rebecca had a cat.

Sweeping the flashlight beam ahead of her, Lainey went quickly to the kitchen, pushing open the swinging door. The flashlight beam reflected shining green eyes, eerily suspended in the air, it seemed. The large black cat sat on the counter next to the stove, looking at her accusingly.

"Well, so who are you?" She reached out a hand tentatively, having a respect for pointed teeth and sharp claws.

The cat sniffed at her hand, apparently found it acceptable, and rubbed its head against her fingers.

"You are a handsome creature." She stroked the shining length of his back, and it arched under her hand. "What's your name?"

He didn't answer, of course, but he butted her hand again and then jumped lightly to the floor, where he pawed at the cabinet door.

"Is that where the cat food is kept?" Silly, to be talking to a cat, but the house was so deadly silent that it was a relief to make some noise. She opened the door and had a look.

No cat food, but there were several cans of tuna. Her visitor seemed to know what that was, because he hooked a paw over one can.

"All right, all right, I get the message. But I can't believe that one of the neighbors isn't feeding you while Aunt Rebecca is in the hospital."

The hand can opener was in the top drawer, and in a few minutes she'd dumped the contents of the can into a bowl and set it down in front of the animal. The cat took one sniff and then began eating.

"I'm not sure what to do with you," she muttered. "Are you supposed to stay inside or go out at night?" She searched the neat, sparsely furnished downstairs to the living room, finding no sign of a litter box. "Out, I guess."

The front windows of the living room looked out on the main road that ran through the village, becoming Main Street on its way. Nothing moved outside. Even when she craned her neck to look down toward the center of town, the streets and sidewalks were empty. Apparently at 3:00 a.m. the citizens of Deer Run were safe in their beds.

A small town would undoubtedly seem even smaller and deader when seen through the eyes of a thirty-year-old, rather than the ten-year-old she'd been when last in Deer Run. But she was here to see to Aunt Rebecca's care, not to socialize.

And afterward? Afterward would have to take care of itself for the moment.

A loud meow interrupted her reverie. She returned to the kitchen to find that the cat had polished the bowl and now stood at the back door, looking fixedly at the knob as if he could turn it with the force of his gaze.

"Okay, I get the message. You want out." She opened the door. The cat spurted through it, disappearing into the shadows as if part of an illusionist's trick.

Lainey stood for a moment in the doorway, looking out. Beyond a large shed, a stretch of weeds and brush led to the woods. There was a stream back that way someplace, as she recalled, and on the other side some Amish farms. That probably wouldn't have changed since…

She lost her train of thought as she caught movement from the corner of her eye. Near the shed, was it? She stared, trying to make out what it was, but nothing stirred.

Her imagination? Lainey frowned. She had plenty of that, certainly. But this had been real enough, she felt sure. If it had been an animal, it was a large one.

A shiver went down her spine. *It's nothing,* she told herself. An overactive imagination and an overtired body made a bad combination. But she locked the door carefully, just the same.

PUNCTUALITY HAD NEVER been Lainey's strong suit, but she arrived at the attorney's office a few minutes before nine the next morning, eager to get this meeting over with and go to the hospital. Why was it necessary, anyway? Jake Evans surely had fulfilled his duty by letting her know about her great-aunt's condition, but he had insisted she stop by.

She wouldn't find out without asking, she supposed. The lawyer's office was in the ground floor of a square, solid brick building right on Main Street. *Evans and Son, Attorneys-at-Law,* the sign read.

Lainey pulled open the door and found herself in a wide entryway, bare except for a mounted moose head that stared down at her rather sourly. She hustled through a second door into a conventional receptionist's space. Four or five padded chairs sat empty against the wall. Two identical doors apparently led to the offices of Evans Senior and Evans Junior.

The receptionist, a gray-haired female with an

unrelentingly stern face, turned from watering the philodendron that overflowed from the corner of her desk.

"Ms. Colton?" Her gaze swept Lainey from top to toe, and a faintly pained expression formed as she took in jeans, boots and tucked turquoise shirt topped with a fringed suede jacket.

"That's right." Lainey forced herself not to fidget. Deer Run must really be behind the times if the woman found this outfit inappropriate. It was probably the most businesslike thing Lainey owned. "I'm supposed to meet Jacob Evans at nine." She brushed her hair back, setting the dangling silver-and-turquoise earrings she'd made jingle.

"I'll let Mr. Evans know you're here." The woman leaned across the desk to press a button on the phone.

In an instant, the right-hand door swung open. The man who emerged was so unlike the image she'd formed from their brief conversation on the phone that Lainey had to stare.

She had expected old, stuffy, businesslike and disapproving. The reality was tall, lanky and probably early thirties, with thick, reddish-brown hair, a long jaw, straight nose and a mobile mouth that looked as if it smiled readily.

It wasn't smiling now. The disapproval, at least, was as she'd imagined.

"Ms. Colton, please come in. I'm Jake Evans, your great-aunt's attorney."

She gave him a cool nod and walked past him into the inner office. There were plenty of reasons why a solid citizen like Jacob Evans would disapprove of her, but she couldn't imagine how he'd know any of them. Maybe he just disapproved of outsiders on general principle. With the quick toss that sent her unruly mane behind her shoulders for a few moments, at least, she took what was obviously the visitor's chair.

"You must have made an early start to get here by nine," Evans said, sliding into the leather executive chair behind the desk. He leaned back, looking for a moment as if he'd prop his foot up on a conveniently open drawer, and then seemed to think the better of it.

"My flight reached Pittsburgh at nine last night. I rented a car and drove straight through, so I got in around midnight."

He blinked. "I didn't expect… Well, that's fine. You stayed at a motel out on the highway, then?"

"I stayed at my great-aunt's house, of course. Why not?"

"No reason." He straightened his tie, drawing her attention to his tie clip. The engraved lion gave him away as a Penn State graduate. "I just thought the lack of electricity might be a problem for you." His lips quirked, making him suddenly more likable.

"I did keep reaching for a switch, I admit." She returned the smile, liking the way his face warmed when he forgot to be stiff and legal. "But the cat and I got along all right."

"Cat?" He looked at her blankly.

"Aunt Rebecca's cat. Big, black, furry, with green eyes?" *Like yours,* she thought.

He frowned slightly. "Your aunt doesn't have a cat."

"She doesn't?" It *was* odd that Aunt Rebecca hadn't mentioned a cat in her letters, since she talked about everything in her life. "Well, I guess I gave the neighbor's cat a middle-of-the-night tuna treat, then."

Although in that case, how had the cat gotten into the house? It couldn't have come in with her. She'd been tired, yes, but not so tired she wouldn't notice a large cat.

Lainey gave herself a mental shake. Not important now. She'd shelve that question until later. Unfortunately that thought reminded her of Phillip, telling her that she must be related to Scarlett O'Hara, with her tendency to worry about things tomorrow.

He'd been more right than she knew. If she'd spent a little more time thinking about where their relationship was headed—

"I don't suppose the neighbors will mind," Jake said, his thoughts obviously still on the cat.

"I'd like to see my great-aunt," she said abruptly. "Can you give me directions to the hospital?"

"Before you head over there, I thought we ought to clarify your position." His tone had shifted back to being formal.

"My position?" she echoed, not sure what he was driving at.

His green eyes narrowed, much like the cat's had. "Didn't your great-aunt speak to you about her arrangements?"

"Arrangements?" She sounded like a demented

parrot, echoing everything he said, but she honestly had no idea what the man was talking about.

Evans rotated a pen slowly in his hand for a moment, and then tried to balance it on its tip. It fell over. "I was afraid of that. You see, your great-aunt has given you power of attorney. Do you know what that means?"

"I know what power of attorney means." He didn't need to sound as if she were a dimwit. "But I'm not sure what effect it has in this situation."

"She should have talked to you," he murmured, half to himself, she suspected. "Basically, it gives you the authority to make any decisions that are necessary in regard to her medical care or finances in the event that she can't make them herself."

"But...she can, can't she? I mean, you said she asked for me, so that must mean she's able to talk and make decisions."

Evans shook his head, his face somber. "She did ask for you, yes. But after that she lapsed into what I suppose is a coma. She's a little responsive, but she hasn't been able to communicate."

Lainey stared down at her clasped hands, absorbing his words. She'd known it was serious, of course—even a mild stroke and a fall would be in a woman her great-aunt's age. But she hadn't imagined it was this serious.

Evans sat quietly, apparently realizing that she needed time to absorb this news.

Lainey rubbed her forehead, trying to think what she ought to do first. "How exactly did it happen?"

He looked startled, as if he'd expected a different question. "No one knows, exactly. Her niece Katie stopped by the house to check on her and found her at the bottom of the stairs. The doctor says there's no way of knowing whether she had the stroke and it caused her to fall or whether she fell and the shock brought on the stroke." He gave her a rueful smile. "At least, that's what he said with the medical lingo stripped away."

The stairs she'd been up and down last night, never knowing...

"But do they think she'll recover?" Lainey discovered she was holding her breath.

He spread his hands, palms up. "Nobody's willing to commit, either way."

"I see." A headache was starting to build, and she pressed her fingertips to her temples.

"That's why this power of attorney has suddenly become so important, and why I insisted that you come immediately." Evans leaned toward her across the desk, eyes intent. "Someone will have to make decisions about her care. There are other relatives who live close at hand, but they can't do anything if you accept the responsibility."

She studied his face, trying to read behind the words. "You mean I could decline?"

He nodded. "Since she didn't consult you, I'm sure everyone involved would understand if you felt you couldn't handle it."

"So what exactly would happen if I declined to accept the power of attorney?" It was beginning to sound more like the power to make a big mistake with her great-aunt's life at stake.

"The court would have to appoint someone. Probably one of the other relatives, I imagine. I'm sure either Rebecca's brother or her late husband's brother would be glad to take the burden off your shoulders."

Evans wanted her to refuse. She could hear it in his voice and read it in his eyes. Why? Because she wasn't from around here? Because he didn't like the way she looked?

Jake Evans's attitude might be annoying, but it wasn't nearly as important as the debt she owed Aunt Rebecca for being an anchor in her life when she had desperately needed one.

She stood up, obviously surprising him. "I'm going to the hospital," she said. "I can't decide anything until after I've seen Aunt Rebecca."

JAKE CHECKED HIS rearview mirror to be sure he hadn't lost Lainey, following in her rental car, when he turned up the street that led to the hospital. He hadn't.

His encounter with Lainey Colton had confirmed all his concerns about the wisdom of Rebecca's choice. His elderly client, like most Amish in the valley, had more relatives close at hand than an *Englischer* like him would find comfortable. Rebecca could have named any one of them.

But she hadn't, obviously. Maybe that plethora of local relatives was exactly the reason she'd chosen to leave her affairs in the hands of an obscure great-niece she hadn't seen in twenty years.

When he'd voiced his concerns to Rebecca, she'd been adamant. According to her way of thinking, you could know everything there was to know about a person's character at ten. He'd thought Rebecca, from the shelter of her quiet Amish life, was underestimating the influences the outside world could bring to bear on a person.

At the time, Rebecca had been in fine health for a woman in her seventies, and he'd thought he would have plenty of time to convince her to reconsider. In retrospect, he'd been wrong. Now he was going to have to deal with the fallout.

He flipped on his turn signal and swung into the visitors' lot. Lainey pulled her car into a slot a short distance down the row from his, so that he had an opportunity to study her as she walked toward him.

Lainey would draw a second glance no matter where she was, he suspected. In conservative little Deer Run, it would no doubt be more like four or five glances.

The October breeze lifted her long mane of curls, blue-black as a crow's wing in the sunshine, revealing beaded earrings that reached almost to her shoulders. Even from several yards away the deep blue of her eyes was startling against her pale skin. She looked…what? Exotic? Artsy? She'd fit in fine at the huge arts festival held over in State College every summer, but not in staid Deer Run.

Whatever. He could only hope Lainey would be able to cope with the tangle she was walking into. Either that, or that she'd have sense enough to get out.

"It's a small hospital, isn't it?" she said, nodding toward the redbrick building that sat at the top of the hill overlooking the town.

"Deer Run is a small community." He fell into step with her as they walked toward the entrance.

"Is my great-aunt getting the care she needs here? I assume there's a larger facility somewhere nearby."

"The doctors would recommend a transfer to a larger care center if they thought it necessary." He couldn't help sounding a little stiff. If she intended to take this adversarial attitude into every encounter, it was going to be a long day.

They reached the portico at the front entrance, and Lainey turned to him with a cool smile. "Thank you for showing me the way. You don't need to come in with me."

Accept dismissal? He didn't think so.

"That's okay. I want to check on my favorite client." He gave her the laid-back smile that usually disarmed people and stepped forward so that the automatic door swished open. He gestured. "After you."

She hesitated, as if she'd like to argue, and then she swept inside, her momentum carrying her right past the pink ladies stationed at their welcome desk.

"Good morning, Jake." Helen Blackwood patted her iron-gray curls in an automatic gesture, her cheeks as pink as her smock. "This must be little Lainey, come to see her great-aunt. You won't remember me, my dear, but I knew you when you were a child. I'm Helen Blackwood."

Lainey looked a bit nonplussed at this welcome,

but she shook the hand Helen held out. "It's nice to see you, Ms. Blackwood."

"Helen, please, dear. After all, we're old friends. Now, be sure you give your dear aunt a kiss for us. We're all praying for her."

"I...I will. Thank you," Lainey added. She tried to pull her hand away, but Helen had her in a firm grip.

"My goodness, I remember how you children loved my gingersnaps—"

"We certainly did," Jake interrupted, taking Lainey's arm and turning her to the elevator. "I'm sure Lainey will look forward to catching up later. And you might let me know the next time you're baking gingersnaps." He propelled Lainey onto the elevator while Helen was still fluttering over his comment.

The door swept shut, and he punched the button for the second floor, grinning at Lainey. "See? I do come in handy."

Her face relaxed in response. "Obviously the little old ladies adore you."

He managed a look of mock hurt. "I'll have you know that the Evans charm extends to females of all ages."

The door opened before she could answer.

"Rebecca's room is just down the hall. The next door on the right."

Lainey stepped into the room ahead of him and stopped so abruptly he nearly walked into her. A look over her shoulder told him the reason. The room seemed full of people in Amish garb.

Easing her into the room, he nodded to those he

knew. "Family," he murmured in Lainey's ear. "How is she today?" He focused on Katie Gaus, one of Rebecca's many nieces, whose round face was made even rounder by her generous smile. The mother of a large family, Katie was comfortably middle-aged, her dress the dark purple color that seemed favored by Amish women her age. Katie had been the one to find Rebecca the day she fell.

"Not much change," Katie said softly. She came to take Lainey's hand. "Little Lainey, all grown up. It is *gut* to see you. *Wilcom.*"

"Thank you." Lainey seemed to struggle to place her. "You're Cousin Katie, right?"

"*Ja,* that's so." Katie smiled again, her gentle face warm. "I am a bit older and wider than you remember, *ja?*"

"You had a son about my age, didn't you?" Lainey was showing more composure than Jake had expected at this horde of relatives. Maybe this was going to be all right.

"*Ja,* that would be Daniel. But *komm.* You are here for Aunt Rebecca, not for all of us." Holding Lainey's hand as if she were still a child, Katie led her toward the bed.

Jake stood back, watching. Now that he had a chance to look around, the room wasn't as full as it had first appeared. In addition to Katie, three other women he recognized as relatives of Rebecca had apparently been sitting with her.

On the opposite side of the room was a small knot of men, their black coats and pants creating a dense spot in the bright room. Zebulon Stoltzfus, the oldest brother of Rebecca's late husband, stood in front of three of his sons.

There was no doubt about who was in charge in that family—Zeb had always ruled his numerous progeny with an iron fist, and rumor had it that the bishop and ministers who shepherded the local Amish congregation had made more than one call on him. That usually meant the person visited had behaved in a manner that went counter to the *Ordnung,* the mutually agreed-upon rules by which the congregation lived. At the moment, Zeb looked like a man with a grievance, and Jake suspected he knew what that grievance was.

Lainey was bending over the hospital bed, drawing his attention. Her hair swung forward, hiding her face at the moment, but his thoughts were arrested by the tenderness in her movement as she took her great-aunt's hand. She bent to kiss Rebecca's cheek, murmuring something he couldn't hear, and as she straightened he saw the tears that streaked her face. Jake had the uncomfortable feeling that all his preconceptions had just been upended.

He shook off the wave of empathy. Even if Lainey had genuine feeling for her aunt, that still didn't mean that she was capable of making life-or-death decisions for her.

Zeb stalked over to him, his face set in a frown that would likely have even his grown sons quaking in their shoes. "Well? What are you going to do?"

Jake managed to keep from glaring back. It was no

part of his duty to Rebecca to alienate her relatives if he could help it. "Lainey Colton is Rebecca's choice to take change of her affairs." He kept his voice even.

Zeb flung out a hand toward the women. "The *Englisch* woman is unsuitable. There is too much at stake."

"She is Rebecca's great-niece." Jake's jaw tightened. "And it's Rebecca's business, not yours."

Obviously Lainey had heard him. She straightened with a toss of her head that sent her black hair flowing back over her shoulders.

"What is he talking about? What is at stake, and why am I unsuitable?"

Jake had hoped he'd be able to avoid an outright confrontation. Once again in this situation, he'd been wrong.

CHAPTER TWO

LAINEY FROWNED AT JAKE, waiting for an answer. When it didn't come fast enough to suit her, she shifted her glare to the other man.

His narrow face was tight with an emotion she couldn't immediately identify—disdain, maybe. Vague memory stirred. An Amish man talking to Aunt Rebecca, looking at the ten-year-old she'd been with just that expression.

"Well?" She wasn't going to start off by letting herself be intimidated. "What did you mean?"

"I'm sure Zeb didn't…" Jake began, but the older man's voice cut across his.

"Chust what I say. You are not suitable to have charge of my brother's wife. You are not Amish. *Englischer.*" He clamped his thin lips together on the word.

Katie intervened, coming quickly to join them. "Onkel Zeb, you must remember that this was Rebecca's decision. It's not Lainey's fault."

Not her fault, Lainey felt the words echo in her mind. Freely translated, that must be that Katie agreed with him but objected to his methods.

They couldn't be any more convinced than she

was that this entire situation was beyond her. Still, she wouldn't give Zeb Stoltzfus the satisfaction of seeing her doubts. She remembered him faintly now—Uncle Isaac's brother, and as sour as Isaac had been sweet, from what she remembered.

"Aunt Rebecca apparently thought I was capable enough." She stated the obvious. "That's why I'm here."

Zeb seemed to be gritting his teeth. He turned to Jake, glowering. "You are responsible for this mess. I told Rebecca she didn't need a lawyer to handle things for her, but she wouldn't listen. And now see what has happened."

"You can't…" Lainey began, but Jake held up his hands to both of them. There was enough command in the gesture to enforce an uneasy silence in the room, broken only by the rhythmic hum of a machine by Aunt Rebecca's bed.

"Enough." Jake looked equally annoyed with both of them. "Rebecca's hospital room is no place to have this discussion."

"That's right." Katie tugged Lainey's arm. "What would your aunt Rebecca think of this *fratching? Komm*. Sit."

She wasn't going to retire from the battle that easily, but Lainey let herself be maneuvered a couple of steps back. Jake, seeming satisfied that she wouldn't interfere, turned to Zeb.

"Why don't you and your boys go on home now?" he said. "I'll stop by the farm this evening and answer any questions you have then. No point in hanging around here, is there?"

Zeb didn't speak. He glared for another moment, then glanced at his sons and jerked his head toward the door. They filed out without a word.

Katie expelled a sigh of relief when the door swung slowly closed, and her round face creased in a smile. "There now." She patted Lainey's arm as if she needed soothing. "You mustn't mind Zeb. He's always been cross-grained, and I believe he's getting worse the older he gets."

"Aunt Rebecca said once that he was sour where Uncle Isaac was sweet." Lainey smiled, remembering.

Katie chuckled. "*Ja,* that's certain sure. Your *gross-onkel* was a kind man."

"Yes, he was." Like Aunt Rebecca, he had made her welcome in his home, although surely he must have had doubts about taking in a waif who'd been no relative of his at all.

"Komm." Katie gestured to the chair next to the bed. "Sit and talk to Rebecca. Maybe she'll hear your voice, even if she doesn't speak."

"I'll be on my way…." Jake turned toward the door.

Lainey grabbed his arm before he could get away. "I'll be right back," she assured Katie, and led him out into the hall for a private word.

He came to a halt a few feet from the door, forcing her to stop as well. He was a bit too large for her to tug very far.

"You mind telling me what you're doing?" His right eyebrow lifted.

"Stopping you. You're not getting away before I understand what going on with Zeb Stoltzfus."

"Later," he said. "After you've had a chance to think about what Rebecca is asking."

"Now." Her fingers tightened on his sleeve. "I can't make a decision without knowing all the facts. Surely an attorney can understand that."

Jake detached her fingers from his sleeve. "Are you always this stubborn?" He sounded more interested than condemning.

"Yes." Stubborn. And impulsive. Those two qualities had landed her in trouble more often than she cared to remember. Pain flickered at the thought of the events of the past couple of weeks.

"All right." His rapid capitulation surprised her. He glanced around. "Come on. We can't talk in the hallway where anyone might hear."

Now it was his turn to grasp her arm and propel her down the hallway. His big hand enclosed her elbow, and she felt his warmth even through two layers of fabric.

Jake stopped at a door and peered through the narrow vertical window. "Good, it's empty." He shoved the door open and led the way inside. "We shouldn't be disturbed in here for a few minutes."

It was a chapel, she realized, carefully non-denominational as chapels usually were in places like hospitals. Light streamed through the abstract pattern of the stained glass window on the outer wall, laying a path of color across beige carpeting. Two short rows of pale wooden benches faced a table under the window, which held a vase of bronze-and-yellow mums.

"Have a seat." He waited until she'd slid into a pew and sat down next to her.

"Now tell me." Almost without thought she lowered her voice. "What does Zeb have against me?"

Jake frowned absently at the vase of flowers, apparently arranging his thoughts. She waited, trying to be patient. She could stand to do some thought-arranging herself, since at the moment her brain felt like a juggler, tossing a handful of colored balls into the air.

"Didn't you wonder why an Amish woman would have an attorney?"

Lainey blinked at the question. "Well, I guess I didn't consider it." Why would she? She hadn't known until he'd called her with the news, and she'd been too shocked to think of anything except getting here.

"It's unusual, to put it mildly." The lines of his face relaxed a little. "Unlike most of the Amish in this area, your great-uncle was actually fairly wealthy, at least in terms of the property he owned. I think it started almost by accident, but Isaac seemed to have a gift for knowing when to buy. As a result, when he became sick, he consulted me, wanting to be sure Rebecca had someone to advise her."

"He didn't trust the family to do so?" Picturing Zeb's narrow, avaricious face, she didn't think she'd trust him either.

"Let's just say that Isaac didn't want Rebecca to have to handle any family disagreements. He felt that having an outsider assisting her would prevent that."

"Okay. But I still don't see what there is in that to make his brother so upset. If, as you say, my aunt's money is invested in land, there surely isn't anything I have to do about it while she's ill. When she gets better…" She stopped, not wanting to think about the alternative.

"Yes." Jake seemed to be answering what she didn't say, and his already deep voice deepened still more in sympathy. "We don't know yet what will happen to Rebecca, and whether she'll ever be able to take over managing the property again. In the meantime I can certainly collect rents and pay taxes, but there's more to it than that."

Lainey's head was beginning to ache as Jake seemed intent on adding even more to the number of balls she was juggling. "You'd better tell me the worst of it. How else am I going to know what to do?"

His firm lips curved slightly. "There's no 'worst,' as you say. It's just that Rebecca owns several farms among other things—farms that Zeb and three of his sons operate."

"They're doing it for her?"

"No, they're doing it for themselves. They pay her a rent that is…nominal, to say the least."

She still didn't quite see what all the fuss was about. "Surely Zeb doesn't think I'm going to raise the rent or evict them or something. Things can just go on the way they are."

"Maybe. Maybe not." Jake's frown told her that despite his words, there was something worse to come. "A week or so before Rebecca's stroke, Zeb had asked her to sign one of the farms over to him so that he could use it for collateral on a loan. She hadn't made a decision yet, so that's in limbo, and I don't know how badly he needed or wanted the money."

No wonder Zeb was upset. "But he could hardly expect to go anywhere with that project while Rebecca is incapacitated, no matter who had the power of attorney."

Jake shrugged. "As I said, I don't know how badly he needs the money. And it is possible for the person with the power of attorney to sell property. In fact, it might become necessary for other reasons."

Lainey glared at him, not liking the way this conversation was going. "Stop trying to break it to me gently. Just tell me."

"I wasn't." His grin startled her. "But you'd be surprised how few people can keep up when a lawyer starts explaining things."

"They teach you that in law school, do they?" That smile of his seemed to touch something inside her.

"Actually, I picked that up from my dad."

The only thing she'd picked up from a long line of stepdads was that she was superfluous. And the assurance that they wouldn't be around for long.

"So why might it be necessary to sell property?" She could feel the weight of responsibility getting heavier.

"I don't know how much you remember about

Amish beliefs, but they don't have insurance. Decisions may have to be made about how to pay for Rebecca's care. As long as her assets are tied up in land, it's not going to be easy to come up with funds."

She stared at him blankly for a few seconds. "But surely, Medicare…"

He was already shaking his head. "The Amish don't pay into Medicare and Social Security, and they don't accept the benefits. In the case of someone needing hospital care, the family pays out of pocket, and when necessary, the church district takes up an offering to make up the difference."

She tried to wrap her mind around it. So in addition to fending off angry relatives and making decisions about Aunt Rebecca's care that she felt very ill-equipped to make, she was also probably going to be landed with a cartload of bills she couldn't pay. She pressed her fingers to her temples.

"Is that all of it? You don't have any more surprises for me?"

"That's it." She thought she read sympathy in his clear green eyes. "Sorry about hitting you with all of this, but you wanted to know."

"I did." Lainey took a deep breath. It didn't help. "Well, thanks for being honest with me."

"It's not an easy situation. To continue being honest, I advised her against choosing you for this responsibility."

"Prejudiced without seeing me?" she asked sweetly.

"It's not that." His tanned face flushed. "I just

thought it made more sense to name someone here, someone who'd have a better understanding of Rebecca's situation."

"Like my great-uncle Zeb?" The momentary connection she'd felt at his sympathy vanished.

"No, certainly not Zeb." His voice was crisp. "Not anyone who has something to gain or lose by the decisions that might be made. But that list still includes other people who…" He let that trail off.

But she could finish it for him. "…who are more qualified than I am? Annoying as that is, you may be right."

Jake's jaw set, and he seemed to censor the words that sprang to his lips. "As I mentioned, you don't have to accept. We could make a recommendation that another person be chosen because you're unable to perform the duties. After all, you have a home and a life elsewhere. No one could blame you for saying no."

Home was something she'd never had, unless she counted one long-ago summer. And her life was such a mess that she wasn't especially eager to return to it.

But neither of those was a good reason for turning down the responsibility Aunt Rebecca had thrust upon her.

"I'll think about it," she said, rising. "I'll let you know what I decide."

Jake stood, too, looking down at her for a long moment, his face giving nothing away. "I'll look forward to hearing from you." He glanced at his watch. "If you'll excuse me, I have to get back to the office."

Without waiting for a response, he walked quickly out of the chapel.

Lainey followed more slowly. Heading down the hall toward her aunt's room, she tried to marshal her thoughts, but they refused to be collected.

She was aware of one overwhelming urge. Escape. That was what she always did, wasn't it? When things got difficult, when relationships grew sticky, she escaped. At least, unlike her mother, she didn't marry her mistakes.

At the moment, her stomach churned with anxiety, with the urge to keep going right past that hospital room where Aunt Rebecca lay, to get on the elevator, to get in her rental car, and get out of town.

She didn't. She turned and walked back into her aunt's room. If she was going to back out of this situation, at least she wouldn't run.

LAINEY GLANCED AT the clock over the refrigerator. Jake had told Zeb he'd stop by to see him this evening. He might be there now. What was he telling the man?

Odd, wasn't it? She'd never heard of an attorney who made house calls, and on someone who wasn't a client, no less. Maybe Jake was just a really nice guy. Or maybe there was more involved in this situation than she realized. In any event, she'd better curb her well-known gift for acting impulsively and consider all the options before making such a big decision.

She dried the plate she'd used for her supper, looking out the window over the sink. The sun was sliding over the ridge, its slanting rays turning the trees in the woods to gold. Beyond the patch of woods, where the land sloped gently upward, she could see cows moving toward a barn, prompted by a small Amish boy whose straw hat didn't even reach the cows' backs.

She'd forgotten how peaceful the valley was. And how beautiful. Of course, it was possible that as a child she hadn't noticed it. She'd been too busy running around all day with those two girls…she blanked out, unable to remember their names for a moment. Then it came back to her, swimming up from the depths of memory. Rachel and Meredith.

Rachel had been the Amish girl from the farm on the other side of the creek, and Meredith the one who lived in the house next door. Apparently she still did, from what Lainey remembered of her great-aunt's letters. It was hard to imagine someone as bright and energetic as Meredith had been settling down in a place like Deer Run.

People did, she supposed. Her thoughts went back to Jake. He had, obviously. Maybe he liked being the big fish in the small pond.

What was he saying to Zeb Stoltzfus? She couldn't help feeling a sliver of uneasiness, despite Jake's assurances. Jake had claimed he didn't support the idea of Zeb controlling Rebecca's assets or her care, but what if he liked the idea of Lainey doing it even less? Despite those few moments when they'd seemed to click, he'd clearly thought Rebecca had made a mistake in naming her.

Lainey's cell phone rang, and her nerves seemed to jangle in tune with it. She'd given the hospital her cell number. Dropping the dish towel, she snatched up the phone.

"Hello?"

For a moment there was nothing. Then a voice, a muffled, hoarse whisper that might have been a man or a woman, muttered a string of the abuse and obscenities that had grown all too familiar in recent weeks.

She yanked the phone away from her ear and punched the off key. Her stomach churned, and her ear tingled as if something ugly had crawled inside.

She wrapped her arms around herself, trying not to shake. She ought to be getting used to it. The calls had come in a steady stream since Joanna Marcus had so publicly attempted suicide. She'd tried reporting them to the police in St. Louis. The officer she spoke with had looked as if he thought she deserved what she got.

But those calls had come on her landline at the apartment in St. Louis. How had someone gotten the number of her cell phone? Of course, anyone who'd worked in the ad agency could easily have access to her cell number. Her stomach churned at the thought that the caller might be someone she knew.

Lainey reached out to turn off the phone and realized she couldn't. That number was the only way the hospital could reach her.

At least she could be smart enough to check the

caller before she answered. After a string of remarkably stupid decisions, surely she could manage that.

Lainey ran her hand through tangled curls. She was not going to go through it all again. But the memories, once started, unrolled in her mind like a disaster movie, where one wrong choice led inexorably to another.

Dating your boss was stupid. She knew that, but she'd let Phillip Marcus charm her anyway. She'd let it get serious, more so than she ever did, believing him when he said he and his wife had been legally separated for a year, that his divorce would be final in a matter of months, that he was free of a marriage both of them agreed was a mistake.

Lainey had bought it all, and now she looked at her actions with disgust. Anyone would think she'd been a starry-eyed eighteen-year-old instead of a cynical thirty.

If it had ended quietly, she'd still have been ashamed, but at least it would have been a private shame. But Joanna, the wife Phillip had insisted wanted to be rid of him, had called in to a radio talk show, announcing she had taken a massive dose of sleeping pills and naming Lainey as the worthless tramp who had stolen her husband.

The paramedics had been in time to save her, thank God. If she'd been anyone else, the whole affair might have passed from the media's attention in twenty-four hours. But Joanna's family was a prominent one—her father a judge, her brother a state senator. Lainey had been completely unprepared for the level of vitriol launched at her.

Maybe she'd deserved it, but she hadn't expected it to follow her here. She'd been wrong, it seemed.

A loud meow, followed by a scratching at the back door, jerked her out of that profitless line of thought. She hurried to open the back door.

"All right, all right. You don't have to make scratch marks on the door."

The black cat walked inside, tail high, with an air of owning the place. He sat down on the exact spot where she had fed him the previous night and looked at her.

"Doesn't your owner feed you?" She opened the cabinet and retrieved a can of tuna. "If this keeps up, I'll have to lay in a supply of cat food. I don't imagine that Aunt Rebecca can afford to keep you in tuna."

The cat followed her every move with unblinking green eyes. When she set the bowl down in front of him he stared at her for another moment and then tucked in.

She couldn't help smiling. "You have a fine sense of your own importance, I'll say that for you." At least he'd announced himself at the door this time, instead of appearing out of nowhere.

A knock at the front door pulled her away from contemplation of the cat. She went quickly to the front of the house and swung the door open. Maybe Jake…

But two women stood on the front porch, looking at her with an expectation that reminded her of the cat.

"Don't you know us, Lainey?" The taller woman brushed a wing of silky brown hair behind her ear. "I think I'd know you anywhere."

The pieces fell into place. "Meredith, of course. And Rachel. I was just thinking about you. Please, come in."

Strange, to see them now when the only images in her mind were of a tomboy in braids and blue jeans and a sweet-faced Amish girl, blond hair drawn back under a *kapp,* dress reaching below her knees. Memories began to filter through the intervening years— of giggling slumber parties and secrets shared in the tree house Meredith's father had built in her backyard. It was as if Lainey had a whole life she'd forgotten, just waiting for her to remember.

"You've changed. Still, I guess we've all grown up, haven't we?" She followed them into the living room. They seemed to know their way around the house as well as she did, which wasn't really surprising.

Rachel chuckled. "You're thinking that I've really changed, right? It's a shock when you're expecting an Amish woman in *kapp* and apron." She gestured toward her jeans and cotton sweater.

"I think Aunt Rebecca wrote to me about it when you came back to Deer Run." Lainey's brain finally caught up. She probably should have reread Aunt Rebecca's letters on her way here. "You have a little girl, don't you?"

Rachel's face lit with maternal pride. "Mandy. We're next door, actually." She gestured toward what was the last house in the village. "I've turned my mother-in-law's old home into a bed-and-breakfast."

"And I'm still on the opposite side of your aunt's house, so we have you surrounded," Meredith said.

"Just like old times." It was oddly familiar to be here with them, even though she'd thought of them so seldom in recent years.

Meredith sat down in a rocker. "I run my accounting business out of my home."

"Accounting?" Lainey shook her head. "It seemed to me you were going to be an astronaut. Or run a dude ranch out West."

"That summer must have been the end of my cowgirl phase," Meredith said, brown eyes smiling at the memory. "It finally occurred to me that I was afraid of horses, something that limited my cowgirl ambitions. As I recall, you were going to live in Paris and be an artist. What happened?"

"I discovered I wasn't that talented." Funny, how easy it was to admit that to them. Maybe the bond they'd formed then was more durable than she would have expected. "I ended up working for an advertising agency." At least, that's what she had been doing. Technically, at the moment she was unemployed.

"Life seldom turns out the way we dream it will when we're ten," Rachel said. "But you were a wonderful artist. We still have the scrapbook from that summer with your drawings."

Meredith glanced at her, frowning almost in warning, it seemed, making Lainey wonder why that would be a touchy subject.

"I'd like to see it sometime." That seemed the polite thing to say, although Lainey would have to admit that her memories of that summer were rather hazy. "It was about some story we made up, wasn't it?"

"Something like that," Meredith agreed. "Have you been to the hospital yet? I was there yesterday, but the nurses weren't very forthcoming about Rebecca's condition."

"That was nice of you." Lainey was reminded that Rebecca had an entire life here, with relatives and friends who were all probably wondering about her. "I don't think they can predict very much about how much she'll recover. She was still…"

She lost the thread when the cat, apparently finished with his dinner, appeared in the kitchen doorway. He stood for a moment, assessing them, and then crossed the room to jump lightly onto Lainey's lap and settle there.

"You have a cat." Rachel reached out to run her fingers lightly along the glossy back. "My daughter, Mandy, will fall in love. She's been asking if she can get a kitten, but since she already has a puppy, I think that's enough."

"She's welcome to come and visit, but I can't guarantee the cat will be here. It's not mine. I supposed it was Aunt Rebecca's, but Jake Evans said she didn't have a cat, so I guess it belongs to a neighbor."

"That's odd." Meredith's forehead furrowed. "I can't think of anyone on the block with a black cat."

"Probably a stray," Rachel said. "Rebecca has such a tender heart that she wouldn't turn it away. He's a handsome creature, isn't he?"

Lainey's cell phone rang, and her hands clutched in the cat's fur. With an annoyed glance, he leaped to the floor and began washing himself.

"If you want to get that, please go ahead," Meredith said, obviously surprised that she wasn't answering.

Lainey pulled the phone from her pocket. A quick glance told her that it was an unfamiliar number. She clicked it off. "It's nothing important. I'll deal with it later."

There must have been something odd in her tone, because both Meredith and Rachel were looking at her with varying degrees of puzzlement.

Well, it didn't matter what they thought, did it? Much as she enjoyed seeing them again after twenty years, that was all—just satisfying a passing curiosity. She wasn't going to be here long enough to make friends.

CHAPTER THREE

JAKE HELPED HIMSELF to coffee and lifted his mug in a mock toast to his father. "Here's to a better day today than yesterday."

Dad raised his eyebrows, and the result was like looking in a mirror. Mom always said that he'd look exactly like his father when he grew older. If so, that wasn't such a bad reflection, he figured. Dad was still lean, still fit, with just a bit of gray at the temples to add distinction.

"I take it things didn't go as well with Rebecca Stoltzfus's relatives as you'd hoped?" As always, Dad was careful not to tread on his cases, but their ritual morning coffee on reaching the office had become a time when Jake could air anything that bothered him.

"Not exactly." He pondered for a moment. How much to say? Dad was safe, of course, and as senior partner, had a right to know. "Rebecca's relatives might have reason to be worried about her decision to leave the great-niece in control."

Dad set his mug down, frowning. "Are you saying the great-niece might make decisions that aren't in Rebecca's best interest?"

An image of the tenderness with which Lainey

had bent over Rebecca's hospital bed slid into Jake's mind. "I wouldn't say that, exactly." He realized he was falling into the careful phrasing his father always used, and he couldn't suppress an interior grin. "Lainey—the great-niece—seems to care about Rebecca. But she hasn't been back to Deer Run in twenty years. How can she know what Rebecca would want in this situation?"

"What did Rebecca say when you raised that point with her?" Dad didn't seem to doubt that Jake would have covered all the bases with his client.

"She insisted that Lainey's good heart would help her make the right decisions. And when I pointed out that she'd only known her as a ten-year-old, she just smiled and said character was as plain at ten as it was at twenty or thirty." He shrugged. "So what could I do?"

His father mused, the fine lines around his eyes deepening. "You had to do as your client wished, of course, but it's an unsatisfactory situation all around. I'm sure we all hope Rebecca's condition improves, but if it doesn't…"

"Exactly." Jake gestured with his mug, realized the coffee was in danger of sloshing out, and set it down. "That's what has me losing sleep over it. As far as I can tell, Lainey Colton knows little or nothing about the lifestyle Rebecca led. What if she should decide to slap Rebecca into a nursing home, away from the rest of her family and friends? Or what if she decided to bail out…go back to her normal life and ignore what's happening here?"

That was the thing that bugged him most. Lainey was such a fish out of water here. She must be longing to go back where she belonged.

"Well, if this young woman is going to walk away from her responsibilities, it's incumbent upon you to gain her cooperation in straightening out the question of the power of attorney. A family fight over it wouldn't be in anyone's best interests."

Dad, at his most professional, was looking at him as if he expected action. Right.

Jake straightened his tie and checked to be sure his keys were in his pocket.

"I'd better talk to Lainey Colton before I do anything else. It's time she made a decision."

Aware of his father's gaze on him, Jake headed for the door. With any luck, he'd catch Lainey before she left for the hospital.

Rebecca's house was just three blocks away, so he decided to walk. Jake headed down Main Street, relieved to be out and moving. The worst thing about being an attorney was the amount of time he had to spend sitting at a desk.

Deer Run looked its best on a sunny October morning. Chrysanthemums bloomed in pots or window boxes in front of most of the businesses, and the maples that were planted at frequent intervals along the street were already turning color.

Several kids from the high school were clearly enjoying a morning out, painting Halloween scenes on the storefront windows for the annual art contest. He paused to watch three girls painting a witch sailing across a stormy night sky. When they noticed him watching, they nudged each other and giggled.

He moved on. Only buckets or planters of mums decorated the fronts of the Amish businesses like Miller's Shop. The Amish didn't observe Halloween, considering it a pagan idea. Still, the town wore a celebratory air as it prepared for the annual Apple Festival.

Small pleasures, he supposed, but he appreciated them. Unlike a lot of his classmates at Dickinson Law, he'd already known the life he wanted. No high-powered law firms in New York or Los Angeles for him. Everything he wanted was right here, where nobody cared if he drove a battered old pickup or spent his fall Saturdays playing touch football or relaxed with a beer at the local sports bar. And it made him proud, though he wouldn't openly admit it, to be in partnership with someone as respected as his dad.

He'd only made one unscheduled detour on his life plan, and it still left a bitter taste in his mouth when he thought of it. That had been the only time he'd acted impulsively in his adult life, and he'd definitely lived to regret it.

No more mistakes of that sort for him. When he decided it was time to marry and start a family, he'd find someone who wanted what he did out of life.

He passed Meredith King's place and started up the walk to Rebecca Stoltzfus's house. What would Lainey Colton think of that peaceful Main Street scene he'd just been appreciating? She'd probably find it boring, he supposed. She'd be used to a bit more excitement in her life.

He tapped on the front door, but no sound came from inside. He knocked again, louder. Her rental car was still in the driveway. He hadn't missed her, then. Why wasn't she answering?

Finally he heard footsteps on the stairs. The door swung open. He blinked.

He'd clearly caught Lainey before she was ready to face the day. Her black hair hung in wild ringlets past her shoulders, and he had to reject the impulse to touch it to see if it would curl around his fingers. *Don't go there,* he ordered himself. She wore an oversize tie-dyed T-shirt and a pair of yoga pants so fitted they showed every curve. He forced his gaze back to her face.

"Sorry," he said. "I shouldn't have come by so early. I wanted to catch you before you left for the hospital."

"What time is it?" Her voice sounded blurred with sleep, but there were dark circles under her eyes.

He glanced at his watch. "Just after nine."

She groaned, turning away but leaving the door open. He took that as an invitation and stepped inside, closing it behind him.

"Coffee," she muttered, heading for the kitchen.

He followed, finding her staring at the old-fashioned percolator on the gas range with what he thought was loathing.

"I'll fix the coffee." He pulled out a kitchen chair for her. "It's the least I can do after getting you up."

She didn't argue, but her expression said that letting him make the coffee was the lesser of two evils. "I suppose you think it's a crime to sleep late."

"Nope. Do it myself on Saturdays." He measured out the coffee. Luckily he'd spent enough time at the family hunting cabin to know his way around a gas range. "You must still be tired from your trip."

She nodded, and then rubbed the back of her neck as if it ached. "That, and the fact that I got very little sleep last night."

"Not used to the quiet?" He adjusted the flame under the coffeepot and then sat down across from her.

"Actually, I find the lack of traffic noises very soothing. I just had a bad dream or two, that's all."

"About your aunt?" He wouldn't have thought she was the kind of person who'd let a nightmare keep her awake.

"No." She clipped off the word, closing the door on that conversation. "I'm sure you had a reason other than making coffee for stopping by at this hour. Did you talk to my aunt's brother-in-law?"

He nodded. At least telling her about his visit to Zeb would let him lead up to what he wanted to say.

"I went by the farm after supper last night. I figured there was no point in going any earlier if I wanted a quiet conversation."

"And was it? Quiet, I mean. Zeb impressed me as the kind of person likely to shout." The drowsy look was gone from Lainey's face, and she seemed ready to do battle. Zeb must have really annoyed her yesterday.

"Yes, well, he can be a bit…dictatorial. His point is that his brother was the one who bought the land, and that he, Zeb, certainly is in a better position to understand about the property than…than someone from outside."

"Putting it in polite terms, are you?" Her eyebrows lifted.

He grinned. "Something like that. And I can understand his feelings, but as I explained to him, it wouldn't be proper for him to have the power of attorney, given that he has financial interests of his own."

Zeb hadn't responded to that line of reasoning very well.

"Did he accept that?" The aroma of coffee brewing seemed to distract Lainey, and she glanced toward the stove.

"Not entirely," he hedged. "I'll talk to him again." When Zeb had had time to cool off. "He'll come around."

Lainey's gaze fixed on his face again, her eyes so deep a blue that they looked almost black. It seemed to him there was a question in them.

"You're going to a lot of trouble over my great-aunt's situation," she said.

It was the last comment he expected. "No more than I would for any of my clients." He hesitated a moment, not sure what she was driving at. "I suppose, in an urban area, a law firm tends to be more impersonal. It's tough for me to stand on ceremony with people who've known me since I was delivering their newspapers. Besides, Rebecca is a special person."

Apparently he'd hit the right note, because she smiled. It was tinged with a little sorrow, maybe, but a smile none the less. "Yes, she is."

He smiled back at her, and their gazes seemed to catch and tangle. He was suddenly aware of how pale and delicate her skin was, startlingly framed by that blue-black hair. Aware of how close she was, with only the small table separating them. Of the soft curve of her lips—

He leaned back, breaking off the gaze. *Whoa. Back off.* That was definitely not the way he should be thinking of Lainey.

Jake cleared his throat, hoping his momentary lapse hadn't been too visible.

Lainey rose abruptly, turning toward the stove and reaching for the coffeepot, as if she didn't want him to see her expression.

"I...I actually came over to ask you something." Since she didn't turn, he plunged ahead. "Have you come to a decision about whether or not to take on this responsibility?"

Lainey turned to face him, her expression guarded. "Can I have a bit more time? I'd like to see how Aunt Rebecca is this afternoon and talk with her doctors before I come to a conclusion. I didn't have an opportunity to meet with them yesterday."

"Yes, of course. That's fine. Only..." He wasn't sure how to say it, but he knew it had to be said.

"Only what?" Her tone had an edge to it.

"If you do decide not to accept the power of attorney, there are some formalities to go through," he said carefully. "It would be helpful to come to an agreement with the other relatives as to who would take on the job."

"I understand that." She all but tapped her foot with impatience.

"You realize it's important that you not just…take off."

Her lips pinched together; her eyes narrowed. "No, I won't just take off, as you put it. What do you take me for?" She made an abrupt, slicing motion with her hand. "No, don't bother to answer that question. It's pretty obvious what you think of me." She spun away from him, bracing her hands on the countertop. "Thanks for making the coffee. You can find your own way out, I'm sure."

Jake opened his mouth to offer an explanation, an apology, but the set of her shoulders and the rigidity of her back dissuaded him. That hadn't turned out well, had it? Still, he'd had to say it. It was Rebecca's welfare he was concerned about, no one else's. If Lainey couldn't understand that, it was just too bad.

LAINEY GLANCED IN the small mirror that hung over the dresser in the bedroom she already thought of as hers. She looked halfway decent, despite the dark shadows under her eyes. She patted a little concealer on and surveyed the result. Too bad she hadn't been ready for that early-morning visit from Jake Evans.

It was his own fault for coming without calling first, and she wasn't remotely embarrassed at his seeing her that way. Was she?

When she'd finally gotten to sleep it must have been nearly dawn. Odd that she couldn't even remember the dreams from which she'd awakened shaking. She'd just had a sense of running, stumbling, sensing something chasing her, something terrible that was growing closer with every step.

Lainey turned away from the dresser and smoothed the handmade quilt over the bed, comforted at the touch. It was the same quilt that had been on her bed when she was ten. Sunshine and Shadows, the pattern was called, and Aunt Rebecca had said it was hers—that she'd made it for her.

Mom had insisted she leave it behind when she'd picked up Lainey to cart her off to another fresh start. They didn't have room for it, she'd said.

But Aunt Rebecca had kept it where it belonged. Lainey remembered kneeling beside it, the hooked rug knobby under her skinny knees, saying prayers with Aunt Rebecca, and her great-aunt's hands tucking her into bed.

She'd declared from the superior height of ten years that she was too old to be read to when Aunt Rebecca made the offer.

"You can read to me, then, ain't so?" Rebecca had replied. She'd sat next to her, a book between them, listening while Lainey read aloud, showing every sign of pleasure in hearing the story. They'd read their way through three of the Little House books that summer. She glanced at the row of books on the bookshelf under the window.

Lainey's hand lingered on the quilt. She'd felt so safe, going to sleep in this room to the soft sound of Aunt Rebecca's and Uncle Isaac's voices drifting up the stairs from the living room. No quarrels, no crying or shouting, just soft-voiced conversation in the Pennsylvania Dutch dialect Lainey hadn't understood. Maybe you didn't need to understand a language to hear love in it.

Pulling herself out of the memories, Lainey headed down the stairs. Then, moved by an impulse she couldn't explain, she went back and took out the first of the Little House books. Silly, maybe, but if she read to Aunt Rebecca, perhaps at some level she would hear and be comforted.

What would Jake think of her, carting a children's book to Rebecca's bedside? He'd never know, and she didn't care what he thought, anyway.

She went downstairs. Her tapestry bag hung from a hook in the back hallway, and she tucked the book inside. She probably should make a list and stop by the grocery store on her way back from the hospital. And maybe pick up some flowers on her way there…

List-making fled from her mind when movement in the driveway along the side of the house caught her eye. An Amish buggy rolled to a halt at the hitching rail by the back porch. Her stomach clenched when she saw the man who held the reins. Zeb Stoltzfus looked as stern and unbending as he had yesterday at the hospital.

She smoothed her palms down the flaring print skirt, glad he hadn't been the one to come to the door before she was dressed. If he was here to renew his argument, he might as well just leave. Nobody was going to force her into a decision she wasn't ready to make.

Zeb approached the door, followed by two other dark-garbed figures. Pushing away the thought that they were ganging up on her, Lainey went to greet them.

"Good morning." She stood holding the door, not at all sure she wanted to welcome him inside if he'd come to argue.

Zeb gave a curt nod, his graying beard looking a bit unkempt in the breeze. "I have brought two of my grandchildren to meet you. Ella has a basket for you."

The young woman behind him stepped toward the door, smiling shyly, and held out a covered basket. "Just some beef stew for your supper. And a shoofly pie. My *mamm* thought you wouldn't have time to cook, running back and forth to the hospital so much, ain't so?"

The smile and the gesture disarmed Lainey. "How kind of her, and of you." She swung the door wide. "Please, come in."

The girl…Ella, he'd said, went straight to the kitchen and set the basket on the counter as if this were familiar territory. Zeb followed her, and the third member of the little party trailed in his wake. The boy must be about fourteen or fifteen, lanky as boys that age often were. He darted what seemed a wary glance at her and then lowered his gaze to his shoes.

Lainey hesitated, not sure whether to hold out her hand to him or not. She settled for a friendly smile. "I'm Lainey. What's your name?"

The boy's blue eyes held a hint of panic, and he glanced toward his grandfather.

"Answer your cousin," Zeb said sharply.

"Thomas," he muttered, a flush mounting to his straw-colored hair. Even the tips of his ears turned red. "I'm Thomas."

She shouldn't have singled him out, obviously, so she just nodded and turned to the counter, lifting the tea towel from it to reveal the crumbly top of the shoofly pie perched on a covered casserole dish.

"It looks wonderful. Thank you."

Ella had removed her black bonnet and sweater, revealing a pert round face and a pair of sparkling blue eyes. She, at least, didn't seem intimidated by her grandfather.

"Ach, we know what it's like when someone's in the hospital. You don't want to be eating that cafeteria food, ain't so?" Ella seemed to be taking it for granted that she'd spend the day at the hospital. "*Mamm* and I stopped by to see Aunt Rebecca yesterday, but it was after you'd left."

"Sorry I wasn't there to speak to you." She felt obscurely guilty. "I was so tired after the flight and then driving from Pittsburgh that I went to bed early."

"Ach, it's a long trip. I went to a wedding last year out in Indiana, and I thought we'd never get there."

Her cheerful face lit with the reminder. "I met lots of new cousins out there."

Ella was probably a couple of years older than her brother, so she wouldn't have been born yet the summer Lainey spent here. The fact made her feel old.

Aunt Rebecca had never let anyone come in her house without offering food and drink, but Lainey had finished the coffee Jake made earlier.

"Would you like to have a piece of the shoofly pie? I could make a pot of coffee." At least she hoped she could.

Ella looked about to agree, but Zeb got in first. "No. *Denke,*" he added. "You will need to leave for the hospital. I chust wanted to stop." He paused, and she imagined that there was a struggle going on behind the thin, leathery face. "I spoke too hasty yesterday. Rebecca picked you. She must have had a reason." He sounded as if he couldn't imagine what that reason might be.

She tried to think of something to say that wouldn't sound antagonistic. "It might have been a good idea for Aunt Rebecca to talk it over with me first."

"Ja." He seized on that idea. "Then you could have explained that it would be too hard with you living in St. Louis and all."

He was jumping to the conclusion that she'd have turned down the power of attorney if she'd known, and that wasn't really what she'd meant. Still, at least he wasn't glaring at her today, and she had to admit that was a step in the right direction.

"In any event, she did choose me, so I'll have to go from there." She kept her tone pleasant but, she hoped, firm.

Zeb stiffened. "You mean you are going ahead with this? Even knowing nothing at all about Rebecca's way of living and her property?"

"She must have thought I knew enough." If people would stop pushing her, she might be able to think instead of react. Unfortunately, reacting won the day, and she blurted out what she hadn't intended to say. "I trust Rebecca's judgment. I'm accepting the power of attorney."

Zeb's face reddened, and Ella touched her grandfather's arm with an air of cautioning him. "That's so. Aunt Rebecca would have a reason. And if you have any problems deciding things, especially about the property, *Grossdaadi* would be the one to help you. He knows all about it."

Zeb seemed to be counting to ten. *"Ja,"* he said, his tone short. "I know more than anyone about my brother's property and what he wanted done."

In other words, he expected her to let him vet any decisions she had to make. Apparently Jake's conversation with Zeb hadn't borne much fruit.

"I'm sure my aunt's lawyer is capable of advising me." There, put the responsibility back on Jake. He was getting paid for it, after all.

"That *Englischer.*" Zeb shook off Ella's restraining hand, his color darkening alarmingly. "No Amish woman needs to have a lawyer to take care of property for her. Her family does that—the kin who have worked long hours in the sun to be sure the land is paying. Not some fancy lawyer who sits in an office all day."

From what she'd seen of Jake, he didn't do much sitting, but that was neither here nor there.

"There's also the matter of making decisions about Aunt Rebecca's care," she said. "Or had you forgotten about that?" She didn't bother trying to hide the annoyance in her voice.

"I have not forgotten." He muttered something in Pennsylvania Dutch that she couldn't understand. "Her family can do that better than you. We see her every week. You haven't come near her in twenty years."

The fact that it was true didn't make it any more palatable coming from him. "But Aunt Rebecca still picked me. I wonder why she trusts me? By the way, she owns the farm you work, doesn't she?"

Zeb's big hands, strong despite his age, clenched into fists. For a moment she feared she'd gone too far.

Ella clutched his arm, murmuring to him urgently in Pennsylvania Dutch. She tugged at him, trying to pull him toward the door.

Zeb glared at Lainey for a moment longer. Then, not speaking, he turned and stamped out the back door. Thomas, blue eyes wide in a white face, scurried after him.

Ella shook her head, pulling her bonnet back on with hands that shook a little. "I'm sorry. He has a temper. He forgets himself. He'll regret he spoke so after a bit."

"I'm sorry, too." She should have handled the situation better. When would she learn not to let her emotions get the better of her? "I do appreciate your trying to help. And the food."

"Ach, it's nothing." Ella clasped her hand. "I must go. Maybe I will see you again soon."

Lainey nodded, but somehow she doubted it. She was suddenly tired and dispirited. How had she let herself get into this situation in the first place? She didn't belong here.

But she didn't belong back in St. Louis, either. There seemed no place where she did belong.

CHAPTER FOUR

IT WAS ONE thing to declare she was the person in charge, Lainey decided, and quite another to sit for hours at her great-aunt's bedside, wishing Rebecca would wake up and tell Lainey what to do.

Fortunately her cousin Katie arrived early in the afternoon, bustling into the hospital room carrying a basket on one arm and what looked like a sewing bag on the other.

"Ach, all alone here?" Katie bent to kiss Aunt Rebecca's cheek and then glanced at Lainey. "Any change?"

"Not that I can see," she admitted. "I'm hoping to have a chance to talk with one of the doctors this afternoon."

"Some things chust take time," Katie said, her tone confident as she took the second chair and opened her basket. "Now, I knew you would be hungry, so I brought a little lunch for you."

"That looks like more than a little." Lainey accepted the paper plate Katie handed her. "I'm fine, really."

Katie eyed her. "You have circles under your eyes and a worried frown on your face. *Komm,* now. A nice sandwich and some potato salad will keep you going. And a walnut brownie to finish off. I brought lemonade, but if you want me to get you a coffee, I will." She looked as if she'd jump out of the chair to do so, and Lainey waved her back.

"Lemonade is lovely." Obviously it would be easier to eat than to argue. "Didn't you bring any for yourself?"

"I ate with the family before I left the house. The men are getting a last cutting of hay today, so they had lunch early." Katie leaned back, watching until Lainey bit into the sandwich.

She'd have said she wasn't hungry, but the combination of fresh chicken salad on what had to be home-baked wheat bread would tempt any appetite. "Delicious," she said around a generous mouthful. "How did you know this was my favorite?"

Katie chuckled. "Homemade food is always comforting when you're having trouble, ain't so? And I remembered you liked chicken. And chocolate." She put a huge slab of brownie on the plate.

"Guilty," Lainey said. She glanced toward Aunt Rebecca's still figure. "It seems wrong to sit here enjoying my food when Aunt Rebecca is so ill, though."

"That is nonsense, and she would be the first one to tell you so." Katie's round face grew serious. "You must take care of yourself so you can take care of her, ain't so?"

"You sound like Aunt Rebecca," she said softly, remembering how her great-aunt always seemed to have a store of solid common sense to share.

"Ja." Katie's smile was reminiscent. "I always thought Aunt Rebecca was exactly what an Amish woman should be, so maybe that's not surprising."

Seeming satisfied that Lainey was going to do as she was told in regard to her lunch, Katie set the basket on the floor and took up the bag. In a moment, scraps of brightly-colored fabric were spread on her dark green skirt.

"What are you making?" Lainey forked up potato salad, enjoying the crisp contrast of pickles and celery combined with the potato and egg.

"Chust piecing the patches for a quilt." Katie's fingers moved dexterously, rearranging the pieces into a square. "Sometimes I use the treadle machine to do the piecing, but I always like to have a project I can work on when I'm sitting."

"It's a log cabin design, isn't it?" Lainey had always been fascinated by quilts, loving the complex patterns and use of color.

"Ja. For my oldest granddaughter's birthday. She's going to be eight already, and such a little *schnickle-fritz.* Always into mischief." Katie's smile suggested she didn't mind that in the least.

"Aunt Rebecca tried to teach me to quilt when I was here." The memory slipped into her mind, making her smile. "I'm afraid I wasn't very good at sitting still, but I did love arranging the blocks."

"A nine-patch, was it?" Katie asked. "She taught me, and that's the first one I made."

Lainey nodded. They'd gone in the buggy to a shop outside town where a pair of Amish sisters ran a quilting business. If you needed anything for quilting, Aunt Rebecca had said, that's where you went.

"Lorena and Lovina," she said abruptly as the names came back to her.

"Ach, imagine you remembering them," Katie said. "Aunt Rebecca got all her fabric from them. She still does, though I think she must have enough for a dozen quilts in the chest in the back bedroom."

"I was fascinated by the rows of fabric. The colors...it was like being in the middle of a rainbow." She'd run from one to another, unable to make up her mind.

Katie nodded as if she understood. Then, without a word, she put the row of fabric pieces she'd been pinning into Lainey's lap and handed her a needle.

Lainey blinked. "You want me to work on your granddaughter's quilt? But I'm not good enough."

"If Rebecca taught you, you know enough," Katie said. "And it's *gut* to keep your hands busy when you're worried. At least then you have something to show for your worrying," she added, her tone practical.

Lainey actually found herself laughing. "If that's the case, I should have a half-dozen quilts done by now." She picked up the pieces and held the needle poised. "Well, we can always rip it out if my stitches are too terrible."

But her sewing wasn't half bad once she started. Thanks to Aunt Rebecca's early tutelage, she'd always been able to do the hemming and mending most of her peers seemed unable to tackle. Tiny, even stitches, she reminded herself.

The routine, repetitive movements were oddly soothing, reminding her of how much she'd always enjoyed the creativity involved in hand arts. Most of her colleagues would dismiss sewing, knitting, crocheting as crafts, insisting they had no place beside the work of a real artist.

But who was to say which was important? Katie's creations might never hang in a gallery, but they clothed her family in garments made by her own loving hands.

They worked in silence for some time, but there was nothing either boring or uncomfortable about it. Lainey glanced at her great-aunt. It seemed to her that Aunt Rebecca had relaxed somewhat, her face turned slightly toward them instead of squarely on the pillow. The room was oddly peaceful.

"Zeb came to see me this morning," she said abruptly. Would Katie have known about his intent?

"Ja?" Katie looked up, her expression guarded. "What did he want?"

Lainey shrugged. "The same as yesterday, I suppose. He just tried a different approach this time. Ella and Thomas came with him, and she brought me food." She cast a rueful glance at the remains of her lunch. If she kept eating everything her Amish relatives pushed on her, she'd gain twenty pounds while she was here.

"Ella's a sweet girl," Katie said. "But young

Thomas is so shy it wonders me that he'd come to meet you."

"I don't suppose his grandfather gave him much choice."

"No." Katie was frowning. "He brought up this business about the power of attorney, did he? I wish he'd leave well enough alone."

"He thinks Aunt Rebecca should have appointed him." She turned in her chair so she couldn't miss Katie's expression. "Is that what you think, too?"

"No." Katie's response was so prompt and firm that Lainey couldn't doubt her sincerity. "Not Zeb. He's too set on his own way." She looked at Lainey, her expression troubled. "But there are other relatives."

Lainey's heart sank a little. Despite Katie's friendliness, she must agree that Lainey wasn't the person for the job.

"I told Zeb I'm going to do what Aunt Rebecca wanted." If that came out sounding a little belligerent, she couldn't seem to help it. "All I can do is my best."

Katie studied her for a long moment. Then she nodded. "*Ja.* All right." She smiled and patted Lainey's hand, but Lainey thought the smile held a tinge of doubt. "Then I will help you as best I can."

"Thank you." Her throat tightened. Maybe that wasn't a wholehearted endorsement, but at this point, she'd take any support she could find.

THE REALITY OF the situation had begun to sink in by the time Lainey was headed back to the house late that afternoon, and she was already having second thoughts despite Katie's promise of help.

As usual, she'd acted on impulse, letting Zeb's antagonism push her into making a decision. Was she ever going to learn?

Lainey pulled the car to the curb in front of Miller's and got out, pausing for a moment as memories crowded in. She had been allowed to walk to the store on her own the summer she'd stayed with her great-aunt, but usually she'd come with Meredith and Rachel, intent on the purchase of candy—real, old-fashioned penny candy, scooped into a small brown paper bag from the glass case.

The store looked larger than she'd remembered, but it still had pots of flowers on either side of the front door and a hitching rail at the side where Amish buggies could be parked. She touched a deep burgundy mum with her fingers, releasing its spicy scent, and went on into the store.

Lainey paused for a moment inside the door, orienting herself. Groceries were on the right, as always, but the left side of the store had been expanded. It was filled with handcrafted items to delight the heart of a tourist. Faceless Amish dolls, quilted place mats and table runners, even a few hooked rugs crowded the counters. The upper shelves held wooden items like napkin holders and even a small train.

The deep, saturated colors of a quilted table runner drew her, but she resisted the impulse and turned into the grocery aisle. Before she could pick up a box of cereal, a voice called her name.

"Lainey? It is you. I heard you were coming back to look after your great-aunt. It's wonderful *gut* to see you."

Anna Miller looked much as she had twenty years ago, with a white apron over a dark blue Amish dress and a wide smile on her round face. The face might be a little rounder, the hair a bit more gray, the curves more generous, but Anna Miller hadn't changed much.

"Mrs. Miller." Lainey walked quickly to the back counter. "I'd have known you anywhere. How are you?"

"Anna, please. You're a grown-up now, ain't so? But you still have a look of that little girl we knew." Her cheerful face sobered. "I'm afraid it's a sad business that brought you back to us."

Lainey nodded. Obviously all of Deer Run knew who she was and why she was here. They probably knew what she'd had for supper last night. "I wish I'd come sooner."

She blinked, a little surprised at herself. With everyone else she'd felt defensive on that subject, but with Anna, one had the sense that, like Aunt Rebecca, she wouldn't judge.

"You're here now, that's what counts. How is your dear aunt today?" Anna leaned on the counter, seeming ready for a long chat.

"I don't think there was much change from yesterday." Her throat tightened. Aunt Rebecca's hands had always been so busy—stitching or stirring or comforting a child. It had seemed wrong to see them lying lax on the white hospital sheet.

"It's hard to see someone we love chust lying there." Seeming to read her mind, Anna reached across the counter to pat Lainey's hand. "But with a stroke, sometimes it takes time for the brain and body to heal. Don't give up hope."

"I won't." That was another thing that was easy to say but perhaps not so easy to do. What if this went on day after day, week after week? What would she do then?

"We are all praying for her," Anna said softly. "She is in God's hands."

Lainey's throat was too tight for her to do anything but nod.

"Ach, I'm talking away and not helping you with your shopping. You aren't here for penny candy this time, ain't so?" Anna's eyes twinkled, and she gestured toward the glass-enclosed case at the end of the counter. The top part contained a variety of obviously homemade baked goods, while below there was the familiar array of bubble gum, Swedish fish, and lollipops.

"No, I think I'll pass on that this time. We used to be awful pests at picking out what we wanted, it seems to me."

"You and Meredith and Rachel," Anna said. "You've talked to them since you came back?"

"Just briefly. They came over for a little while last night. It was nice to see them after such a long time."

Nice, but odd. Maybe even a bit awkward. What

did you say to people you hadn't seen in twenty years?

"You were always together that summer, ain't so? It's quite a reunion, with first Rachel coming back to Deer Run and now you. Meredith never did leave, what with taking care of her mother and all." Anna shook her head, a mournful look sitting oddly on her cheerful face. "I won't say Margo King was a pleasant woman, but it was terrible, her being killed and Meredith coming that close to losing her own life as well."

The words jolted, and Lainey could only stare at her. "I didn't know. What happened to Meredith's mother? An accident?" She envisioned a car smash-up, with Meredith barely surviving. But Meredith had seemed well enough last night.

Anna shook her head. "They didn't tell you? Well, it would be a lot to take in, and you having plenty of worries on your plate as it is. No, Margo was murdered, and Meredith nearly so, and all because of poor Aaron Mast's death that summer you were here. If Rachel hadn't come back, maybe we'd never—"

Her words cut off abruptly as the bell on the door jangled. Two women came into the store—one tall, angular and businesslike, the other so fair and frail that she looked as if a breath would blow her away.

Lainey's gaze crossed that of the taller woman and met a look so malevolent that she was reminded of Zeb Stoltzfus for an instant. Apparently this was yet another person who didn't think she should be here. Lainey gripped the edge of the counter and managed a pleasant smile. She wouldn't let herself be unnerved by a stranger's hostility.

Anna, after standing motionless for a moment, came from around the counter and went quickly to take the blonde woman's hand. "Laura, it is *sehr gut* to see you. I didn't know that you were home from… home already."

Lainey watched them, surprised by what seemed embarrassment underneath Anna's hearty welcome. Laura, she repeated the name, memories coming back from the distant recesses of her mind. Laura had been a teenager that summer Lainey had spent here. Pretty, popular…what had happened to her? Her face was still beautiful, but thin and somehow empty-looking. She stood motionless next to the other woman like a doll.

"Yes, Laura is home." The other woman's tone was brisk. "She's doing very well, aren't you, Laura?"

Laura nodded, and the resemblance to a mechanical doll increased.

"We're glad to hear it." Anna's hearty tone didn't ring quite true, Lainey thought. "And look who else has come home to Deer Run?" She waved an ample arm at Lainey. "Here's little Lainey Colton, all grown up. Lainey, you maybe wouldn't remember Laura Hammond. And Jeannette Walker. She runs the bed-and-breakfast across the street from your aunt's house."

Lainey nodded. "The Willows, of course. It's lovely." The front yard and flower beds were manicured to within an inch of their lives, and the large Victorian house was immaculately kept up.

Just the same, she wouldn't say she'd look forward to staying there. It was a bit on the formal side for her.

It was time for Jeannette to say that she was glad to see Lainey, or to ask about her aunt. She did neither. Instead she handed a list to Anna.

"Those are the things Laura would like. We won't wait. You can have them delivered to Laura's house."

"She's not staying with you, then?" Anna seemed to be trying to untangle something in her mind.

"No." Jeannette snapped off the word. She gave Lainey a cool nod. "We'll be going. Come along, Laura." She touched the woman's arm.

Laura turned obediently and moved toward the door. But before she left she glanced back. She gave Lainey a long look, her forehead creasing as if with an effort to remember.

When the door closed behind them, Anna let out her breath in a whoosh. "Ach, I am so clumsy. But there seems nothing to say around the woman that won't bring up things that are better left unsaid. At least she didn't recognize you."

"Who? Laura?" Jeannette had certainly known who Lainey was, regardless of her actual words.

And Laura? Well, Lainey didn't know what to make of Laura, but one thing struck her. Her fingers itched to draw that lovely, empty face, and she had a sense that she had drawn it before.

"You don't remember?" Anna looked at her questioningly. "I shouldn't say—" She let that trail off.

"I think you'd better," Lainey said briskly. "I can't go around Deer Run walking on eggshells, not knowing who I'm going to offend next."

Anna shook her head. "I can't tell you all of it. Not about the part that happened when you were here. You'll have to hear that from Meredith and Rachel. But Laura…the reason I was surprised to see her is that she's been in a mental hospital for more than a month. And she was there because it was her husband who killed Meredith's mother."

Lainey's mind spun. Laura's husband a killer? Meredith's mother his victim? That didn't make sense.

And the thing that made the least sense of all was Anna's implication that the crime had its roots in something that had happened that long-ago summer.

Well, one thing was certain. She'd have to talk to Rachel and Meredith again, and soon.

JAKE SUSPECTED LAINEY wasn't going to appreciate an unannounced visit from him this evening. On the other hand, if he'd called her first, she could so easily have made an excuse.

He'd made up his mind to drive over after supper. He didn't want this decision put off any longer. Having a client's affairs in disarray pounded on his nerves like a jackhammer. He might be relaxed and informal in the rest of his life, but when it came to his profession, he dotted the *i*'s and crossed the *t*'s. The school buddies who saw him as a typical good old boy would be surprised.

Only six o'clock, and it was growing dark already, with lights appearing in the houses and shops along Main Street. Fall was drawing in, no matter how nice the weather had been.

A string of orange pumpkin lights decorated the house he was passing, and in the next yard the sheet of a makeshift ghost fluttered from the branch of an oak tree. Halloween wasn't until next week, but each year the decorations started earlier and grew more elaborate. The adults, it seemed, had taken over a holiday that used to be for kids.

There were no Halloween decorations at Rebecca's house, of course. But every kid in town knew there'd still be whoopee pies waiting if you knocked on Rebecca's door. Not this year. The thought depressed him.

He parked at the curb and got out. The glow of a gas lamp came from the front windows, so Lainey must be there.

He toyed with the thought of what she'd do for Halloween if she were back in St. Louis. A party, no doubt. She'd go as a gypsy. Or a witch. Either of those suited the somewhat wild quality of her beauty.

He reached the porch, raised his hand to knock, and nearly hit Lainey in the face as she swung the door open and charged through. For a moment both of them froze, probably equally startled.

"Sorry." He lowered his arm, trying to look harmless. "I didn't come to attack, honest."

"My fault. I was just going out." The way she said it invited him to leave.

"I'll just take a few minutes of your time." And then he could cross this job off his list and move on to a consideration of who would best care for both Rebecca and her property.

Lainey stared at him, maybe deciding whether or not to make an issue out of his unscheduled visit. Finally she shrugged and turned away from the door. "You may as well come in, I guess."

Not a very gracious invitation, but he'd take it. He stepped inside quickly, before she could change her mind.

Lainey headed into the living room, and he followed. She slipped the handbag strap from her shoulder and tossed the bag onto the table next to Rebecca's favorite chair. "You might have called."

"Sorry." He raised his eyebrows, feeling an urge to annoy her. "Have a hot date?"

For an instant he thought she'd snap at him, and then a reluctant grin tugged at her lips. "So far the only males I know in Deer Run are Uncle Zeb and young Thomas. Not exactly eligible, either of them."

"You know me," he pointed out. "I'm generally considered eligible."

"And that's according to the local newspaper, from what Aunt Rebecca said in one of her letters. Most eligible bachelor in the county, or something like that." Lainey looked as if she felt she'd scored.

"Ouch. I hoped Rebecca didn't know anything about it." He grimaced. "How I let myself be talked into that idiotic contest I can't see."

"Someone caught you in a weak moment, no doubt," she said.

"Something like that. Well, much as I enjoy having my follies paraded to the immediate world, maybe we'd best get down to business, so you can meet your date."

"I planned to drop in on Rachel. Or Meredith." She shook her head slightly, as if to clear it. "I'm not sure. There's something I need to find out from them."

Lainey's eyebrows drew together, and she raised one hand to press her fingertips between them, as if to clear her thoughts. The urge to annoy her left him abruptly.

"What's wrong?" He took a step closer, surprised by the strength of his concern.

Lainey blinked, seeming to make an effort to focus. "I was going to ask Meredith or Rachel, but actually I guess you would know it, too. What does the death of Meredith's mother have to do with the summer I spent here when I was ten?"

He hadn't expected that, and maybe he should have. Once she was back in Deer Run, Lainey was bound to hear about the events that had been a nine-days-wonder just a month ago. Not enough happened in Deer Run to eclipse something as dramatic as murder, attempted murder and suicide.

"I can, yes," he said slowly, trying to think how to frame the story. "What did you hear about it? And how?" Obviously not from Rachel or Meredith, or she wouldn't have been ready to seek them out tonight.

"Sit down, for goodness' sake." Lainey waved a hand toward the rocker that was drawn up close to Rebecca's seat.

He obeyed. They were practically knee to knee, sitting in the two rockers. Rebecca always liked to have her visitors close to her, especially as her hearing worsened in recent years.

"Well?" he asked, a little too aware of how near she was—enough that her elusive, exotic scent touched him.

Lainey shrugged. "I don't see why it matters, but I was in Miller's Store today when two women came in—Jeannette Walker and Laura Hammond."

Jake sent a startled glance out the front windows to the Willows, which sat diagonally across the street. "Laura? Laura's back in town?"

She nodded. "I thought she looked unwell, and after they left, Anna told me why. She said Laura had been in a psychiatric facility. That her husband had killed Meredith's mother." Her eyes grew shadowed. "She said it had something to do with that summer I was here."

How much to tell her? Maybe he'd have been better off not to interrupt her visit to Meredith and Rachel. They'd do a better job of this than he would.

"Well?" She interrupted his thoughts. "Is it true?"

"More or less. How much do you remember about the summer you were here?"

She considered. "I remember a lot about some things, not much about others. I've started to remember more about Meredith and Rachel since I talked to them last night. But there are holes."

"Natural enough. You left here, went back to your normal life. I stayed here, but I still don't remember much about the summer I was ten." He grinned. "Except that I probably spent most of it playing basketball."

"The years do run together. But..." She frowned. "I should remember more about that summer, I'd think, because it was the only one I lived here."

He didn't know whether that theory was true or not. "What makes one thing stay in your memory and another fade? I can remember every single detail of a Saturday afternoon I worked on a science project with my dad and nothing at all about the class I was in."

She gave him a look. "That must gratify your teacher. Anyway, just tell me. Don't assume I know anything."

"That makes it harder. The important thing about that summer was a romance between Laura Mitchell, as she was then, and an Amish boy, Aaron Mast. Ruffled the feathers of both sets of parents, I suppose."

Lainey nodded, looking a little surprised. "I remember him. Blond, blue eyes." She smiled suddenly at whatever it was she saw in her memory. "He was our knight."

"You recall the game you girls played, then."

"Bits and pieces. We made up a kind of fantasy world, and the three of us played it all that summer. Aaron was the noble knight, and Laura...of course.

Laura was the beautiful princess." Her eyes lit with the memory, and for an instant her face was the face of the little girl she'd been. "Everyone wanted to marry the princess, but she had eyes only for Aaron."

"That's it, from what I heard from Meredith and Rebecca." He hesitated. "Do you remember how it ended?"

"Ended? I went away. My mother came, out of the blue, and took me with her. I didn't even have time to say goodbye to people." Lainey's words were underlined with resentment and something else...resignation, was it?

"Surely you must have heard that Aaron died—drowned in the pond back by the dam." He nodded toward the rear of the house, seeing in his mind's eye the stretch of lawn, the narrow belt of brambles and tall grass, and then the strip of woods that bordered the stream where it tumbled over Parson's Dam—only three feet high, but deadly when a day or two of rain turned it into something like a riptide.

Lainey put her hand to her head. "I...I don't think so." Her face paled. "How could I have forgotten something that terrible?"

She looked so white and distressed that he reached out and clasped her hand. Her fingers curled around his.

"Apparently the day after his death your mother took you away. You weren't here to have any reminders."

"Even so." She seemed to realize she was clinging to his hand, and she let go, drawing back in her chair. "But I still don't understand. How could that have anything to do with Meredith's mother's death?"

This was the complicated bit, trying to piece the story together. "I guess it began when Rachel came back to Deer Run in the spring. She and Meredith got together, and they started remembering things from that summer. And they started asking questions."

She nodded, and it surprised him that she seemed to find that normal. "They would, wouldn't they? It seems impossible to me, coming into it cold, that Aaron could have drowned that way. He was sensible, and a lot more responsible than most teenagers. He even warned me about the dam one day when he found me down by the creek. How could he have an accident there?"

"You have a lot in common with those two, you know that? You're reacting just the way Rachel and Meredith did. So, as I say, they started asking questions."

She looked pleased at being told she was like the two girls who'd been her friends. She brushed a strand of thick, curling hair back from her face, and again he wanted to touch it, to feel it twist around his fingers.

"What did they find out?" She seemed to take it for granted that they would have uncovered something.

"At first it seemed they'd found a reason for Aaron to have killed himself. As you can imagine, that opened up his family's grief all over again. But they dug deeper and learned that someone had been with him at the dam that night. That it wasn't an accident or suicide. That knowledge nearly cost Meredith her life."

Lainey considered his words, staring down at her hands, clasped in her lap. Then she looked up. "Laura's husband, I understand. Victor Hammond. I remember him now. Kind of pudgy, anxious, eager to please. One of Laura's followers. Are you seriously saying he killed Aaron? And why Meredith's mother?"

"Margo King had seen or heard something at the dam that night, and she made the mistake of letting Victor know she had. She was drowned, same as Aaron. And when Meredith got too close, he tried the same to her."

Lainey shuddered. "Thank heaven he failed."

Jake nodded. He'd been there, that day, arriving with the police and Zach, Meredith's fiancé, in time to save her. He didn't like remembering how close it had been.

"No wonder Laura looked as if she's…" Lainey hesitated, apparently considering the word. "Empty. That's how she looks. Empty."

"That describes it pretty well. If she knew, and I think she must have at some point, she wasn't strong enough to cope with the knowledge."

"Poor woman. And poor Meredith, losing her mother that way. I'm surprised they didn't say something about it last night."

He considered. "It's a pretty complicated story to hit you with the first time they see you after twenty years. But I'd guess they're eager to talk to you about it. They even have the scrapbook you kept that summer. You were quite an artist for a ten-year-old."

Her gaze slid away from his, as if she were embarrassed. "Kid stuff. Not enough talent for the real world."

He wasn't sure what to say to that comment. It was revealing, and he suspected she'd regret it if he got too close.

Maybe she thought so, too, because her expression changed and her chin came up. "You didn't come here to tell me this story, Jake. So why did you come?"

Jake had to do some rapid reordering of his thoughts. "Right, that. I was hoping you'd come to a decision about Rebecca's wishes, so we can move ahead."

Her eyebrows lifted. "You mean you hope I've decided to give up the power of attorney."

"No." It had sounded that way, hadn't it? Why was he so inept in dealing with this particular woman? "Not at all. I just need a decision, one way or the other."

"Fine, you've got it." Her face firmed. "I told Zeb Stoltzfus today, so I'll tell you. Aunt Rebecca wanted me to do this, so I'm doing it."

"Right." She wouldn't be leaving, then. He had a certain sneaking pleasure in the thought. "That's all I needed to know." He stood. "We'll go from there, then."

"Really? No arguments? No pointing out that I don't know anything about Rebecca's way of life?"

She stood, which put her very close to him. "Aren't you going to tell me that I'm…" She looked up into his face, and their gazes caught. She seemed to lose track of what she was saying.

And he didn't think he could utter a coherent sentence to save him. His eyes traced the line of her cheek, the curve of her lips. It was all he could do to prevent his hand from following along. She leaned toward him, as if some force of gravity pulled them together.

With an effort of will and muscle, he drew back away from her.

"Right," he said, not pleased to discover that he was breathless or that he was repeating himself. Couldn't he think of something else to say? "I…I'll have to talk to you about business in a day or two if Rebecca doesn't improve. In the meantime, you can refer to me anyone who has a question about finances."

"Yes, all right." She turned and walked a few steps away. Maybe she felt the need to put some distance between them as well. "Thank you, Jake. And thank you for telling me."

She'd thanked him twice in one meeting. That had to be a record. Now he'd better get out of here before he did something foolish, like checking for himself how those lips tasted.

CHAPTER FIVE

IF SHE HAD to worry, Lainey decided after Jake left, she ought to be obsessing over how to manage Aunt Rebecca's care, now that she'd committed herself. Instead, she found herself going over and over that strange story Jake had told her about Aaron Mast's death.

Trying to push it out of her mind, she finished putting away her supper dishes, turning on the kitchen gaslight with what had already become an automatic motion. Strange, how quickly one adapted to the lack of electricity. The only continuing issue was charging her cell phone and notebook.

The cell she'd been keeping charged up with the car adaptor, but the notebook was a more difficult problem. She'd actually found herself eyeing the electrical outlets in the hospital room today. It might have been logical, but somehow she couldn't bring herself to do it with Aunt Rebecca lying motionless in the hospital bed.

Both Meredith and Rachel had urged her to use their homes like her own when they'd left last night, but that seemed an imposition. She might have to get over that feeling if things went on as they were for much longer.

Lainey glanced out the window toward Meredith's house. The front room was dark, but a light was on in the kitchen. She couldn't see the other side of the house, of course, where Meredith had mentioned her office was.

Why hadn't they said something to her about Aaron Mast's death and its terrible aftermath? Perhaps the memory of Meredith's mother's death was still too fresh and painful for her to talk about. It was hard to imagine the past coming back to haunt one in so dangerous a form. Lainey had plenty of things to regret in her past, but certainly nothing dangerous.

Well, she now had the story from Jake, so she wouldn't need to bring it up to Meredith and Rachel. If they did decide to confide, that was fine, but unlikely.

Lainey closed a cabinet door, glancing around the kitchen to be sure everything was as tidy as her great-aunt would have left it. At first glance it looked like any slightly old-fashioned kitchen. Only a closer inspection showed the lack of electricity. Whatever reasons the Amish had, and she had to confess she'd never looked into the subject, they had been ingenious in adapting to other means of cooking, light and heat. Batteries, generators and gas appliances seemed to fill the gaps except, of course, for things like computers and televisions. But then, maybe those were the very things the Amish preferred not to have in their homes.

Her cell phone rang as she walked into the living room. Lainey picked it up, careful to check the caller. Her stomach clenched into a hard knot. She'd thought of regrets, and one of the biggest ones was calling. Phillip.

Lainey's immediate instinct was to switch off the phone. This was the first time he'd attempted to contact her since everything blew apart.

Still, she wouldn't be a coward. She clicked to answer.

"Lainey? Where on earth are you?" Phillip sounded aggrieved. "I couldn't find you."

Anger swept away the nerves at speaking to him again. "You can't have tried very hard. This is the first time you've called."

"I had to be careful. You should know that. But I had Bobby check your apartment, and no one had seen you there."

Bobby was his assistant, a young man so quiet it was easy to forget he existed. His job was to keep Phillip's life running smoothly, and in this case, apparently that meant managing her.

"I'm out of town." She hadn't the faintest desire to let him know where.

"Where?" His voice softened to the caressing tone she knew so well. "I've missed you, Lainey. We have to talk."

"So you can tell more lies?" It was surprisingly easy to harden her heart against that voice. Maybe she was cured.

"Lainey, don't say that." Now he sounded hurt.

"How is your wife?" she asked deliberately.

"At home with her family. She doesn't want me back. She never did. It was just her typical play-acting. And you don't need to sound so holier-than-thou. You…"

Lainey stopped listening. She doubled-checked her emotions. Phillip blamed his wife. He blamed Lainey. He blamed the media. He'd never think of blaming himself.

And she'd imagined she loved him. Yes, she was definitely cured. She wasn't even angry with him any longer, just deeply ashamed of herself.

When he stopped for breath she spoke quietly. "Don't ever call me again." She cut the connection.

She sank down into Aunt Rebecca's rocker, the cell phone in her hand. Over. She wouldn't have believed, a week ago, that she could stop loving him so easily. Maybe the dismal truth was that she, like her mother, wasn't capable of lasting love.

She'd barely thought the words when the cell phone sounded. If Phillip thought he could get around her…

She snapped the phone on. "I told you not to call me."

It wasn't Phillip. It was a hoarse whisper, impossible to identify as male or female, pouring out a string of obscenities and threats. Stomach churning, she yanked the phone away from her ear, fumbling to end the call. But not fast enough to keep from hearing one last line.

"You can't hide from me. I know where you are."

Lainey barely kept herself from throwing the phone on the floor. She dropped it on the table instead and wrapped her arms around her body, trying to shove the repellent sound out of her head.

Something brushed against her leg, and she nearly jumped out of her skin. "Cat." She managed a shaky laugh. "Am I glad to see you." She stroked the glossy fur.

The cat arched his back against her hand, turned in a circle, and then leaped to her lap. He kneaded his paws on her legs and then tucked them under him, closing his eyes and purring.

It was amazing, how soothing the sound and the warm weight proved to be. Lainey leaned back, suddenly exhausted. The house was quiet, too quiet. Cat's presence, the sense of something else warm and alive nearby, was comforting.

The cat's head jerked up, ears pricking.

"What? Can't we relax for more than a minute? Do you hear a mouse?" Soon she'd be expecting him to respond to her questions.

And then she heard it, too…the faintest rustle of sound outside. Tensing, she peered through the nearest window, realizing that with the light on, she might as well be on a stage.

Something struck the window. She jumped, the cat dug his claws into her jeans and flew off her lap, and there was a rattle outside, as if hail struck the porch.

It wasn't until a second window was hit that she identified the noise. Thrown corn. Halloween was fast approaching. It had to be kids, out for some early mischief. She could follow their progress along the side of the house by watching the direction of the cat's gaze. His hearing was obviously keener than hers.

Nothing to worry about, but she wasn't going to make herself a target, either. She went quickly from window to window, pulling down the shades, masking herself from the night.

Then, when that didn't bring the measure of assurance she wanted, she double-checked the front and back doors, making sure no one could get in.

Lainey paused, hand on the kitchen door, looking at the cat, and her certainty drained away. She hadn't let the cat in, had she? He'd done his mysterious appearance act again. If he could get in…

She stared at the cat. "I wish you could talk. How are you getting in here?"

And more importantly, if the cat could get in, what else could?

Dr. Yvonne Morrissey frowned a little as she checked Aunt Rebecca's chart, and Lainey found herself wishing Katie had stayed a bit longer today. If her great-aunt's doctor was about to deliver bad news, some support would be welcome.

But when she turned to Lainey, the woman was smiling again, hazel eyes crinkling. Far younger than Lainey would have expected, Dr. Morrissey had a mop of short brown curls and a pleasantly freckled face that reminded Lainey of a mischievous kid.

"Don't look so worried," she said. "Rebecca's vitals are strong, and I see some signs that she's becoming aware of things around her." She nodded toward Rebecca's face, turned slightly toward Lainey. "You see it, don't you? That's a response to your presence."

"You think she knows it's me?" Lainey couldn't quell the hope that bubbled up at the thought.

"I wouldn't go that far." Dr. Morrissey grew cautious. "There's no way of knowing that, but certainly she realizes someone is with her."

Lainey took her aunt's hand in both of hers. "Still, that is encouraging, isn't it?" She'd have to try to hold on to the good thought instead of focusing on her fears, something she'd done too much of during a long and mostly sleepless night.

The woman nodded, folding her arms as she leaned against the foot of the bed. "I'm making every effort to justify keeping Rebecca here as long as possible, but the hospital is starting to make noises about moving her soon."

"Moving her where?" She shouldn't be surprised, she supposed. Hospitals seemed as eager to rotate patients out as restaurants were to turn their tables quickly.

"Ideally, I'd move her straight to the rehab facility that's attached to the hospital." The doctor gestured vaguely in the direction of the parking lot. "But—"

"But? If that's the best place for her, then that's where she should go." Jake's caution about the lack of insurance or Medicare was a burr in her thoughts. Still, surely they could find the money somewhere if that was the issue. "If it's a matter of money—"

The doctor held up her hand to stop the flow of argument. "Not entirely that. All of us are aware of the special circumstances involved in treating our Amish patients. In addition, Rebecca will have to be a bit farther along before she can benefit from rehab."

"And if she's not?" It was better to know all the options, she supposed.

"Then a nursing home, I suppose." Dr. Morrissey shrugged. "It's not ideal, but it's probably the only solution."

Everything in her rebelled at the thought. "We can't give up and do nothing." She patted her great-aunt's hand, hoping she could sense the reassurance. "How long before you have to move her?"

"Probably the beginning of next week." The woman looked unhappy but resigned. "I'll send a social worker in to talk to you about the possibilities. That's really their department, not mine." She leaned over Rebecca, clasping her hand for a moment. "I'll stop in to see you tomorrow, Rebecca. Meantime, I know your niece is taking good care of you."

If the doctor knew that, she knew more than Lainey did. Well, all she could do was try. She'd committed herself to this, and she had to go through with it.

By the time Lainey had finished with the social worker and left the hospital, her doubts had reached epic proportion. The doctor might assure her that they understood dealing with Amish patients, but that didn't seem to make a difference to what the business office expected. Somehow, she was going to have to manage a payment to the hospital in order to take Rebecca out, to say nothing of another payment to get her aunt into the rehab facility. The amount mentioned was easily out of Lainey's range.

She'd have to go to Jake. There were no two ways about it. He'd have to be persuaded to find a way to access Aunt Rebecca's assets, and quickly.

JAKE PICKED UP his jacket and the tie he'd shed once his father and their receptionist had left. It was time for him to get out of here, as well. He'd spent so much time dealing with Rebecca's affairs that he'd fallen behind on other work.

He was just reaching for the light switch when the outside door opened. Lainey looked at him with a question in her eyes.

"Are you leaving?"

He shook his head, tossing jacket and tie onto the nearest flat surface. "Not if you need to see me. Come in."

He went ahead of her into his office to switch on the light, turned to her, and took a second look. Purple shadows marred the delicate skin under Lainey's eyes, and her shoulders sagged.

"You look tired." The words were out before he considered that they might be ill-advised.

Her chin snapped up. "No woman wants to be told that she looks tired."

The flash of anger was evidence of frayed nerves, he'd guess. "Sorry," he said cautiously. "I didn't mean—"

But Lainey was already shaking her head. "No, I'm the one who's sorry. You're right. I look tired because I am tired." She stopped. Then, seeming to think something more was warranted, she continued. "I didn't sleep well, that's all."

Concerned about her great-aunt? Or just the stress of her new responsibility? He gestured to the padded visitor's chair.

Lainey sat, dropping her bag to the rug. He perched on the edge of the desk, not wanting to have it between them.

He studied her face. She was looking down at her hands, and now that she was here she seemed to have forgotten why she'd come.

"Worry about Rebecca keeping you up?" He kept his voice neutral, sensing that this might be a sore point, since he'd been a bit too obvious that he didn't approve of Rebecca's choice initially.

She glanced up, eyes startled. "Aunt Rebecca? No, that wasn't…" She let that peter out, maybe feeling that it was leading in a direction she didn't want to go. Then she shrugged. "If you must know, I've been bothered by a couple of crank calls lately. Stupid, to let that keep me awake."

"On your cell phone?" Well, obviously. There wasn't another phone in the house.

Lainey nodded. "I can't imagine how people like that get cell phone numbers."

"They probably just dial at random." But he was sure there was more to this that she was saying. She didn't seem the type of person to be thrown off balance by a chance crank call.

"I suppose." She looked unconvinced.

"You could change your number, if it's really bothering you. Or at least check the number before you answer."

"I won't let some anonymous crank make me change my number." She had a flash of spirit at the thought. "And of course I normally do look to see who's calling. I just thought a…a friend was calling me back."

She looked uncomfortable enough at that to make him wonder. A boyfriend? He could hardly ask that, no matter how curious he was.

"I suppose you have a lot of people missing you back in St. Louis."

"A lot? No. I haven't been there all that long." She seemed to turn inward for a moment. "I may not go back at all, at least not to stay."

"But you said you hadn't been there very long." He tried to decipher what lay behind the wary expression on her face.

Lainey lifted her hands, palms up. "Maybe I get bored. Maybe I'm as much a gypsy as my mother was. Anyway, that's hardly why I'm here."

Jake bit back the urge to ask her about her family. That last comment was plainly a no-trespassing sign. "What can I do for you?"

"I need to know how Aunt Rebecca stands financially."

He was still trying to assess her meaning when she went on.

"Not to the penny, of course. But I talked to the doctor today, and then the social worker stopped by. There's going to be pressure soon to move Aunt Rebecca somewhere else."

"I knew that would happen, but I didn't expect it this early." He had hoped Rebecca would regain consciousness and control of her own affairs before it came to this.

"Her doctor was very nice." Lainey seemed momentarily distracted. "I must confess, I didn't expect Aunt Rebecca to have a young, female doctor. I pictured someone grandfatherly. Anyway, Dr. Morrissey says that she can justify keeping my aunt where she is a little longer, but by sometime next week, we have to make a change. To a nursing facility if she's not improved, or to a rehab place if she is. Either way, it can be costly, from what the social worker told me."

He nodded, sliding off the desk. "Let me grab your great-aunt's files. I have them right here, and I'll go over them with you." He glanced at the clock. "Unless—"

"I don't want to keep you after hours," Lainey said. "Just give me the files, and I'll look over them tonight."

"I wasn't trying to skip out on you," he said mildly. "We'll have to go over this together before you can make any decisions anyway. I was just going to suggest we do this over supper."

Lainey looked instantly wary. Before her lips

could form the *no* he saw hovering, he went on quickly.

"A business dinner on the firm, of course. I'm sure you've had an even longer day than I have."

She hesitated for a moment and then shrugged. "I suppose so. Where do you want to go?"

He considered. "Let's try the Stone Grill. It's out on the edge of town and shouldn't be too busy on a weeknight. We'll want a bit of privacy and space to spread out if we're going to get through this bunch." He hefted the two thick files.

Again the hesitation. What, did she think he was Jack the Ripper? But finally she nodded.

"All right. I have my own car, so I'll follow you."

A business dinner, he reminded himself as he followed her out, aware of a totally misplaced elation that he'd persuaded her to have dinner with him. Just a business dinner.

THERE WAS REALLY no reason why she shouldn't have dinner with Jake. Lainey kept saying that all the way to the edge of town.

When they'd reached the restaurant, a small cement block building with a gravel parking lot, she had her doubts. It looked like a dive. But the inside was bright and clean, the rear wall of the dining room decorated with a mural of fields and farms and an Amish buggy bowling along a dirt road.

The hostess, a fortyish blonde, took one look at Jake and rounded the counter. "Jake! We haven't seen you in an age. Come here, you." She grabbed him in a hug, pressing her rather obvious attractions against him.

"Hey, Wendy." He disentangled himself, color deepening. "Nice to see you, too. Listen, can you give us a quiet table? We need to work."

"Anything for you, Jakey." She leaned across the counter with an ample display of leg and retrieved two menus. "Right this way."

Bemused, Lainey followed her to a table in a small alcove, well away from the few other diners.

"Here you go." The woman—Wendy—swished the menus in front of them, resting her hand on Jake's shoulder. "Your server will be right with you."

When the woman had finally swayed off to her station, Lainey raised her eyebrows at him. "Jakey?" she asked.

"Call me that at your peril." He grinned. "Sorry about Wendy. She's a bit…overly enthusiastic."

"You could say that." Her momentary cynicism, if that's what it was, vanished in the face of his beguiling grin. The warmth that swept over her sounded all her alarms. Business, she reminded herself. "About the papers…" she said.

"Sure thing." Jake pulled out the file and fanned its contents in front of her. "Let's order first and then we can talk."

Lainey nodded, relieved to flip open the menu and remove her attention from Jake's disturbing presence.

Once the preliminaries had been gotten through and they'd placed their orders, Jake turned to the business at hand. Even a cursory glance at the pa-

pers he spread out showed Lainey that she did indeed
need his explanations. He went through her great-
aunt's assets quickly, giving her a bare overview,
she supposed.

"Wait a second," she said, when he'd shoved a list
of leases under her nose. "My great-aunt and uncle
owned all this property?"

He nodded. "I explained that, didn't I? Isaac had
an eye for a deal, buying up land when it came on
the market, renting some, reselling others. I have the
impression it was all kind of a game with him. Certainly they didn't live any differently than any other
Amish. They'd never want to be thought proud."

Lainey nodded. She might not remember a lot, but
she did have a firm sense of the humility that had
governed her great-aunt's life. "It's funny...." She
stopped, not sure she wanted to speak her thoughts
in front of Jake.

"What?" His gaze probed.

Luckily the server arrived with their meals, dis-
tracting him, and by the time he might have followed
up on his question, she was pretending absorption in
her pasta primavera.

She might be able to keep her balance better if she
wasn't so tired. When she'd finally gotten to sleep
last night she'd expected nightmares after the ugly
phone call and the untimely Halloween tricksters.
Instead, her subconscious had reverted to the odd
story Jake had told her.

She eyed him, thinking of what he'd said about
the death that long-ago summer and its tragic after-

math. Intent on his steak, Jake seemed to have given up on business for the moment.

Strange, that she hadn't remembered Aaron Mast's death. Had she known? Surely she would have heard something, no matter how the adults tried to protect her from the tragedy.

The emotions that accompanied the nightmare were still vivid, although the memory was as jumbled as dreams tended to be in the light of day. She'd had a disjointed sense of terror at being alone in the dark, trying to run, and of something following her.

Lainey knew, suddenly, that she was breathing too fast. She glanced up to find Jake studying her face.

"All right?"

"Yes, fine." Her voice was too bright, but it was the best she could do. "Please, finish your steak. The business can wait."

"Okay, no business. Just finish what you started to say before the server came. What's funny?"

She might have known he'd be persistent. She shrugged. "That my mother was actually related to Great-aunt Rebecca. She didn't have a humble bone in her body."

"Maybe it's learned, not inherited. The way I understand it, Rebecca's younger sister left the Amish when she was eighteen and never looked back. By the time your mother was born, she was a long way from being Amish."

"She certainly was." Lainey had long since lost any illusions she might have cherished about her mother. Deanna Colton had been too self-absorbed to notice much of anything about Lainey. "I've never really understood how I ended up here that summer."

Jake's level brows drew together, as if he considered his words. "Rebecca isn't the kind to forget about kin. I suppose she thought you needed her."

"My mother certainly didn't hesitate to ask a favor. She had to put me someplace so she could go on her honeymoon." As she remembered, the honeymoon had lasted longer than the rest of the marriage.

"When I drew up the papers for her, I tried to point out that she hadn't seen you in years. She said that as far as she was concerned, you were her granddaughter. You'd do the right thing."

That left her speechless and struggling. Certainly Rebecca was the closest thing to real family she'd ever had, but she had never imagined Rebecca thought of her in that way.

Granddaughter. The word seemed to spark a flow of warmth in her heart. A sense of belonging that had been missing most of her life.

But she couldn't seem to control the fear that Rebecca might have made a mistake in thinking Lainey would know the right thing to do.

Once the plates were cleared away and the coffee cups refilled, Jake drew the file toward him and shuffled through the contents. "Here's the statement for your great-aunt's savings account. She always kept enough in it to cover the taxes and a little more."

Lainey glanced at the balance, glad to focus on the mundane. "I suppose it might cover enough of the hospital bill to keep them off our backs, but nothing more."

"I suspect you're right, and the trouble is that the property taxes come due the end of the month." Jake grimaced. "Bad timing, but there you are."

Lainey set her cup down before she could spill it. "So soon? I didn't realize."

"You've probably never been in a situation to consider it," he said. "The penalty for late payment isn't very high, so we can put off doing it until January, but no later." He put his hands flat on the papers. Long-fingered, tanned and strong, they looked more like the hands of someone who spent a lot of time outdoors. "The only answer I can see is to sell some of the property. It's not as if Rebecca has any particular attachment to most of it. The question is, which?"

"Not any parcels that are rented to family members. Aunt Rebecca wouldn't want it." That she was sure of. "What else is there?"

Jake studied her face for a moment. Apparently convinced she meant it, he turned to the property list, going down it quickly and making check marks against five or six of them.

"You understand, of course, that the farms are the most valuable. Without considering them, these are the parcels most likely to sell."

Lainey glanced down the list, but the locations and descriptions meant nothing to her. "I suppose I'd better have a look at them before deciding."

Jake nodded. "I'll take you around to see them."

"You don't need to—"

He put his hand over hers on the table. Lainey's breath caught, and she lost the rest of the sentence. She met his eyes, saw them darken, and felt the attraction surge between them, strong and unmistakable. Unmistakable, too, that he felt it just as much as she did.

For a moment neither of them moved. Then Jake seemed to shake himself, like a dog coming out of the water.

"Well." He cleared his throat. "I'll pick you up about one tomorrow, if that works for you. Okay?"

Arguing, she reasoned, would be admitting she… well, never mind. She wouldn't think about that now.

"Fine," she said.

CHAPTER SIX

By THE TIME Lainey reached the house after supper, the sun had slipped behind the ridge. She parked at the curb and got out, feeling as if she'd come home.

Odd. Where was home, exactly? Not the furnished apartment in St. Louis, nearly as anonymous as a hotel room. She'd never felt the need to burden herself with a lot of possessions. Certainly home wasn't with her mother, currently living in Arizona with her eye out for husband number five.

Dismissing the fruitless subject from her mind, Lainey headed for the house. She'd have to visit the hospital in the morning, in order to be free in the afternoon for her appointment with Jake. By then, she should have regained her balance where he was concerned.

It was the height of stupidity to imagine herself attracted to Jake so quickly after the collapse of her last disastrous love. She had no intention of turning into her mother, jumping impulsively from relationship to relationship.

Before Lainey could allow herself to be caught up in that old, familiar battle, she saw Rachel coming toward her across the lawn of the bed-and-breakfast. Lainey paused, smiling.

"I was just on my way to pick up Meredith's mail when I saw you pull up," Rachel said. With her long blond hair drawn back into a single braid and her simple denim jumper, she still looked a bit like the Amish girl she'd once been. "How is Rebecca today?"

"There isn't much change. The doctor thinks the coma might be a little lighter. I hope she's right."

Rachel reached out to touch her arm in sympathy. "I'm sorry. This must be very worrying for you."

"Especially after a talk with the doctor and the social worker today." Lainey grimaced. "I'm sure the Amish have good reasons for not taking Social Security or getting insurance, but it's causing some problems now."

"It's a matter of depending on God and the church, not the government," Rachel said. "I guess it does seem strange when you're not used to it."

"Not to you, I guess," she said, remembering again Rachel's Amish roots. "You obviously feel at home here, even after living away."

Rachel smiled. "I used to envy you all the places you'd been and the things you'd seen, but I didn't find the big wide world quite so great."

"I probably exaggerated my adventures a bit." They hadn't actually seemed that adventurous to her when she'd been constantly starting over at a new school and trying to make new friends. "I envied you and Meredith, as I remember. You seemed to belong here."

Rachel chuckled. "The grass is always greener, in other words." Then she sobered. "About your aunt, though. But if the bills are pressing, you should talk to the bishop. Members of the church district would help. I could take you to see him...."

"No. Or at least, not at the moment," she added quickly. "Aunt Rebecca trusted me with this situation, so I'll try to figure it out. Jake suggests selling some of the property my great-uncle had acquired."

Rachel nodded as if she knew all about it. "I'm sure you can trust Jake. He's a good lawyer, and a good man to have on your side."

Lainey could only hope Jake was, indeed, on her side. She suspected he was as long as she did what he thought was right for Rebecca.

"I take it Meredith is away, since you're picking up her mail?" She had a feeling she'd talked about Jake as much as she ought.

"She went down to Pittsburgh to see her...well, her fiancé, but it hasn't been announced yet. With her mother's death..." Rachel let that trail off, as if wondering whether to embark on explanations.

"I'm glad Meredith found someone." Lainey hesitated, but it only made sense to bring the subject out in the open. "Jake told me. About Meredith's mother, and how it was related to Aaron Mast's death that summer I was here."

Rachel looked relieved. "I was wondering whether

I should explain it to you or not. I didn't want you to worry about it."

"Why would I worry?" The little matter of her persistent nightmares seemed to answer the question. "I just can't understand why I don't remember anything about it."

"You don't?" Rachel's blue eyes widened. "But we were all heartbroken when we found out."

Lainey shrugged. "I left so soon afterward that I guess the move wiped everything else from my thoughts. It would be harder for you and Meredith, being here."

Rachel nodded, but a doubt seemed to linger in her face. "I suppose so. It's still difficult to believe everything that happened. Meredith..." Her voice trembled slightly. "Meredith was nearly killed. If Rebecca hadn't seen her going with Victor toward the dam and come to me about it—" She shivered. "Another few minutes would have been too late."

Rachel was obviously reliving the incident too vividly, and Lainey regretted bringing it up. "I'm sorry," she said, knowing how ineffectual that was.

"Don't be silly," Rachel said quickly. "It's over now, thank goodness." She glanced up at the sound of a door closing across the street, and Lainey followed the direction of her gaze. "But I'm afraid it will never be over for Laura," Rachel said quietly. "That's Laura Hammond, getting into the car with Jeannette Walker."

Lainey nodded. "I ran into them at the store. Anna

introduced me. Or reintroduced me, I guess. Apparently they knew me back then."

She found she was staring at the two women, and tried to force her gaze away. Jeannette had helped Laura into the passenger seat as if she were an invalid. But as she walked around to the driver's side, Laura's door popped open again. She slid out of the car and came running lightly across the street to where they stood watching.

"It looks as if Laura wants to see us," Lainey murmured, not sure how to respond to someone who'd been through what Laura had.

"I hope she's all right." Rachel sounded concerned. "Laura can be…well, a little off-key sometimes."

She couldn't say more, because Laura had reached them already, with Jeannette hurrying after her.

"It is you." Before Lainey could move, Laura had grasped her hand. "I thought it was when I saw you in the store, and now that I see the two of you together, I'm sure."

Lainey could only nod, hoping that was the right response. Up close, the woman's face was oddly youthful, as unlined and beautiful as the face of a girl. It was as if she'd removed herself from the stress of life that usually marked the face of a woman nearing forty.

"It's nice to see you, Laura." Rachel's smile was strained. "You must be happy to be home."

Considering that the woman had been in a mental

institution since her husband's death, Lainey thought that was an understatement.

Jeannette hurried up to them, glancing from one to the other as if she'd like to wish them away. "Come, Laura. I'm ready to drive you back to your house." She put her arm around Laura as if to guide her away. Laura's fingers bit into Lainey's arm.

"Not yet. Don't you see? It's the third one. You are, aren't you?" She turned an appealing face on Lainey.

"Laura remembers the three of us from that summer you spent here," Rachel said, her voice soft. "We've all grown up since then, Laura." She seemed to be trying to placate the woman.

Jeannette grasped Laura's fingers, detaching them from Lainey's arm. "Come along, now, Laura. It's getting late. I'll take you home."

Laura's face clouded. "People keep coming back," she said. She shook her head. "I don't understand."

"It's all right. I'll explain everything." Jeannette patted her shoulder, her voice gentle. "Come along."

"Good night, Laura." Rachel seemed to make an effort to sound normal. "We'll see you again soon."

Jeannette led Laura toward the car, arm around her waist, their heads close together.

Lainey let out a breath she hadn't realized she'd been holding. "That was…odd." To put it mildly.

"Yes. Laura hasn't been well for a long time, and after seeing her husband kill himself—" Rachel shivered. "I'm not sure she ever will be again. Do you remember her at all?"

"A bit, I suppose." It had begun to seem that it

was some failure of hers that she remembered so little from that summer. "Laura is the vague image of a make-believe princess in my mind. Did Aaron's death affect her that badly?" It seemed incredible that a broken teenage romance, even one that ended tragically, should result in such damage to the woman.

"That was apparently the beginning of her problems." Rachel frowned. "There was so much that we didn't know at the time—so much that we just finally learned in the past few months. I sometimes wonder—"

Her words were cut off by the crash and tinkle of broken glass, the sound coming from the rear of Aunt Rebecca's house. For an instant Lainey was too startled to react, and then anger sent her racing around the house.

"Lainey, wait—"

No waiting, and no hiding behind drawn shades in the house. Throwing corn was one thing, but if Halloween pranks had escalated to breaking a window, she was going to call a halt.

Lainey rounded the back corner and stopped, fists clenched, scanning the area. Sure enough, a star-shaped hole marred the bottom pane of the kitchen window. The perpetrator had to be somewhere nearby, surely. But the shed door stood closed as always, and the tall grass beyond it stretched unmarked to the band of trees.

"Where did they go?"

"Maybe around the house," Rachel said, hurrying

on to the far side, where a gravel drive led from the back yard to the road in front.

Lainey joined her, staring uselessly at the empty drive and beyond it at the deserted street. "How could they disappear so fast?"

Rachel shook her head. "If it was a kid, I suppose he threw the rock or whatever it was and then ran. But this is unheard of in Deer Run. Nobody would break Rebecca's window. People love her."

"Somebody did." Lainey spun, scanning the area back toward the dam again. "Do you suppose they could have gotten out of sight in the woods that quickly?"

She took one step in the direction of the path behind Meredith's house, but Rachel grabbed her arm.

"Don't."

Lainey stared at her in surprise, and Rachel's color heightened.

"Sorry. But I don't see how anyone could have gotten that far without our seeing them. And the dam…"

"Has some negative connections for you, obviously." A shiver moved across Lainey's skin. Apparently she wasn't immune to that feeling. "Well, I guess I'd better go in and check on the damage."

"We can probably fit some cardboard over the window for tonight," Rachel said, seeming automatically to include herself in the problem. "I'll send my brother over to repair it properly tomorrow."

"I can call a repairman…." Lainey began, but Rachel shook her head.

"Nonsense. What are neighbors for? Anyone in town would do that for Rebecca."

Lainey fished out the key ring and let them in the back door. As she moved to turn on the lamp over the table, the glass crunched underfoot.

"A rock," Rebecca said, stating the obvious. They both stared at the jagged, golf-ball-size stone that lay on the floor. "It could have been picked up anywhere."

"Like the creek, for instance?" Lainey said.

"I suppose." Rachel went to the closet and fetched a broom and dustpan. "I think you'll find a few cardboard boxes in the hall closet. Rebecca usually kept some there."

They worked together silently, disposing of the broken glass and patching the hole with a square of cardboard.

"There," Rachel said, putting the last strip of tape in place. "That should do to keep out any wildlife until tomorrow." She shot a glance at Lainey. "Are you going to report this to the police?"

Lainey's first impulse was to say yes. No one should be allowed to escalate simple Halloween pranks to the level of destruction of property.

Unfortunately, she couldn't dismiss from her mind that whispering voice on the phone. *I know where you are.*

Impossible. Wasn't it? Still, how extensive would a police response be? She didn't want her problems in St. Louis to become public property in Deer Run.

"I don't think so," she said slowly. "No point in stirring up trouble."

It was always possible that trouble had found her, whether she did any stirring or not.

JAKE MENTALLY RAN through the property list as he drove down Main Street to pick up Lainey. Rebecca was, as many Amish were, rich in land but poor in terms of cash.

He'd already decided on the best property to put on the market. Now he had to convince Lainey to follow his judgment, and this afternoon's little trek would be crucial in that regard.

The truth was that he still didn't know where he stood with the woman. Her attitude toward him seemed to change from moment to moment, and that totally inappropriate flare of attraction he felt for her simply complicated matters.

Business, he told himself. This afternoon was strictly business. Anything else would be both ethically wrong for an attorney and a serious mistake personally. He'd already caused enough problems for one lifetime by plunging into a relationship with someone who didn't share his values.

Jake pulled into the gravel drive and stopped by the front porch. Rachel's younger brother, Benj, a straw hat pushed back on his head, was heading toward the back of the house, a toolbox in one hand. Like most Amish boys in their early teens, he had a look of growing out of his black pants and light blue shirt. Benj raised a hand in greeting and disappeared around the corner of the porch.

The front door clicked and Lainey came toward him, a patchwork bag swinging from one shoulder. Today she wore a skirt that fluttered around her calves, seeming to invite a second glance despite its length. Or maybe that was just him.

Jake reached across to swing the door open for her. "All set?"

"I guess so." She slid in, her expression shielded by the dark glasses she wore.

"Looks like Benj Weaver is doing some work for you." He backed out onto the street.

"Yes." The reply was short. Perhaps Lainey realized that, because she shrugged slightly and took off the glasses, dropping them in her bag. "There's a broken window in the kitchen. Rachel volunteered her brother to fix it, and he seems to know what he's doing."

"You don't need to doubt that. Amish boys his age have already learned all sorts of handy things that the rest of us would struggle with." He cast a sideways glance at her face as he took the road out of town. Lainey seemed tense out of proportion to a broken pane of glass. "What happened to the window?"

She hesitated a moment before flicking a guarded glance his way. "Somebody pitched a stone through it. Halloweeners, I suppose."

"Halloweeners?" His fingers tightened on the wheel. "I'm not saying that kids don't get into trouble in Deer Run, but that sort of vandalism is rare. When did it happen?"

"Last evening, just as it was getting dark. I was outside, talking to Rachel, when we heard the noise. We ran around to the backyard, but whoever did it had vanished by the time we got there."

He frowned, not liking the sound of this. "Did you call the police?"

"For a broken window? Of course not." She shrugged. "Anyway, I'm sure it was Halloweeners. They'd thrown corn at the house the evening before."

"There's a big difference between tossing a handful of dry corn and pitching a rock through a window." His concern deepened. What was going on in his quiet little town? "Vandalism directed specifically against the Amish is rare here, but it does happen. I think you should report it."

"No. I appreciate your concern, but I'd rather not."

Lainey's words had been spoken normally enough, but her fingers twisted against one other in her lap, as if she were fighting with herself. She spoke again before he could press her, maybe to head him off.

"While Rachel and I were talking, Laura Hammond came out of the house across the street with the woman who owns the B and B."

"Jeannette Walker," he supplied the name. "Jeannette seems to be looking after Laura since Victor... now that Victor is deceased."

"Laura ran over to us before Jeannette could head her off." Lainey gave a little shiver, as if shaking something off her skin. "She was...odd."

"That's Laura, all right." He tried to keep his voice light and wasn't sure he succeeded. "Some people seem to remind her of Aaron's death and just—" he took his hand from the wheel to gesture "—just set her off. It's as if she's never gotten past what happened that summer. I hope she didn't upset you."

"Of course not." The emphasis she put on the words seemed overdone.

Should he pursue the subject? Before he could decide, he spotted the lane he'd been looking for. He slowed the car, flicking the turn signal.

"To return to the business at hand, I thought you should at least have a look at one of the farms Rebecca owns." He eased the car down the gravel road over the ruts made by the milk trucks. "This is Zeb's place." He reached the top of a gentle grade and stopped. "You can see it's a dairy farm. Zeb usually has sixty to seventy cows, and that's considered a large herd by local standards."

Lainey shot him a quick glance and her lips quirked. "I suspect you realize that no, I couldn't have told you it was a dairy farm. I don't mind admitting that I'm out of my depth here."

If she really accepted that, it might make her more amenable to following his suggestions. Somehow Jake thought that might be too easy.

Lainey leaned forward, one hand against the dash, to gaze at the pastures and cornfields, the large barns and the twin silos. "My uninformed opinion would be that it's worth quite a bit."

"Upwards of a million, I'd say. Prices for farmland have been going up steadily." He hesitated, but this may as well be said. "I agree with you that Rebecca wouldn't want to sell out from under any of her family. But if her condition drags on for an extended period, it may be time to think about the rent Zeb is paying. At the moment, it's a pittance in comparison to what it should be."

Lainey's eyebrows lifted. "And which of us wants to be the one to tell Zeb that?"

"Neither, I guess," he admitted. "But if the situation requires it, I'll deal with him."

"Thanks. But I have a feeling he'll know who to blame anyway."

He couldn't help but smile at her expression. "Cheer up. Maybe we can make a quick sale of a parcel nobody cares much about."

"I wish I knew what Aunt Rebecca would do." Her shoulders moved restlessly. "She may have been putting too much faith in my judgment."

Since that was his opinion, he couldn't argue, but at least Lainey seemed aware of the issues. That was progress.

Jake turned the car carefully in a spot where the lane widened out a little, mindful of the blackberry brambles that grew rampant on either side. As he drew out onto the highway, Lainey glanced toward Zeb's place.

"Are the other farms Aunt Rebecca owns similar to this one?"

He shrugged. "Similar, yes. Zeb's is the largest and most successful. In some ways, he's as clever about finances as your great-uncle had been. He's been able to put his money into stock since he hasn't been paying off a mortgage, and from what I've heard, he has an eye for a good deal, too."

Lainey nodded, pushing her hands back through her hair, a move that had him noticing how it curled against the smooth skin of her neck. "And to think I had the idea that life was less complicated here."

"Less complicated?" He repeated her words, thinking of all that had transpired in the past few months. "I suppose a town like Deer Run has its share of issues and tragedies. They're just on a smaller scale, for the most part, than in the city."

"You're thinking of Aaron Mast's death," Lainey said. "It certainly had far-reaching consequences, didn't it?"

He nodded, sending a quick glance at his map, propped on the console between them. The old grist mill property was just a couple of miles down the road, so they'd stop there next. He brought his mind back to her question.

"If Rachel hadn't returned to Deer Run and started talking to Meredith about what they remembered from that summer, I don't suppose the truth would ever have come to light. And Meredith's mother..." He let that die out.

"Poor woman. So much tragedy to grow out of a simple summer romance."

"Not so simple. Romantic relationships between Amish and English are always difficult. Romeo and Juliet stuff, I guess."

Lainey frowned. "When Laura spoke to me last night, it was as if she thought we'd been a part of that."

He glanced at her in some surprise. "Weren't you? I mean, from all I've heard from Meredith and Rachel, it sounds as if the three of you were like little shadows, following Laura and Aaron around that summer."

"I don't remember." Her blue eyes darkened with concern. "That's strange, isn't it? Rachel and Meredith seem to recall every day of that summer, and for me it's just a haze, with a few little bright spots here and there. And a few bad…" She stopped, as if she'd said more than she intended.

He studied her face, considering. "Bad what? Memories?"

Lainey looked down, her dark hair screening her face. "Bad dreams. Nightmares. Not remembering anything, just knowing something bad happened."

He hesitated, not sure what to say. "If it bothers you…have you looked at the scrapbook you girls kept that summer?"

She shook her head, still not looking at him.

"That might bring back some memories," he said. "As I mentioned, it's full of your drawings."

Lainey finally met his gaze, lips quirking. "I might be embarrassed to see them."

He let that slip away. What difference did it make to him, anyway, whether she remembered that summer or not? Trouble was that he couldn't seem to stop feeling responsible for her.

Lainey glanced up, seeming startled, when he pulled the car off the road under the trees. "Why are you stopping?"

"Next spot on the tour," he said. "Rebecca has a parcel of about five acres that includes an old grist mill."

Lainey glanced ruefully at her sandals. "I'm not very well dressed for tramping through the woods."

"It's just a hundred yards or so to the mill. We may as well take a look at it as long as we're here."

He got out and walked around the car. Lainey slid out with a certain amount of reluctance.

"If I get poison ivy, I'm blaming you," she said.

He touched her arm, leading her toward the path. "I'll buy the calamine lotion," he said. "Come on. In my opinion, this is the most logical property to put on the market, so I want you to see it."

The path was narrow, so Jake led the way, on the lookout for poison ivy or snakes, either of which, he figured, wouldn't endear him to Lainey.

"Maybe I will ask Meredith and Rachel if I can see the scrapbook." Lainey's words startled him.

He halted, turning to look at her. A shaft of sunlight, slanting down through the leaves, gilded her face, and her eyes were very serious.

"And maybe that was a dumb suggestion of mine," he said. "If you're already having bad dreams about what happened—"

"I'd rather face it than hide from it, even so." Her chin came up on the words. "And after all, it's all

over now. The truth has come out, and the person
who killed Aaron is dead himself."

He nodded slowly. That was right, wasn't it? Still,
he couldn't quite squash the single doubt remaining
in his mind. "I suppose...."

It was no good. He'd have to tell her the possibility
that troubled him, especially since Laura had started
showing an interest in her. It seemed he couldn't
maintain a businesslike detachment where Lainey
was concerned.

"As far as the rest of the world is concerned, that's
true. It's all over." He hesitated, frowning. "The trouble is that I was there when Victor killed himself. I
saw his face, and Laura's. And I can't quite rid myself of the thought that he might have been covering
up for someone he loved. That the person who actually killed Aaron might be Laura herself."

CHAPTER SEVEN

FOR A MOMENT Lainey just stood, aware of Jake's gaze on her face, trying to accept what he'd said. She couldn't.

"Laura? Kill someone?" Lainey saw in her mind that almost childlike face. "That seems impossible. She's so…" Words failed her, and she gave an amorphous gesture.

"Now she is," Jake agreed. "But that's not who she was twenty years ago."

"But why? I might not remember much, but I do know she loved Aaron. Why would she do such a thing?"

He shrugged, beginning to walk again. The trail was narrow, forcing her to stay behind him, and her skirt brushed against tall weeds on either side. The trees seemed to hem them in, creating a sense of privacy.

"Maybe he wanted to break up with her." Jake tossed the words back over his shoulder. "Maybe she wanted to break up with him. There could be a lot of reasons."

"Romances end all the time, but most of them

don't result in murder." Or suicide attempts, her mind taunted.

"From what I've been told, their relationship was pretty intense." He paused, turning to look at her. She hadn't stopped as quickly as he had, and her stride had taken her a bit too close to him for comfort. Somewhere ahead of them there was the sound of running water…a stream, probably.

"I don't know if Rachel mentioned it, but apparently Laura was pregnant. Add that into the mix and—" He shrugged. "Look, I'm not saying I'm sure of anything. But if Laura is showing an interest in you, it might be best to be on your guard."

As if she didn't already have enough people who seemed to see her as a threat. "I doubt I'll ever see her again. Certainly not if Jeannette Walker has anything to say about it. The woman's like a mother grizzly with one cub."

Jake's face relaxed in a grin. "She is, isn't she? And not above pulling some dirty tricks to get what she wants, if all I've heard about her is true."

"Since I don't have anything she wants, that should be no problem." He was probably exaggerating the whole thing. After all, Laura's husband had confessed. What more did he want?

"You think I'm making a mountain out of a molehill," he said, as if reading her thoughts. "Maybe I am. Just—be careful." He circled her wrist with his fingers, and her skin seemed to warm at his touch. "Okay?"

"Okay." She sounded a bit breathless, but he was

turning away already, dropping her hand. Maybe he hadn't noticed.

"Well, there's the grist mill, or what's left of it."

She stood next to him, staring. They'd come out of the trees into an open space—a narrow valley with a stream running through it. Beautiful, the way the sun filtered through the leaves and touched the water with light. She'd love to draw it, but that wouldn't do justice to the effect of the light. It reminded her of the quilt Aunt Rebecca had made. Sunshine and Shadows—that was the perfect description of the scene as well.

The building seemed to loom over them, providing the shadows. Three stories high, of weather-beaten planks that had long since lost any paint they possessed, it squatted next to the stream like some prehistoric monster.

A shiver went through her, and she regretted her too-active imagination. "What did you call it?"

"A grist mill." A glance at her face apparently told him that further explanation was needed. "Years ago there were grist mills all through the area, wherever there was a stream with enough water force to turn a wheel. Local farmers brought their grain to be milled, and since they couldn't travel very far, there were usually mills every ten miles or so."

Lainey stared, trying to figure out what it must have been like. "So there would have been a water wheel?"

"There." He pointed. "It's long gone now, but you

can still see where it was. A sluice gate would have controlled the flow of water to the wheel."

"And Aunt Rebecca owns this?" She jerked her mind away from the images of horse-drawn wagons and bustling figures with which she'd been populating the quiet valley.

"The mill and about five acres of land around it. There's been some interest from time to time in buying it, so it might be the logical site to put up for sale."

"Can we go inside?" Before she made any decision, she'd need to take a closer look.

"I guess so." He held out his hand. "Better watch yourself in those sandals. We have to cross the stream on the stepping stones."

She took one look at the flat stones in the running water, decided a twisted ankle or a wet shoe wasn't worth it, and took his hand. Jake went sure-footed across the stone and she followed, holding on to him.

Once on dry ground, she drew her hand free. The sense that the mill loomed over them intensified as they went closer to the structure.

"It's not going to fall down on us, is it?"

Jake shook his head, smiling. "I had a look at it a few months ago, because there were some rumors that the township might try to force Rebecca to pull it down. The overall structure is sound enough, so I was able to discourage the township board from starting a fight they'd lose. But that was another reason I thought she ought to sell."

"Aunt Rebecca didn't agree with you, obviously. So why are you so eager to convince me?"

"I'm not eager." He sounded exasperated. "I just think it's the most likely possibility to sell quickly and bring in the money you need. And your aunt didn't want or need to get rid of anything at that point."

She considered that as he handed her up several rickety steps and into the first floor of the mill. It was dimmer inside, of course, but enough light streamed through the empty windows and between the boards to see the open, echoing space. A stairway led up to the second floor.

"The question still applies," she said. "Why didn't she want to sell?"

"I don't suppose she saw a need to." Jake was looking around, apparently satisfying himself that nothing had changed since his last visit. "I had the impression she wasn't ready to sell what her husband had bought. And then there's the difficulty of having too much money."

"Too much?" she echoed. "Most people wouldn't see that as a problem."

"Most people aren't Amish," he replied. "There's a sense in which humility depends on not possessing a lot more than your fellow Amish. As long as Rebecca's wealth, if you want to call it that, is tied up in land, no one would think anything of it. She preferred the status quo, I guess."

That accorded with what she remembered of her great-aunt, Lainey realized. So what had Rebecca thought of Lainey's job, producing ads to convince people to buy things they didn't need? The question made her vaguely uneasy.

"Look, if that's how she felt, maybe we shouldn't be considering selling," she said abruptly.

"Changing your mind again?" The filtered sunlight seemed to stripe Jake's body as he turned to her. "You've already said you have to raise the money for Rebecca's care. You can't just impulsively reject the only way of doing that out of sentiment."

Lainey's hands curled into fists at his tone. Impulsive? Sentiment? "It's not impulsive or sentimental to try and do what my aunt would want, especially since she's incapable of telling us."

Their gazes clashed, but it was his that fell. "I'm sorry. That was a bit strong, I guess. If you see any other way of doing this, I'm open to it."

He'd disarmed her, leaving her feel a little foolish.

"No, I don't. I just don't want to make any hasty decisions and then regret them."

Jake tilted his head as if in acquiescence. "Right. I doubt the property would sell quickly in any event. We'll take whatever time you need." He paused, studying her face. "It seems Rebecca made a wise choice after all."

For an instant they looked at each other, and she felt the intensity of his gaze on her skin. She turned abruptly, tilting her head back to peer up the staircase, just as glad to change the subject. The building soared above her to what seemed a dizzying height.

"What's upstairs?"

"The second floor is where the millstones are. Or were. There's only one left of the pair."

"Can we go up?"

Jake nodded. "I didn't have any trouble the last time I was here. Just watch your step."

Lainey climbed the stairs, very aware of him close behind her. The railing was loose, so she kept well over against the opposite side.

She reached the top, and Jake stepped up next to her. "There's the remaining millstone," he said unnecessarily. The stone was placed in the center of the floor, a massive circle about four feet in diameter and probably a foot thick.

She approached cautiously, but the floor seemed solid. It would have to be, to support the weight of the stone. "So there would have been another stone on top of this one?"

Jake nodded, bending to touch the grooved surface with his palm. "The grain would have been hoisted to the third floor and then poured down through a hopper to the stones, which ground it."

"How do you know so much about grist mills?" She studied his face. Clearly this fascinated him, perhaps more for the technology than what she saw as the romance of this reminder of the past.

"My dad's something of a local history buff. You don't grow up in our house without acquiring a lot of fairly useless knowledge."

"On the contrary, today it's become useful," she said. She went to the stairway that led up to the third floor. It was almost more of a ladder than a set of stairs, and looked more rickety that the first set.

"There must be a beautiful view from the top." She put her foot on the first plank and grabbed the railing.

"Wait a second. That third step—"

Jake reached her just as she put her foot on the third plank and heard a resounding crack. Before she could tumble, Jake had lifted her down.

He stood holding her, his laughing face very close. "...isn't safe," he finished, his voice low. "I noticed the last time I was here. Like I said, impulsive."

Her palms rested on his biceps, and she felt his unexpected strength. His skin warmed her hands right through the fine cotton of his shirt. Her breath caught.

Jake's eyes seemed to darken, and she couldn't look away. It felt as if the very air was pushing them together, and she didn't want to resist. She wanted to lean into him, to feel his arms go around her—

Realization hit her like a dash of cold water in the face. She couldn't do this.

And Jake must be feeling exactly the same. His expression seemed to close, his hands dropped from her waist, and he took a deliberate step back.

"Maybe we should get moving." His voice grated.

She nodded, mute, and headed for the way down.

LAINEY LET OUT a breath of relief as they neared Aunt Rebecca's house late in the afternoon. She and Jake had been reduced to an awkward silence when they'd walked back to his car after that charged moment at the old mill.

For the remainder of their property tour, their conversation had been limited strictly to business matters. That said, didn't it, that he'd been as appalled as she had at that burst of mutual attraction?

Or maybe she was misinterpreting his reaction entirely. Maybe she'd imagined that he'd even had one, and that he'd thought she was coming on to him.

Lainey let out a breath of relief as Jake turned the car into the drive. Right now, all she wanted was to get out of the man's disturbing presence.

Jake drove to the back door and then shook his head. "Sorry. I'm just used to coming in the kitchen when I come to see Rebecca."

"That's fine," she said, opening the door before he could back up. "I want to check anyway to be sure Benjamin locked up in back before he left."

Jake reached out a hand to detain her. "So you'll think over the property situation and give me your decision?"

"Yes." She got out and stood holding the door. "I realize it's a matter of the sooner the better. I don't want to start juggling hospital bills. Tomorrow all right?"

"That's fine. Just give me a call." He paused, his hand extended toward her, looking as if he had something else to say.

Lainey closed the door and lifted her hand in a gesture meant to combine goodbye and thanks. She turned away and heard the car reverse out the drive.

Finally she could breathe again. One difficult afternoon over with, thank goodness. She'd have to figure out a way to deal with Aunt Rebecca's business without putting herself into any more close encounters with Jake. Of course, he'd probably see to that himself.

Mounting the back porch steps, Lainey forced herself to focus her thoughts elsewhere. The kitchen window looked fine, and she stopped to take a closer look at Benjamin's work.

She ran her finger along the frame of the window. It was as if it had never been broken. In fact, Benj had apparently cleaned the window as well as fixing it.

She'd have to figure out a way of repaying him. He'd turned red to the tips of his ears when she'd tried to give him money, refusing with such determination she hadn't had the heart to press him. Probably he thought of it as Rebecca's window, and he wouldn't take money for being neighborly to another Amish person.

True enough, but she'd still like to show her appreciation.

Fishing the key ring from her bag while juggling the folder of property listings Jake had given her, Lainey turned to the door. That was odd. A broom was propped crossways against the frame of the door, as if to block entry.

That was ridiculous. Benjamin had probably used it to clear up bits of glass. Maybe he'd locked the door and then realized the broom was still outside, so he'd left it where she'd be sure to see it.

"Ms. Lainey, Ms. Lainey." The high young voice was accompanied by the sound of running feet. "Hi. I'm Mandy."

Lainey smiled at Rachel's daughter. Mandy's blond hair had been plaited into two inexpert braids, leading her to suppose Mandy had done it herself. Her Lab puppy danced around her feet and then launched herself at Lainey's sandals.

Lainey bent to ruffle the soft fur. "Your mother told me about you, Mandy. And about your puppy, too. How was school today?"

"Okay." She shrugged with typical eight-year-old disregard for the dumb questions grown-ups asked. "Mommy says will you come to supper? I was supposed to watch for you and tell you it'll be ready whenever you are." She delivered the last part of her speech as if it had been memorized. "Please come," she finished, smiling.

Lainey hesitated. She might have said something about not wanting to impose if Rachel had come herself, but somehow she couldn't say that to a child.

"That's nice of you and your mommy. Just let me put these papers away, and I'll be ready. Do you want to come inside and wait for me?"

"Sure." Mandy glanced at the broom she was still holding. "Were you sweeping?"

"This? No, I was just going to put it away." Lainey pushed the door open, following child and dog into the kitchen and propping the broom in the small closet. "I think Benj…your uncle…must have used it after he fixed my window."

"It's okay. I don't call him uncle, even if he is one. He's not old enough for that, do you think?" Mandy tilted her head to the side, considering.

"Probably not," she said, smiling, wondering how Rachel, whom she remembered as the shy one of their little trio, had gotten such an outgoing child.

Lainey walked quickly through to the dining room, where she'd been using the table as a desk, and dropped the folder, then stopped. Hadn't she put the list of nursing homes into the file with the other papers from the hospital? Apparently not, since it was lying next to the pad where she'd been making a shopping list. Shrugging, she put it away and returned to Mandy.

"Okay, I'm ready." They went out together, and Mandy waited while she locked the door, chattering about the new trick she was trying to teach the dog, who Mandy had said was named Princess.

This was a good idea, Lainey decided. The little girl's bubbling conversation was an excellent antidote to the brooding she'd probably have done if she'd been left alone in the house right now.

Supper in Rachel's cozy kitchen really was the break she needed. Lainey leaned back in the chair, feeling stuffed. "The chicken potpie was scrumptious. How did you turn into such a good cook?"

"My mother." Rachel poured coffee into two mugs. "You don't grow up with an Amish mother without learning how to cook."

"*Grossmammi* is teaching me, too," Mandy said,

putting her plate and silverware in the sink without being asked. "I helped her make an apple pie."

"You're lucky to have your grandparents living so close." Lainey smiled at the child. Mandy probably didn't realize how fortunate she was to be so surrounded by family. Lainey couldn't remember her mother teaching her how to do anything remotely domestic.

"You'd better get busy on your homework," Rachel said. "I'll look it over before you go to bed."

Mandy made a face at the prospect but trotted off with only that mild complaint.

"She actually loves school, but apparently it's not acceptable to say so." Rachel sat down across from her with her own cup of coffee.

"So I hear, not that I'm around kids much."

Rachel's lips curved in a smile. "Someday," she said. "Don't I remember that you wanted to have a big family?"

"If I said that, it was probably because I was an only child." Maybe her friendship with Rachel and Meredith had awakened a yearning to have sisters. "It's lovely that Mandy has so much family close at hand."

"It was a little difficult when we first came back." Rachel stared down at her cup. "After all, no Amish parent wants to see their child leave the faith. But they've adjusted to it now, I think. And they do like Colin."

Colin, Lainey knew, was Rachel's fiancé. "When are you getting married?"

"Not soon enough for Colin," Rachel said, eyes twinkling. "But I want to be sure Mandy and Colin's father are both ready for the change. And I'll have to decide how I can run the bed-and-breakfast if I'm not living here."

"Those don't sound like insurmountable problems. Not that I'm one to dream about marriage myself, but it's pretty obvious that you're ready."

Rachel studied her face. "No thoughts of finding the one and settling down?"

Lainey's thoughts inevitably turned to Jake. Attraction, she reminded herself, was a long way from happily ever after.

"My mother hasn't exactly set a good example of the joys of marriage. I'm not sure I'm suited to settling down."

"You will be," Rachel said. "When it's the right guy."

The conversation was getting a little too close to the bone. Maybe she'd better change the subject.

"Did I tell you Jake took me to see some of Aunt Rebecca's property this afternoon?"

Rachel nodded. "You mentioned it. How did it go?"

"Fine. But Jake told me something that surprised me," she said, setting her cup in the saucer with a little clink of china. "About Laura and all that happened that summer."

"Really?" Rachel hesitated. "I suppose it is still on his mind, to some extent. You know he represented Meredith and Zach when the police suspected him."

"No, I didn't." Maybe that explained Jake's intensity on the subject.

Rachel smiled. "Jake was an absolute rock during that time after Meredith's mother's death. I don't know how we'd have done without him."

"So you think his judgment is reliable?"

"Of course." Rachel seemed surprised that there could be any question.

Lainey frowned, not sure she wanted to bring it up but sure Jake's suggestion would bug her if she didn't. "Jake said that he thought it might actually have been Laura who caused Aaron's death. That Victor was just trying to cover it up with all he did."

She could see the idea was new to Rachel. Rachel didn't immediately respond, seeming to turn it over in her mind.

"In all the talking we've done about what happened that summer, I don't think we ever seriously considered Laura," Rachel said. "She was…well, you remember, don't you? She was so in love with Aaron. And she was apparently pregnant with his child."

Lainey hadn't suspected that complication before Jake mentioned it. "That could have been a wake-up call for her, realizing she was pregnant."

Rachel shook her head. "It makes it all the more unlikely that she'd harm him, it seems to me. They were going to run away and get married—"

"Were they? Wasn't she underage?"

Rachel shrugged. "In Pennsylvania, I guess, but they could have crossed the state line to Maryland. Still, her parents would probably have raised the roof.

I suppose it's possible that things started moving too fast for Laura. She might have reacted, tried to push him away—it would have been an accident. The dam can be dangerous, and the water was running high that week."

Lainey found her mind shying away when she tried to picture the scene. Maybe it was time she went back to the dam and saw it for herself again…. Her stomach cramped at the thought.

"You're right, I'm sure," she said firmly. "If Laura did it, it was an accident. She couldn't possibly be a threat to anyone now."

Rachel's clear blue eyes seemed troubled. "I wish Jake hadn't thought of it, even so."

"Me, too." Lainey patted her hand. "I'm sorry. I shouldn't have brought it up. I didn't intend to worry you."

Rachel clasped her hand for a second. "What are friends for? We have a twenty-year-old friendship, remember?"

"I remember." Funny. She didn't have all that many friends in her life. Moving around as much as she did tended to discourage building relationships. Oh, there were people she stayed in touch with via Facebook and Christmas notes, but that wasn't like having a female friend to confide in, one she'd known long enough to trust. It was nice, having a childhood friend.

Lainey glanced at the clock and then pushed her chair back. "I should go home. I'm sure you'll be getting into Mandy's bedtime routine soon."

Rachel glanced toward the window. "True. Now that it's getting dark earlier, it's a lot easier to get her settled. Do you want a flashlight?"

"I have a penlight on my keys," Lainey said. "That should do me." She wasn't afraid to be out in the dark. That would be silly. "Thanks again so much for the invitation. The chicken potpie was delicious."

"I'll be glad to share my mother's recipe," Rachel said, seeming to glance toward the farm that lay across the covered bridge. "Oh, wait. Here." She thrust a bag into Lainey's hands. "Take this."

"What is it?" She grasped the handles of the shopping bag automatically.

"The scrapbook we kept that summer. I knew you'd want to see it." Rachel flipped on the porch light and opened the door.

If Rachel knew that, she knew more than Lainey did. She wasn't at all certain that she wanted to delve any deeper into the events of that childhood summer. But she could hardly refuse to take the scrapbook. She didn't have to look at the blasted thing, after all. She could just keep it for a few days and then return it. "Good night," Rachel said.

"Thanks." Lainey fished for her penlight.

The air was chilly, and she pulled her sweater around her more closely. Once she stepped off the back porch, the comforting yellow glow of the porch light slipped away behind her. Lainey switched on the penlight, realizing its narrow beam only illuminated the way a few yards ahead of her feet.

Well, she was just going next door, after all. She'd be there in two minutes.

But she couldn't help noticing how much darker it was here than it ever got in the city. The bulk of the ridge on the other side of the creek was an added layer of blackness against a gray sky, and the band of trees seemed to have crept closer than they ever were in daylight.

Stupid, scaring herself that way. Lainey hurried her steps across the grass. This end of Deer Run petered out into the country almost immediately, and it was so quiet she could hear the splashing of the water over the dam. Shivering a little, she ran the last few feet to the porch.

Shoving the key in the lock, she stumbled inside. Why on earth hadn't she thought to leave a light on? She fumbled for the overhead gas lamp, the penlight swinging randomly as she moved, until it caught and reflected two green eyes glowing in the dark.

Lainey stifled a cry as she touched the control on the light. Just the cat. It was only the cat.

When she finally managed to get the lamp on, he came to weave his way around her legs, purring insistently.

"Yes, I'm glad to see you, too." She stooped to stroke the glossy back. "But how are you getting in here?" She had checked the entire house, including the cellar, and she hadn't come up with a single space big enough to let a cat squeeze through.

He looked up at her and let out a single meow, as if that should be an answer.

"Your name should be Houdini," she said crossly, but she had to admit she was glad to have company in the house. "Let me get some light on in the front room, and then I'll find some supper for you."

Exchanging the penlight for one of the large flashlights Aunt Rebecca kept handy in a kitchen drawer, Lainey went through the dining room into the living room, where she turned on another lamp. There, that was better. She didn't like to be fumbling around in a dark house, and—

She stopped, staring. Placed diagonally across the front door was the broom.

Her heart gave a lurch. She had put the broom in the back closet, she knew she had. How did it get to the front door?

Seizing the shreds of her common sense, she told herself firmly that it couldn't be the same broom. She grabbed it, double-checking that the front door was locked, and marched back through the house to the closet.

Sure enough, the broom she'd found on the back porch was there. She wasn't going crazy. She picked it up, comparing the two. Both were straw brooms, the sort you could buy at a discount store. Nothing particularly alarming about either of them.

Lainey stuffed both brooms in the closet and closed the door. Unfortunately, that didn't help her state of mind. She had come up with a perfectly logical explanation for the broom at the back door. But she couldn't think of any, logical or not, for the appearance of the second broom.

CHAPTER EIGHT

JAKE PULLED INTO the hospital parking lot the afternoon after his excursion with Lainey. He really needed to check on Rebecca for himself. The possibility of having to move her to another facility troubled him. Whatever decision Lainey made, somebody wouldn't like it.

For that matter, he didn't relish getting into the middle of a family fight himself. Still, his responsibility was to Rebecca, no matter who else was involved.

And Lainey? His mind queried.

When he reached Rebecca's room, he opened the door quietly, not sure what to expect. No crowd today—just Lainey, sitting in the green plastic chair next to Rebecca's bed, a book open on her lap. She was reading aloud to Rebecca.

He stood where he was, reluctant to disturb her. Lainey's expression was absorbed, as if she'd entered into the story world as she read. He had to smile as he recognized the book. It was one of the Little House series, especially loved by the Amish for its themes of hardships overcome by the love of family and faith.

What meaning did it hold for someone like

Lainey? As far as he could tell, she'd spent her life in one city after another. Was she longing for something she'd never known?

He glanced at Rebecca, his gaze sharpening. She'd moved—the tiniest turning of her head toward the sound of Lainey's voice.

He took a step toward them, and Lainey looked up, her voice stopping.

"Go on," he said softly. "She's responding to you."

Lainey turned to her great-aunt. She must have seen what he had, because the guarded look she'd worn for him softened into an expression of such love that it nearly rocked him back on his heels.

Careful, he told himself. His experience with Julie had certainly shown him the danger of getting involved with someone who wanted different things from life than he did. And that certainly described Lainey, didn't it?

He came to a halt, keeping the width of the hospital bed between them. Rebecca seemed to sigh a little, her body relaxing under the thin blanket. Her hand moved, groping toward Lainey.

Tears spilled onto Lainey's cheeks, and she let the book fall into her lap. She clasped Rebecca's hand.

"I'm here, Aunt Rebecca. I'm here." Lainey looked up at him, cheeks flushing. "She's responding, isn't she? That's a good sign."

"Yes." Jake couldn't help it. He reached across the bed to put his hand over theirs. "It is a good sign."

Something pushed against the door with a thump, and Jake wasn't able to straighten before Zeb was in the room, followed by one of his grandkids—Ella, he thought it was. Zeb was eyeing him with disapproval, to say the least.

"You've come at the right time," Lainey said, a lilt in her voice. "Aunt Rebecca is beginning to respond."

"She is?" The girl hurried across to join Lainey at Rebecca's bedside. "Ach, Lainey, I am so glad." She caught Rebecca's hand in hers. "You are getting better, ain't so?"

Rebecca's eyes fluttered a little, her hand moving.

"You see?" Lainey grinned at the girl. "She's starting to come out of it."

Ella shed her bonnet and then bent to give Lainey a hug that seemed to surprise her. "This is a *gut* day."

Jake glanced at Zeb, and the older man's expression wiped the smile from his face. Zeb didn't seem inclined to join the celebration.

"Rebecca's doing better," he prompted.

Zeb gave a curt nod, his expression softening slightly as he looked at his sister-in-law. *"Gut."* Then his head swiveled back toward Jake. "I went to your office. They told me you were here."

So this was a business call, not a visit to the sick. "I'm sorry I missed you," he said, moving a few steps away from the bed. "What can I do for you?"

Zeb followed him, frowning. "You can tell me what you and that woman were doing on my property yesterday."

He should have known someone would have spotted the car, he supposed. Sometimes he thought you couldn't sneeze without half the township offering you a tissue.

He decided not to respond by pointing out that it wasn't really Zeb's land. No point in starting a useless quarrel.

"I was showing your great-niece around, that's all. Sorry we didn't have time to stop and visit," he added, suspecting they wouldn't have been particularly welcome.

Zeb's face tightened. "She is no relative of mine. Or my brother's."

"Maybe not, but she's in charge of Rebecca's property for the moment, and I thought she should see what it involved."

"The farm is mine." Zeb grated out the words. "I am the one who has worked it all these years. I am the one who has made it prosperous. Rebecca intended to sign it over to me."

Jake's eyebrows lifted. "I didn't know she'd made that decision yet."

"She was going to do it, because it was right." Zeb looked at Lainey again, with what seemed speculation in his face. "The *Englisch* woman—she would be able to do it?"

Jake wasn't pleased with the direction of Zeb's thoughts. "She would have the authority, but I certainly wouldn't advise her to do any such thing."

"You are not part of the family."

"And you just pointed out that Lainey isn't either, according to you." Jake took a firm hold on his temper. "In any event, now that Rebecca is beginning to respond, it doesn't matter. If all goes well, she'll be able to make decisions for herself before long. If, as you say, Rebecca had decided to sign the farm over to you, she'll be able to take care of that herself."

Zeb just stared at him. Then he turned and walked over to the bed.

Jake watched him, his mind busy. What was going on with Zeb? He'd always seemed fond of Rebecca in a nondemonstrative way, of course. Ready to put any members of his large family at her disposal when there was work to be done. So what was he thinking now?

Zeb and Ella exchanged several comments in Pennsylvania Dutch, much too quickly for Jake's slight understanding. Then Ella turned to Lainey.

"My grandfather has to leave. He says I can stay longer if you can take me home."

"I'd be glad to," Lainey said. "It will do Aunt Rebecca good to have you here."

"I will leave you, then." Zeb gave her a curt nod. He stood for a moment, looking down at Rebecca, and then walked out.

The atmosphere in the room improved with Zeb's absence, it seemed. Jake caught Lainey's eye.

"Can I have a moment? Then I need to get back to the office."

She nodded, skirting the bed to join him. "What is it?"

He drew her over to the window. "Have you made a decision about the property yet? Or do you want to wait, now that your aunt is showing signs of improving?"

Lainey glanced back toward Rebecca and shook her head. "I wish I knew for sure if it's the right decision, but I think we'd better move ahead with putting the mill property on the market. The doctor said that if Aunt Rebecca showed signs of improving, they'd want to move her to the rehab facility. That will mean settling some bills with the hospital."

He nodded. "We won't make a sale immediately, of course, but we can use the money in her account for the hospital and settle the taxes when the property closes." He hesitated. "I think you're doing the right thing. It may still be a long haul before Rebecca's able to make these kinds of decisions."

"She's getting better. That's what counts. Besides, if I put the mill property on the market that may assure Zeb and the others that their farms are safe."

"I'm not sure that would be my first consideration," he said, his tone dry.

Lainey's smile lit her face. "He is difficult, isn't he? But I'm sure Aunt Rebecca would want to see that family is taken care of. Anyway, soon she'll be able to tell me what she wants."

She looked at him for agreement, so he nodded and smiled. Unfortunately, he wasn't quite as optimistic as Lainey was. Some people never really recovered their full functioning after a stroke. And as for reassuring Zeb…well, he suspected that Zeb wouldn't be totally reassured until he held the deed to the farm in his hands.

IT SEEMED TO be her day, Lainey decided, to run into members of Zeb's family. She'd just returned to the house from dropping Ella at the farm next to her grandfather's when she glanced across the street to see Ella's brother, Thomas, working in the flower beds at the Willows. Amish boys that age tended to look alike at first glance, but she couldn't miss Thomas's narrow face and thin, wiry body. He was weeding the border of purple and yellow mums along the inn's front porch.

Lainey hesitated, her hand still on the car door. Should she go across and speak to him or not? But she'd liked Ella, with her naïve outlook on life and her obvious affection for Aunt Rebecca, and it seemed standoffish to go inside and ignore him.

Besides, maybe getting to know Zeb's family would help to disarm the enmity that had sprung up between them. For Aunt Rebecca's sake, she should try.

Lainey went quickly across the road and up the walk. The boy was on his knees, intent on the weeds he was tossing into a wheelbarrow.

"Thomas." She touched his shoulder.

The boy spun around, losing his balance and ending up sitting in the grass. He scuttled crabwise away from her, his blue eyes wide, almost frightened.

What on earth was wrong with the boy?

"I'm sorry." She smiled. "It's just me. Lainey. I saw you were working over here and stopped to say hi."

Thomas stared at her, not responding. Didn't he understand her?

"You know who I am, don't you?" She kept her voice gentle.

He nodded. Swallowed. *"Ja."*

They didn't seem to be making much headway. "I didn't know you worked for Mrs. Walker."

Thomas nodded again. He got slowly to his feet, looking everywhere but at her. "I work here." He grasped the handles of the wheelbarrow. "I must go." With that, he trundled the barrow around the house and out of sight.

That hadn't gone as planned. Lainey stood, staring at the spot where he'd vanished. Was there something wrong with Thomas that she hadn't been aware of?

The sound of a step made her look up. Jeannette Walker came out of the house, letting the screen door close behind her. It was clear from her expression that she'd overheard.

"I'm afraid I interrupted Thomas's weeding," she said. "I'm sorry."

"It's not a problem." Jeannette actually seemed friendly, in contrast to their first two encounters. "I'm afraid Thomas is rather shy. I've found it works much better if I just leave him alone to get on with his work. Anything else just seems to upset him."

"I didn't realize. I suppose I shouldn't have put him on the spot that way."

Jeannette came to stand by the porch railing, resting one hand on it lightly. She might have been posing for a photo of the Willows and its proprietor. As always, it seemed, her hair was almost aggressively neat, her skirt and blouse tailored and vaguely old-fashioned.

"You couldn't have known," she said. "All my negotiations are done with Thomas's father or older brother. They make sure he gets here on time and pick him up when he finishes." She sighed. "It's difficult, watching out for someone who's not quite responsible. I should know."

That seemed to invite a question, surprising her. She wouldn't have expected Jeannette to discuss Laura.

"You mean Laura Hammond, I suppose? I've gathered that she's been ill."

Jeannette nodded, the firm waves of her hair never moving. "Poor thing. She's had troubles for years, and now that her husband is gone, she only has me."

Lainey tried to find something tactful to say that wouldn't reveal the fact that they'd been talking about Laura. Jake's face slid into her mind, his expression grave and troubled. *I think the killer might have been Laura herself.*

"It must be difficult for you," she said. "Feeling responsible."

Jeannette stiffened, probably meaning she'd said exactly the wrong thing. But as quickly as it had come, the impression vanished.

Jeannette shrugged. "I do what I can," she said. "I can't complain. And you certainly have burdens enough of your own with your aunt in such a condition." She paused, her gaze on Lainey's face. "I suppose you're eager to get everything settled here and get back to your job and your friends in St. Louis."

Since she currently had neither job nor friends to speak of, that was hardly an issue. The few women she'd sometimes gone to lunch with had worked for the firm, and once she'd been let go, they'd hardly wanted to ally themselves with her and risk making an enemy of the boss. "I'm not really in a hurry. I'll be here as long as Aunt Rebecca needs me."

"Your aunt is fortunate to have such a dedicated great-niece," Jeannette said.

Was that a sarcastic remark? Lainey couldn't be sure, and she'd certainly spent enough time being social with the woman.

"I must be on my way. Again, I'm sorry I interrupted Thomas at his work." She turned, going quickly back across the street, feeling as if Jeannette was staring at her all the way. But when she reached her own door and glanced back, Jeannette was nowhere to be seen. Overactive imagination, she diagnosed, and pulled a handful of envelopes from the mailbox.

Heading into the house, she shuffled through them. Several were probably get-well cards, judging by the shape of the envelopes. Lainey set those aside to take to the hospital. The next one—she stopped, staring.

It was addressed to her. At this address. And the postmark was St. Louis. She stared for a long moment at the block printing, her stomach twisting. Nobody she knew would address an envelope to her this way, even if they'd known where she was.

Lainey resisted an impulse to throw it in the trash unread. That would be cowardly. Better to face it, no matter how ugly. She ripped it open.

I know where you are. You can't hide from what you've done.

It ended with a string of obscenities that made her stomach twist even tighter. She crunched the paper in her hand and walked quickly into the kitchen. A moment in the gas flame of the stove would reduce it to ashes.

One step into the kitchen, a plaintive meow distracted her. Apparently for once Cat's appearing act hadn't worked—he was outside the back door, demanding entrance.

The familiar sound dissolved the tension induced by the anonymous letter. Smiling a little, she dropped it on the counter and headed for the door.

She swung it open, and the smile died on her face. The cat sat there, looking at her with a wide, unblinking green stare. But between them, propped across the doorway, was another broom.

LAINEY FINISHED THE last of the supper dishes. She turned toward the living room and then, reluctantly, went to the closet door and opened it. The three brooms stood there, mute and unnerving. She shut the door on them, making a determined effort to shut them out of her mind at the same time.

In the first moment of discovery, she'd made a

mistake. She'd called Jake. Luckily, his phone went straight to voice mail, and by then she'd reconsidered.

She could tell him about the appearing and vanishing cat, and the repeated business with the brooms, but she certainly wasn't going to reveal the anonymous letter with its trail that led directly to what had happened in St. Louis. And that, after all, was why this whole situation had her so rattled.

Really—brooms? It was laughable, wasn't it? But she didn't seem able to find the funny side.

At least she hadn't blurted everything out to Jake. She'd had sense enough to leave a noncommittal message, just saying she had a question and would call him tomorrow. By then, she'd think of something to say.

Wrapping her arms around herself, she wandered into the living room. If Aunt Rebecca owned a television set, she could turn it on and watch something mindless. All this Amish simplicity gave a person too much time to think. Maybe she ought to start the project that had been in the back of her mind since she'd helped her cousin Katie with the quilt. She could start one of her own.

Katie had said that Aunt Rebecca's extra fabric was in a chest in the back room. Lainey went upstairs, locating the piece of furniture without difficulty. She lifted the lid to find that it was filled to the brim with fabric.

Lainey ran her hand over a rainbow of colors, remembering that day in the quilt shop with Aunt Rebecca. This was a treasure trove of material. She squirreled through the trunk, an image forming in her mind—a simple pattern, of course, but made in a variety of jewel tones. The deep, saturated colors were typical of Amish quilts, she knew.

It wasn't long before she had an armload of material. Half laughing at her own enthusiasm, she carried them downstairs to the dining room table. Aunt Rebecca had always laid her sewing out on the long table to cut things out. Time slipped away as she tried out one color against another, looking for the perfect combination. The process—touching, comparing, fitting pieces together, seemed to satisfy some need in her.

The cat, sitting on the braided rug, let out a loud meow. Then, abruptly, his head swiveled toward the front of the house. He stared unblinkingly at the window. Lainey's hand seemed to freeze on the scissors she held.

A second later Lainey heard it—a footstep on the porch. Thank goodness she'd drawn the shades. At least she wasn't lit up like an actor on a stage. If something hit the window...

A knock sounded. She hesitated for a moment and then walked quickly to the door. Drawing back the curtain gave her a view of Jake's face, looking mildly impatient. She swung the door open.

"I didn't expect you to come by. I intended to call you tomorrow." Feeling a little foolish at her caution made her brusquer than she should have been.

"No problem. I checked messages after leaving

an extremely dull meeting in Williamsport and figured I might as well stop by." His eyebrows lifted.
"May I come in?"

"Yes, of course." Regaining her poise, she stepped
back, gesturing him into the living room.

Jake looked at her, a question in his face. "You
wanted to ask me something?"

"Tell you, I guess." She realized she was fiddling
with a strand of hair and pushed it back. What to tell
him? And how much?

Jake grinned. "I'm trustworthy. Honest. Just spill
it, whatever it is."

"Right." She took a breath. "This is going to sound
stupid, but…" She stopped. Shook her head. "Come
on. I'll show you."

She led the way quickly into the kitchen, with Jake
on her heels, and swung open the closet door. With
a gesture, she indicated the brooms.

He stood staring for a moment. "Three brooms
seems a little excessive, but I don't quite see—"

"I found the first one propped across the back door
when I got home the other day. I assumed Rachel's
brother had left it there after he finished fixing the
broken window. But later, I discovered the second
one across the front door, like…like some kind of a
warning. And tonight when I went to let the cat in,
there was another one across the back door. If this
is some kind of local joke—well, I told you it was
silly." She glared at him, feeling on the defensive.

Jake lifted his hands, palms up. "Hey, I didn't say

anything about it being silly. As for a local joke…" The words trailed off as something seemed to strike him.

"Well, is it?"

"Wait a sec. Do you have a flashlight?" He was frowning now.

Lainey nodded, fetching one of the torches from the kitchen drawer. "Must you be so mysterious?"

"Just give me a minute." He opened the back door and stepped out onto the porch. "So you found two of them here? Only one at the front?"

She nodded. "What difference does that make?" She stepped outside, shivering a little when the cool air hit her.

Jake was shining the light on the porch floor as if looking for something, and for a moment she thought he wasn't going to answer.

"The broken window was in the back, as well. Easier for someone to escape being seen here." He followed the circle of light to the steps and then stopped, seeming to focus on the top step. "Take a look at this."

"What?" Lainey moved next to him, peering down at the wooden step. "It looks as if something is marked on it." Her stomach lurched when she thought of the anonymous letter.

"It's a cross," Jake said. "Chalked on the step."

He turned so quickly they nearly collided. "I'll bet—" He shone the light along the floor in front of the door, shook his head, and shifted it to the window. Reaching out, he touched something white and granular along the outside frame.

"What is it?" Lainey could hear the tension in her voice, and she wrapped her arms around herself protectively.

Jake touched his fingertip to his lips and tasted.

"You shouldn't—" she began, but he shook his head.

"Salt," he said, turning to look at her, his face quizzical in the dim light. "You didn't put it there?"

"Of course not," she snapped. "Don't be ridiculous. What does it mean?"

Jake took her arm, steering her into the house and shutting the door.

"Jake," she said, warning in her voice. "Unless you want me to start throwing things, you'd better answer. What does it mean?"

Jake frowned, shaking his head. "I don't get it," he said. "But I know what it means. It means someone thinks you're a witch."

CHAPTER NINE

JAKE COULD SEE by the expression on Lainey's face
that she hadn't the faintest idea what he was talking
about. For that matter, he wasn't sure whether to treat
the situation as a prank or something more serious.

"If this is your idea of a joke, I don't think it's very
funny." Lainey, hands planted on her hips, looked
ready to take on the world.

"Not a joke—or at least, I'm not joking."

He frowned, glancing toward the window. Now
that he was looking for it, he had no trouble spotting the salt glistening on the outside sill in the soft
glow of the overhead gaslight. The outside of the
window…that suggested something to him, but he
couldn't seem to pull the idea out.

"I suppose this might be someone's notion of a
Halloween prank, but it seems rather fanciful for
that."

Lainey's belligerent expression eased, and she
shook her head. "I don't get any of this. Start at the
beginning. What makes you suppose anyone thinks
such an absurd thing?"

Jake gestured. "The salt on the windowsill, the
broom across the door, the cross chalked on the

step—those are all old Pennsylvania Dutch charms to keep out witches."

"Witches." Her voice invested the word with a suggestion of the ridiculous. "Are you telling me the Amish believe in witches?"

"No, of course not. And I said Pennsylvania Dutch, not Amish."

"Isn't it the same thing?"

"Pennsylvania Dutch refers to the culture of the German-speaking settlers of Pennsylvania. That included plenty of people besides the Amish."

She frowned, looking as if she were scrambling for something to grab onto. "So you're saying that a lot of people around here might be familiar with this…this superstition. Not just the Amish."

Jake nodded, his mind busy with the implications. Should he treat it seriously or dismiss it? He'd rather err on the side of caution.

"Odd little remnants of hexerei exist, strange as that sounds. You ought to hear my dad on the subject—that's one of his interests in local history. Even wrote an article about it for the local historical society."

"Hexerei?" She repeated the word. "So you're pretty well up on the subject, I take it." A trace of suspicion showed in her voice.

"I haven't been sneaking around the back of your house with a saltshaker, if that's what you mean. My point is that anyone might know, including teenagers out for a little Halloween mischief."

"Or the Amish," she said again.

"You're thinking of Zeb, I suppose." He considered. "The Amish are more likely to visit powwow doctors, but witchcraft..." He let that trail off, seeing her confusion. "You've never heard of a powwow doctor? You'd say an herbalist, I suppose. Someone who practices the old remedies for minor ailments. The Amish are more inclined to try a simple home remedy than rush off to the doctor every time someone sneezes."

"Are salt and broomsticks part of the traditional medical lore?" Her jaw firmed. "I still think it was probably Zeb. He'd like nothing better than to see me leave town and give him a clear field. As for anyone thinking me a witch..."

The black cat chose that moment to twine itself around her feet. He couldn't help grinning.

"You have to admit that you look the part. Black cat and all."

Lainey bent and picked up the cat. It responded by nuzzling her neck, rubbing its head against the line of her jaw. Lucky cat.

"So you think I look like a witch?" Lainey lifted her eyebrows, a faint smile teasing her lips.

"A beautiful witch," he said softly. He gave in to the impulse and ran his finger along an errant strand of her black hair, letting it brush her cheek.

Her head tilted, eyes darkening. A step closed the distance between them. He cupped her face, feeling the skin warm beneath his hand, and his lips found hers. She tasted sweet and spicy at the same time. For an instant she seemed to hold back—an onlooker rather than a participant. Then she leaned into him, kissing him back—

A sharp hiss was accompanied by the sting of claws penetrating his shirt. They broke apart, the cat baring its teeth at him.

"Cat!" Lainey yanked the animal away from him. It sprang from her arms, sat down, and began washing itself furiously.

"That's quite a guard cat you have there." *Keep it light,* he warned himself. That might have been the best thing that could have happened.

"I'm so sorry. I don't know what got into him. Did he tear your shirt?"

He brushed at the snag, dismissing it. "No harm done. Actually, it's reassuring to see that you're not defenseless."

"I wouldn't be defenseless even if I didn't have the cat." Her eyes narrowed, much as the cat's had done. "My self-defense class was very thorough."

"I believe you," he said quickly, suspecting her prickliness was due to the same cause as his own discomfort. Neither of them had expected the passion of that kiss. "But despite your prowess, maybe you ought to have the locks changed, just to be on the safe side."

Lainey frowned, turning to stare at the door. "I hate to make changes to Aunt Rebecca's house when she can't approve them. Anyway, the…well, vandalism, if you want to call it that, came from the outside."

"True. Actually, that was what seemed odd about the salt. I'd expect it to be on the inside."

"That proves it, doesn't it? Whoever is badgering me, they can't get in. And I refuse to believe I have to watch out for villagers carrying torches."

He smiled at the image. "No, I don't think you need to worry about that. Still, I don't want to ignore this business. Someone is showing a lot of ill will toward you, for whatever reason."

"Zeb, trying to chase me away," she said promptly. "No one else could have any reason for trying to scare—" She stopped abruptly, seeming to turn inward to examine some possibility.

"What? Did you think of someone else who might want to make your life uncomfortable?"

"Certainly not." She said it sharply, but she didn't look at him, planting a small sliver of doubt in his mind.

Maybe best to let it go for the moment. "If you don't mind, I'll ask my dad about anyone practicing hexerei in the area. That might lead to some answers. In the meantime, I think you ought to be sure the dead bolts are fastened whenever you're in the house alone."

"Dead bolts?" Her eyebrows lifted. "The front and back doors have old-fashioned slide bolts, that's it. But yes, it makes sense to lock up when I'm here alone." She glanced toward the door, and he suspected that was his cue to leave.

"You're sure you wouldn't rather stay elsewhere? I'll bet Rachel would be glad to find a room for you, and you'd be right next door." And he'd feel better, knowing she wasn't alone at night.

She shook her head with decision. "I'm staying here. It's as much home as anywhere else I've lived." As if thinking she'd given away too much, she spun and walked swiftly to the front door, forcing him to follow. "Thanks for coming by, Jake. I appreciate it."

He lingered, his hand on the knob. "I'll see what I can find out. Stay safe, will you?"

"I'm not worried." She looked at the door so pointedly that he had to open it.

Jake stepped outside, taking a quick look around the front. But the joker must have exhausted his energy, or maybe his salt, on the back of the house.

"Good night, Jake. And thank you."

Before he could move, she closed the door, and he heard the sound of the bolt sliding over.

She was safe. There was no logical reason to be worried about a series of pranks that had caused little damage.

But he couldn't help thinking that the situation ran deeper than they'd guessed, and he didn't like it one bit.

LAINEY MADE AN effort to dismiss thoughts of both Jake and witchcraft from her mind as she stepped off the elevator at the hospital the next day. Maybe not so oddly, Jake was the more stubborn of the two.

She couldn't, she absolutely couldn't, let herself get involved with her great-aunt's attorney. Besides which, he was the last man in the world who would suit her—a conservative, small-town professional who was as rooted here as the maples along Main Street. If Jake—

The door to her aunt's room swung open, and Zeb barreled out. His gaze focused on her.

"You. You said Rebecca was better. That she was starting to wake up. But she's not." He seemed far more upset than she'd have expected. Perhaps she'd been misjudging him.

"Aunt Rebecca is doing better, really. She's starting to move and respond to voices. It will just take time. You'll see."

"Time," he repeated.

"That's right." She tried an encouraging smile. "I'm sure you'll see the changes soon."

"Then why are you thinking to put her in a nursing home?" His graying beard seemed to bristle with antagonism.

"I'm not." A conversation with Uncle Zeb always seemed filled with potholes. "But a rehab facility—"

"Rebecca belongs with family. We will take her." He said the words as if they were a command from on high. Then he walked away, not waiting for any further input from her.

Lainey watched him stab at the elevator button. Should she go after him and try to explain?

Before Lainey could make up her mind to try, the elevator doors had swished open. Zeb disappeared inside, and they closed again.

Maybe that was just as well. She'd be better off

communicating the plans for Rebecca to a less antagonistic member of the family.

Lainey turned to the room to find her cousin Katie standing at the door. Obviously she'd heard, and dismay was written plainly on her round, normally cheerful face.

"You heard?" Lainey took her arm and guided her back into the room. She didn't intend to have another family wrangle in the hallway where anyone might hear.

"Lainey, you are not thinking of putting Aunt Rebecca in a nursing home? You wouldn't."

"No, I'm not. Really." She ought to try and have some members of the family on her side, and Katie was a good place to start. "The doctor said that if she improved, she should go to the rehab center. That's where she'll get the help she needs to start walking and talking again. You see?"

Katie nodded a little doubtfully. "But couldn't we do that at home? I'm sure she'd rather be in her own house while she gets better."

"I know how you feel." She pressed Katie's work-roughened hand. "But we haven't been trained in how to help someone who's recovering from a stroke. The rehab place has people who understand all that, and they have all the equipment, as well."

"*Ja,* I see that, all right. But Aunt Rebecca should have people who love her around her."

"I'm sure the nurses and therapists will let us help. They can even show us what to do when Aunt Rebecca does come home."

Some of the worry eased out of Katie's face. "I would like that, that's certain sure." She glanced toward the hospital bed. "But I don't see that she's much better today."

"She was yesterday," Lainey said, moving to the bed. She leaned over to kiss her aunt's cheek. "Aunt Rebecca, it's me, Lainey. And Katie is here, too. Won't you open your eyes for us?"

Nothing happened. Katie clasped Rebecca's hand in hers. She murmured something softly in Pennsylvania Dutch.

Rebecca's eyelids fluttered. Her brow creased a little, as if she struggled to understand something. Then she opened her eyes.

"There, see?" Pleasure mingled with relief. "It wasn't just a fluke yesterday. She's getting better. You are, aren't you, Aunt Rebecca?"

Rebecca's hand moved, and Lainey clasped it warmly in hers. She glanced at Katie.

Tears were spilling down Katie's face, and she didn't make any effort to wipe them away. "Ach, Rebecca, I am *sehr* glad you are waking up."

Rebecca's frown deepened. Her gaze flickered around the room.

"You're in the hospital," Lainey said quickly. "It's all right. You had a bad fall, but you're better now."

Aunt Rebecca's lips curved in a smile. "Lainey," she murmured.

"That's so," Katie exclaimed. "She's come all this way to take care of you." Her smile glowed through her tears. "Ach, it's a shame she didn't open her eyes when Zeb was here."

Lainey nodded, although it occurred to her that Rebecca might not have been eager to see her brother-in-law. But that was probably just prejudice on her part.

Katie was talking in Pennsylvania Dutch again, leaning close to Rebecca. Lainey studied her face, showing such pleasure at the smallest step. Katie was probably about her mother's age, but there the resemblance ended.

Her mother's face had been *touched up* as she'd said so many times that she could no longer show much emotion at all. Perfect hair, perfect makeup, perfect weight—Mom was fighting every inch of the way to stay young.

Katie was frankly middle-aged, and it didn't seem to bother her in the least. Her face, free of makeup, showed the life she'd led in her plump cheeks, natural color and honest wrinkles.

Katie returned her gaze suddenly, her eyes filled with tears. "You were right," she said. "Rebecca must go to the place where they can help her best, and we'll do all we can."

Lainey could practically feel her longing to do something positive for Rebecca. "You know, they might need someone who speaks Pennsylvania Dutch to help with her speech."

"Ach, that would be a joy to do." Katie's face beamed. "I'll come every day."

She looked ready to start any second now.

"We'll have to talk to the doctor about when they'll be ready to switch Aunt Rebecca to the rehab unit," Lainey cautioned.

Katie nodded. "That's so. But I think it'll be soon." She smiled at Rebecca and got a smile in return.

Rebecca still clasped Lainey's hand, and Lainey was heartened by the strength of the grip. Her aunt really was doing better. Maybe Lainey ought to bring up the possibility of selling the mill property.

Still, that might just worry her, and there wasn't a need to have an answer so quickly. Even once it was advertised, the property would take time to sell.

"I don't know where Zeb got that idea about a nursing home." Katie shook her head. "Just getting upset for no reason—that's Uncle Zeb all over."

That was an interesting question, it seemed to Lainey. She hadn't discussed it with any of the family, so what had made him make that accusation?

A memory slid to the surface of her mind—of herself hurrying into the dining room, getting ready to go to Rachel's for supper, and finding the folder with the list of nursing homes misplaced. She might have done it herself, of course. Or—

"Do many people have keys to Aunt Rebecca's house?" she asked.

Katie looked surprised. "All the family does, that's certain sure. So we can get in when she needs help. Is something wrong?"

"No, nothing." She thought fast, not eager to offend Katie, of all people. "I'm just accustomed to locking the door when I leave and at night, and I wouldn't want to lock anyone out."

"Ach, no need to worry about that. Goodness knows how many keys there are floating around the family." Katie was cheerfully unconcerned.

Lainey wished she could have that reaction. No doubt Zeb had a key, and if he'd wanted to take a look at Lainey's papers, he could do so easily.

And not only that. There was Thomas, his grandson, working right across the street, in a perfect position to keep an eye on her.

JAKE PERCHED ON the edge of his desk, nursing a mug of coffee and watching his father pace to the window and back again. It was obvious Dad had something on his mind, and his conversation about the weather had been a sort of verbal throat-clearing.

From lengthy knowledge of his father, Jake suspected that meant there was something Dad wanted to bring up but was reluctant to do so. If Jake didn't make an effort to move this along, they could be here all day.

"What's up, Dad? Did I insult a client or behave in a manner inappropriate to an attorney?"

Dad blinked. "No, of course not. Sorry. I have to confess to a bit of curiosity about the situation with Lainey Colton. Has she indicated how long she intends to stay in Deer Run?"

"Not really." Jake made setting his coffee mug down an excuse not to meet his father's eyes, afraid his face might betray too much of his feeling about

Lainey and that kiss. "But she seems committed to help her great-aunt as long as she's needed."

He glanced up to find that his father was studying his face.

"You find her…um…attractive, do you?"

Jake tried to hide a grin. Dad had been so reluctant to discuss the facts of life that he'd handed off the traditional father/son talk about sex to Jake's mother, which had been embarrassing for both of them.

"Lainey is attractive, yes." Beautiful, even. Was Dad assuming something based on the amount of time Jake was devoting to her? "I don't plan to do anything inappropriate with a client, though."

That wasn't a lie. He hadn't exactly planned on that kiss.

"Properly speaking, it's Rebecca who is our client. Our responsibility is to her."

Jake studied his father's face. Poor Dad, tiptoeing around the subject.

"Look, whatever it is that's bothering you, why don't you just come out with it? It's obvious you have some reservations about the situation."

His father sighed. "I suppose you're right. I may be misjudging the young woman, but given her mother's behavior, I can't help being concerned."

"Her mother?" Jake's eyebrows lifted. "What does her mother have to do with anything?"

"Maybe nothing. Maybe…" Dad sighed. Shook his head. "Deanna Colton was always a problem. Rebecca worried about her, and Isaac worried about Rebecca's caring for her."

"I've gathered that Lainey isn't especially close to her mother." Now that he thought of it, he wasn't quite sure how he had come by that impression, but there it was.

"That might be all to the good. Deanna was hardly a candidate for mother of the year. She made several efforts to get money out of her aunt, and more often than not, Rebecca shelled out. She couldn't bear to think of the little girl—Lainey, that is—doing without, from what Isaac told me."

"He talked to you about it?" That was surprising.

Dad nodded. "I don't suppose he'd have brought it up, but he wanted to be sure that if something happened to him, Rebecca would be protected." Dad shrugged. "Unfortunately, there wasn't much I could suggest that he was willing to do."

Jake considered that. "The summer Lainey came to stay—how did that come about?"

"That was a perfect example of the woman's attitude." He father sounded annoyed, even after all these years. "She just showed up with the child in tow, no notice, no letter, nothing. She claimed she'd just dropped by for a visit. And then she slipped away in the night, leaving the child behind."

"Does Lainey know that?" Jake asked, his tone sharp.

"I doubt it. Certainly Rebecca and Isaac wouldn't tell her. They made her welcome, of course, but Isaac worried about how attached Rebecca became. He was afraid she'd be upset if Deanna turned up and took the child away. Which, of course, was exactly what she did."

"Poor kid," Jake said softly, an image of a small Lainey in his mind. "She got shortchanged in the parent department, didn't she?"

Dad nodded. "Apparently the father was completely out of the picture, and as for Deanna…well, she was a taker. Always was, always will be, most likely."

"You're probably right," Jake said. "But what does all this have to do with what Lainey's doing now?"

Dad looked unhappy. "It's not that I don't trust your judgment. I'd just like to know you'll be cautious in your dealings with her. Rebecca is our responsibility, after all. And Lainey…well, what if Lainey turns out to be just like her mother?"

CHAPTER TEN

I⊤ HAD BEEN a mistake, Lainey decided, to start looking through the scrapbook when she was going to bed last night. She glared at her reflection in the mirror. A night haunted alternately by sleeplessness and nightmares didn't do much for one's appearance.

She patted a touch of concealer on the dark circles under her eyes, decided that looked worse, and wiped it off again. People would just have to take her the way she was.

People, in this case, referred to whoever she might find visiting in Aunt Rebecca's room, followed by the physician and the social worker again this afternoon. If all went well, they'd be able to finalize Aunt Rebecca's move to the rehab facility, tentatively set for Monday.

She turned away from the chest of drawers and her gaze fell on the scrapbook where she'd left it the night before, lying open on the oval hooked rug next to the bed. Stooping, she picked it up, smoothing the page. Rachel probably wouldn't appreciate it if the scrapbook was damaged while in her care.

The page facing her was one of her drawings from that summer. She'd apparently imagined a castle scene, with an unmistakable Laura dressed as a princess and Aaron her handsome knight. There was a certain amount of subtlety to the drawing that surprised her. She'd only been ten, but she'd managed to suggest that Aaron and Laura saw only each other, ignoring the supporting figures that looked on.

Too bad that early talent hadn't matured as she might have hoped. Dreams of being an artist in Paris had been shunted aside by the necessity of earning a living, and her imagination had been channeled into commercial art, persuading people to buy certain products and eat at certain restaurants.

Lainey frowned. The picture seemed to be trying to tell her something. The jester was apparently meant to be Victor Hammond. A bulky guard with a vacant face stood behind the princess, while in the shadows lurked a wizard. Laura and Aaron saw none of them—only each other, caught in their romantic dream of happily ever after.

Lainey closed the scrapbook firmly and slid it into the top drawer of the dresser. Happily ever after was a child's dream—not something that occurred in real life unless, perhaps, one was either very lucky or very good. And she wasn't either of those.

Trotting down the stairs, Lainey grabbed her handbag and jacket from the hook in the front hall and hurried outside, locking the door carefully behind her.

Making a mental list of all that had to be done, Lainey hurried to the car. As she reached for the door handle, she stopped, heart sinking. Both tires on the driver's side were flat.

Both tires? This was stretching the long arm of coincidence a bit too far. It might be time to report this harassment to the police.

A door closed, and she turned to see Meredith coming toward her across the lawn. "Problems?" she asked.

Lainey gestured. "As you can see." She ran a hand through her hair. "I could change one, but two—"

Meredith's gaze flicked from one tire to the other. "This can't be an accident."

"No." It couldn't be.

"Rachel told me about the problems you had while I was away." Meredith's frown deepened. "I don't like this. Halloween pranks are one thing, but deliberate vandalism is another. Do you have any ideas?"

Lainey shook her head. Oh, she had ideas, but none she wanted to share. "I had hoped not to involve the police, but I think I'll have to."

Meredith's smile was strained, reminding Lainey that she'd apparently been under suspicion at the time of her mother's death. She sought for something tactful to say, but nothing came to mind.

"Yes, I think you should. In the meantime, let me call a local garage for you. All right?" Cell phone in hand, Meredith raised her eyebrows in a question.

"That would be great, thanks. I don't really know anyone." And she suspected that Meredith, with her take-charge manner and businesslike incisiveness, might get better results.

Meredith was crisp and brief on the phone, and she clicked off with a satisfied smile. "I called Armstrong's Garage. Someone will be right out." She paused. "Would you like me to wait with you?"

Lainey shook her head. If was obvious, given the neat pants outfit Meredith wore and the portfolio she carried, that she'd been heading out on business.

"I'll be fine. Thanks again so much." She paused, but surely Meredith would realize Rachel had told her where she'd gone. "I hope you had a good time in Pittsburgh."

Meredith's face softened, eyes sparkling. "Wonderful. You'll have to meet Zach. He's coming here in a couple of weeks."

Lainey managed a smile. Would she even be here in a couple of weeks? She felt oddly adrift at the thought.

"I'll look forward to it."

"Good." Meredith started toward the garage on the far side of her house, and then turned back. "By the way, Rachel and I are hoping you'll go to the Apple Festival with us on Saturday. It's a Deer Run tradition you shouldn't miss."

"Sounds like fun. If I don't have to do anything for Aunt Rebecca, I'd love to." Doing something just for fun? That would be a break from routine.

"Good. I'll check with Rachel and set up a time. See you later." With a quick wave, Meredith hurried off.

Lainey wasn't sure what happened at an apple festival, but she appreciated the offer, though she had to admit that she still felt as if this friendship with Rachel and Meredith was rather lopsided. They seemed perfectly ready to pick up where they'd left off twenty years ago, while her memories weren't much clearer than the night she'd arrived back in Deer Run. Still, despite that lack, she felt a bond with them that she'd seldom experienced.

A blue pickup with *Armstrong's Garage* emblazoned on the side pulled up a few minutes later. The man who climbed out wore the usual blue-and-white pin-striped coveralls with a black-and-gold Pirates ball cap. Coveralls, she decided, must come in extra-large sizes, because the man was massive—big, broad-shouldered, and running to flab.

"Hear you have a flat." He approached, fixing her with the curious stare that she'd begun to get used to.

"Two of them." She pointed out the obvious. "I could have changed one, but I don't have an extra spare."

"Don't s'pose so. Let's see what we got here." He squatted, peering at the nearest tire. "Not so bad as all that. Looks like somebody just let the air out."

The relief that swept over her took her by surprise. "Just a prank then," she said.

He stared at her for a moment. "Not a very nice one." He took the ball cap off, wiped his forehead, and settled it again. "Kids are getting meaner about Halloween and starting earlier, seems like. Shoot, it's not until Monday."

"I'm glad they didn't damage the tires any worse." She glanced at her watch, mindful of her appointment with her aunt's doctor and social worker. "Will it take long to fix, Mr....?"

"Armstrong," he said, nodding to the name on the truck. "You can call me Moose. Have it done in a few minutes. Just let me get the pump."

That was the name embroidered in red on the coveralls, then. Moose. It seemed familiar. He seemed familiar, for that matter.

And then she realized. Of course he seemed familiar. She'd just been looking at her own drawing of him. He'd been the guard in the picture of Laura.

"I think I remember you," she said as he knelt to attach the pump. "I'm Lainey Colton, Rebecca Stoltzfus's great-niece. I remember you from the summer I spent here when I was ten."

Was she imagining it, or did his hands stop moving for a moment? His only response was a grunt that might mean anything.

"You were a friend of Laura's, I think. I happened to see her a day or two ago."

Still no response. Moose finished the front tire and hauled the pump over to the back one.

Odd, wasn't it? Surely it would be more natural for him to say something.

She watched the tire inflate slowly. Moose had been one of Laura's admirers, she realized, like the others in that picture. Moose finished the job, tightening the cap on the valve. She couldn't tell anything about his reaction to her questions—not when all she could see was his back.

"I have to admit that I had a crush on Aaron that summer. It was so tragic when he died. Wasn't it?"

The hubcap he held clattered to the ground. He stood, and suddenly he was looming over her, a jack handle still in his grip.

"What're you driving at with all these questions?" His broad face reddened alarmingly.

Lainey took an involuntary step back and then wished she hadn't. She didn't want him thinking she was scared of him, but there was a kind of dumb malignance in his glare that was unsettling.

"I wasn't questioning you. Just making conversation, that's all."

"Yeah? I don't want to talk about it." He fingered the jack handle. "It's done with now. Aaron's dead and Victor's dead and that's an end to it."

"I'm sorry. I didn't mean to bring up something painful."

"Nosy kids." He glared at her. "That's what you were. I remember. For all I know, you might've been the ones told the chief about me getting the beer for the parties."

"We didn't. How could we know that?" And why on earth would that bother him after so many years? Maybe he was the sort who'd hold on to a grudge forever.

"Lots of kids did that. I wasn't the only one."

"I'm sure you weren't."

"Anyway, it didn't have anything to do with Aaron getting drowned." He turned away, apparently satisfied he'd made his point, and tossed the jack handle into the truck, where it landed with a loud clang.

Lainey couldn't help venturing another question. "Did the police say it did? If Aaron had been drinking—"

He swung back toward her, his big fists clenching. "If you want to stick around Deer Run, you better learn to keep quiet about stuff."

He tossed the rest of his gear in the pickup, climbed in, and backed out of the drive without, as far as she could tell, even a glance behind him. His truck was out of sight before she realized she hadn't paid him.

That had been an odd reaction. In fact, Deer Run seemed full of people who reacted oddly to talk of Aaron Mast's death.

By evening, Lainey felt a sense of accomplishment. Aunt Rebecca's situation was settling down, and plans had been made to transfer her to the rehab facility on Monday. She couldn't remember when she'd felt so optimistic about Aunt Rebecca.

Or, for that matter, so satisfied with her own actions. In the ordinary routine of her life, no one depended on her. She'd thought she liked it that way. Being responsible for Aunt Rebecca might be a bit scary at times, but it was also oddly fulfilling.

As Lainey had expected, the hospital billing department had begun making noises about being paid. Given the amount Aunt Rebecca had in the bank, she could handle that as long as they deferred the property tax payment for the moment.

She'd considered talking the matter over with some other member of the family, but who? Certainly not Zeb, and Lainey was reluctant to burden Katie with it, fearing she'd feel responsible. No, Aunt Rebecca had trusted her, and she'd begun to feel worthy of that trust.

At least they'd seen some positive steps today. She and Katie were both convinced that Aunt Rebecca understood what was said to her, even though she did have some difficulty in expressing herself.

That would improve. She'd assured her great-aunt of that, reading the frustration in Rebecca's face plainly.

The only unresolved issue at the moment was exactly how she was supposed to access the funds to pay the bills. Lainey had called Jake's office somewhat reluctantly. Exposure to Jake had been risky to her emotional balance.

As it happened, he hadn't been in, so she'd left a message with his secretary explaining what she needed and requesting the woman call back with the information.

Lainey double-checked her phone to be sure she hadn't missed a call and then returned to sorting the papers she'd spread out on the dining room table. One good thing—living as simply as she did, Aunt Rebecca had few bills. Lainey jotted down the figures, not wanting to miss anything. It had grown dark outside while she worked, and the overhead fixture glowed gently. The house was quiet.

Too quiet, it seemed to her. Did it bother Aunt Rebecca to be alone here? Probably not, since she was used to it. Still, even with the best of outcomes from her stroke, could Rebecca really go back to living on her own?

The cell phone sounded loud in the stillness. Lainey checked the caller ID with a caution that had become almost automatic. It was Jake.

She paused for a moment and then picked up the call.

"Jake. You could have just had your secretary get back to me."

"True enough." His deep voice seemed to hit an answering chord in her. "But I thought you might want the information before Monday."

"I do get the feeling the hospital would like to see some payment before they sign off on Aunt Rebecca for the move to rehab. But I don't suppose they'd hold her hostage."

His low chuckle disarmed her. "It never does to take anything for granted where billing offices are concerned. In any event, it's very simple. All you have to do is stop at the bank with the copies I gave you of the power of attorney information. They'll need a sample of your signature, and that's about it."

"Good." She put her great-aunt's bankbook on top of the folder so she wouldn't forget it. "I'm glad one thing is simple."

"You sound relieved. You haven't had any more trouble with vandalism, have you?" His tone sharpened.

"Nothing but two flat tires," she said.

"When? Did you call the police?"

"This morning. And no, I didn't, because they weren't damaged. Someone had just let the air out of them."

"I still think you should—"

"Wait a second." Lainey held the phone away from her ear, focusing on a sound from the rear of the house.

A familiar meow could be heard even through the door, and Lainey smiled. Cat was persistent.

"What's wrong?" Alarm threaded Jake's tone.

"Nothing. It's just the cat." She headed for the back door, still talking. "I probably should try to find the owners. They might not like my adopting him."

It was a good thing she'd left the gaslight on in the kitchen. Fumbling for it in the dark wasn't her favorite thing. The plaintive meow sounded again, and then turned abruptly to an earsplitting shriek. Something thudded on the porch. The cat gave a yowl that made the hair on her nape lift. Something was wrong.

Dropping the phone, she raced to the door, fragments of news stories about animal cruelty flashing through her mind. The black cat, Halloween—the possibilities repelled her. She flung the door open. The cat streaked inside, fur ruffled, tail standing on end, and took refuge under the table.

Fury coursed through Lainey, swamping caution.

Grabbing a cast-iron skillet from the rack above the counter, she charged outside. If some kid thought he could get away with terrorizing a defenseless animal, he'd soon learn otherwise.

She plunged down the porch steps, scanning the yard. Too dark to see much—surely he or they couldn't have gotten away that quickly.

A faint rustle had her swinging toward the overgrown bush at the corner of the porch. Something made the branches move.

Holding the skillet like a weapon, she approached. "Get out of there," she ordered. "Now!"

Nothing. She prodded the edge of the shrub. "You'd better come out. I've already called the police," she lied.

The night was silent, save for a faint sound that was probably Jake, shouting into the phone. Branches moved. Suddenly a figure exploded from the bush, barreled into her, knocking her flat. It loomed over her, black and menacing.

The cat leaped to the railing, hissing and spitting. Lainey drew breath to scream. The figure turned and bolted into the shadows, disappearing in an instant.

Lainey let out a shaky breath, then another. She was still in one piece, and the ground was harder than one might think. Rolling to her side, she got to her feet and stumbled up the steps.

Cat leaped from the railing to her arms, apparently confident she'd catch him. Holding him close, she went inside. Closed and locked the door. And realized she'd left Jake hanging on the phone.

When she bent to pick it up, the cat scrambled out of her arms and began washing himself furiously, as if to wipe away every trace of the intruder. Lainey understood how he felt. The shock of the attack—

She put the phone to her ear. "Jake?"

No answer, but the call was still open. Frowning, she clicked off and began to hit the number again when she heard pounding on the front door.

Lainey hurried to the door, pulling it open without bothering to look. It had to be Jake.

He surged inside, grasping her arms. "Are you all right? What happened?"

"I'm okay." Her voice sounded shakier than it should. "How did you get here so fast?"

"I was in the car when I called you, ready to head home. Tell me what happened."

"Someone out back. I heard the cat yowl as if in pain. I thought—well, I didn't know what to think. Kids, maybe." She took a breath, trying to calm herself. "When I opened the door the cat raced in, obviously terrified. It made me so angry I charged out without thinking."

"You should have locked the door and called the police. Or told me what was going on."

She tried to muster up annoyance at his tone. "Listen, there's no point in telling me what I should have done. Do you want to hear this or not?"

Jake's lips quirked, his obvious rush of adrenaline ebbing. "I guess you are all right. Yes, please. Tell me what happened."

"Well, I grabbed a skillet, just—well, I wanted

to have something in my hand. I couldn't see anyone, but how could they have gotten away that fast? And then I saw something moving behind that big forsythia at the corner of the porch. I yelled at them to come out."

His eyes closed for a split second, as if in pain. "It didn't occur to you…" He let that trail off with a warning glance.

"Anyway, nothing moved, so I said I'd called the police. Then a figure burst out, running right into me and knocking me flat."

"A figure?" He frowned. "Man or woman?"

"I couldn't tell." She rubbed her arms, suddenly cold. "It wore black and had something over its face. Anyway, he or she seemed big, but maybe that's because I was lying on the ground looking up at it." She managed a shaky smile. "Among the worst ten seconds of my life. Then the cat jumped up on the railing, spitting and hissing, and he-she-or-it ran."

Jake was silent for a moment, frowning. He reached out to touch her arm in a tentative gesture. "You're sure you're not hurt?"

"I'm fine." Lainey put as much confidence in her voice as she could produce. "Really." Now it was her turn to frown. "But what was the point of it? What did he want?"

"I wish I knew." The cat stalked into the room and gave Jake a disdainful look. Jake stared back. "He looks for all the world as if he's reminding me that he protected you and I didn't."

Lainey's heart gave a slight lurch. "It's not your job to protect me."

Jake seemed to study her face, as if probing for meaning. "If you want me to apologize for kissing you, I will. It was unprofessional, to say the least. But even leaving that aside, I'm the one who brought you here. That gives me a reason to look out for you."

Lainey wasn't sure how to react to that. Was he regretting the kiss? It was a bit late to deny that they were attracted to each other.

"I don't need an apology. As for looking out for me—well, I've been doing that myself for a long time."

Jake looked as if he thought that was a sad commentary on her life, but he didn't say so.

"Well, whatever is going on here, we're in this together." He glanced at the cat again. "Were they after that cat? Or did he just get in the way?"

"I don't know." Lainey shoved her hair back away from her face. "At first I thought it was kids. You hear about cruelty to animals—cats especially—around Halloween."

Jake's frown deepened. "I suppose, although the pranks have always been pretty benign around here. But it seems more likely that it would be a group of kids, not a lone individual. And why the attack on you?"

She shrugged, wrapping her arms around herself. "Just trying to get away, most likely. I was in the way."

"Could be," he conceded. "But what if all this—

the broken window, the witchcraft signs, what happened tonight—what if it's really directed at you?"

"If so, I'd think it has to be Zeb." She spread her hands wide. "There isn't anyone else who'd want to scare me."

Other than her anonymous caller, of course. But he or she couldn't be here.

"Could it have been Zeb tonight?" His gaze sharpened on her face.

Lainey tried to picture the image in her mind. "I don't think so," she said reluctantly. "The beard—the size—it's all wrong."

"But if the mask or clothing covered the beard—" he began.

She shook her head. "Come here." She went quickly to the dining room table, pulled the pad she'd been using toward her, and sketched with rapid strokes, the image becoming clearer in her mind as she did.

"See? It looked big looming over me, but that beard couldn't have been hidden. This was a black or navy sweatshirt with a hood, I think. Can you imagine Zeb in something like that?"

"No, I guess not." He leaned over her, his hand planted on the table next to hers. "What's this?" He pointed to a drawing farther up the page, next to the list she'd been making.

"I was doodling while we talked on the phone, that's all." She didn't even remember doing it, but she'd sketched a small picture of trees, arching together, reaching out in an oddly menacing way. There seemed to be an impression of a stream behind them.

"It looks like Parson's Dam." Jake's voice was flat. "Where Aaron died."

She shoved the pad away with a quick movement. "How could it be? I haven't been back there since I returned. Anyway, what if it was?"

"I don't know." The words came out slowly, and Jake's expression was troubled. "But there have been a string of problems growing out of Aaron's death, starting when Rachel came back to Deer Run. Rachel, Meredith, now you." He shook his head. "It sounds stupid even to say it. But what if that's not over?"

She'd like to dismiss that idea, but she couldn't, not entirely. Not when it still haunted her dreams.

She clasped her hands in front of her on the table. "Are you saying I should leave?"

"No." Jake put his hand over hers, enveloping them in a firm grip. "I'm saying be careful."

Someone was trying to scare her away from Deer Run. Given all the times she'd packed up and moved on because of something relatively minor, one would think that was her automatic response to trouble.

Maybe automatic responses could change. She wouldn't leave. She was going to stay, do what she'd come here to do, and find out who was behind all this. She was done running.

CHAPTER ELEVEN

JAKE HAD FINALLY talked Lainey into calling the police the previous evening. Now he was beginning to wonder whether that had been a mistake.

He walked toward the fire hall grounds on Saturday morning. The young patrolman who'd come in answer to the call was now busy directing Apple Festival traffic into the parking area. That job was probably far more suited to his talents, Jake considered.

Maybe he was being unfair. The kid probably wasn't much more than eighteen or nineteen, with little experience.

He'd been polite enough, listening gravely to Lainey's story. He'd asked questions and carefully jotted down the answers in a small notebook.

And in the end he'd ventured the opinion that it was most likely Halloween-inspired vandalism. Kids, he'd opined from the height of his eighteen or nineteen years, were copying things they ran across on social media, thinking it made them cool.

Jake had had to bite his tongue to keep from spilling out the whole complicated story of who might want to hasten Lainey's departure from Deer Run and why. Neither she nor Rebecca would thank him for involving family members with the police.

Jake joined the stream of people moving onto the fire hall grounds. The Apple Festival was one of the highlights of life in Deer Run, and no one who called himself a resident would miss it.

But he had an ulterior motive for his presence today. Lainey had mentioned she was coming with Meredith and Rachel. He wanted Lainey's cooperation for a little experiment he planned to try, and at least if he spoke to her in the midst of a crowd, he wouldn't be tempted to kiss her.

His jaw clenched at the thought of how difficult it had been to keep his hands off her last night. He'd left so abruptly that she'd probably thought him rude.

Stupid. He wasn't a teenage boy, easy victim to raging hormones. He'd never found it difficult to maintain a respectful distance from a client before.

Well, he'd have to figure out a way, because if she agreed to his suggestion, they'd be spending even more time together in the near future.

He stood still for a moment, scanning the crowd for Lainey and earning an annoyed look from an out-of-towner with a camera. Murmuring an apology, he let himself be caught up in the slowly moving stream.

Apple fritters, apple cider, apple-flavored ice cream, craft items of every description decorated with apples—and people were buying, locals and visitors alike. After all, a big share of the profits went to the volunteer fire company, and everyone benefited from its good work.

Keeping an eye out for Lainey, he worked his way along one side of the row of stands. The trouble with knowing everyone in town was that he was naturally expected to buy at every booth. Faithfully promising to come back after he'd made the rounds, he managed to keep himself unencumbered until he spotted his quarry.

Lainey stood among the small group gathered around the apple-butter making demonstration, listening intently to Rachel's little girl, Mandy, who was apparently explaining the process, to judge by her gestures. Meredith and Rachel looked on, smiling either at the child's enthusiasm or at Lainey's questions.

Jake sidled through the group of onlookers to them, inhaling the rich, spicy aroma of cooking apples. "Mandy's giving the lecture today, is she?" he asked.

Mandy looked up and grinned. "I helped my *grossmammi* and *grossdaadi* and the aunts and uncles make it last week."

"That means you're an authority," he said gravely.

"She probably knows more than you do," Rachel teased.

"Come on, now, I've taken my turn stirring the kettle a time or two in the past." He studied Lainey's face, trying not to stare. She was looking a bit worse for the wear this morning, the lines of strain around her eyes accentuated. The wave of protectiveness he felt at the sight was probably inappropriate.

"Mind if I borrow Lainey for a few minutes? Not

long, I promise," he added quickly, as Lainey seemed about to refuse. "Just a couple of questions."

Rachel answered before Lainey had the chance, catching Mandy's hand. "No problem. We promised to stop by the apple dumpling stand my cousin is running." She tapped her daughter's nose. "I'm sure she had an apple dumpling with your name on it."

"I'll catch up with you there, then," Lainey said as they moved off. She turned back to Jake, a question in her eyes. "Problems?"

"No new ones," he said. "Let's walk." He didn't want to begin a private conversation where so many people were standing close to them, no matter how wrapped up they were in the making of apple butter.

She nodded, falling into step with him.

"I take it nothing else happened last night, since you didn't call me." Not that he'd felt at all sure she would. After all, she'd gone after the last threat with a skillet in defense of the cat.

"Everything was quiet," she said. Her smile flickered. "I did have my watch-cat inside."

"Good. I wouldn't want to get on the wrong side of those claws. To say nothing of the cast-iron skillet. If you'd hit anyone with that, I'd be bailing you out of jail today."

"That's all right." She smiled. "It seems I know a good attorney."

"You must mean my dad." Jake shook his head in response to a hail from a friend at the basketball toss stand. "Not now," he called. "Later."

"Wimp." Jase Morgan grinned. "I'll spot you a couple and still beat you."

Lainey raised an eyebrow at him. "Don't let me interrupt your fun."

"That's the trouble with knowing everyone," he said. "I'll go home with empty pockets and an armload of things I have no use for."

"Big man on campus?" she suggested. "Football team, homecoming king, class president?"

He shrugged, suspecting she was laughing at him. "That's small-town life," he said. "I like it." If he'd married Julie, he'd have been ground up in her father's law firm, probably commuting back and forth from the city to the suburbs every day, with little time for anything but work. It hadn't been her father he'd wanted to emulate, but his own. Dad might not have a Rolex or a vacation home in the Caribbean, but he had the respect of everyone he knew.

"I don't suppose that's what you wanted to talk to me about," Lainey said, looking with apparent fascination at a bin of dried apples.

"No." He didn't bother reminding her that she was the one who'd brought it up. Maybe she was trying to redraw the rather shaky boundaries between them. "My questions about hexerei practitioners finally bore fruit. I've found someone local. An elderly woman known as Doctor Mary."

Lainey blinked. "Not really a doctor, I assume."

"Healer, herbalist, practitioner of the traditional lore. The point is, if someone around here is interested in hexerei to the point of putting witch signs around your house, she probably can at least make a guess as to who it is."

Lainey studied his face, as if trying to convince herself that he was serious. "You know, it's hard to believe we're really having this conversation."

"I know," he said impatiently. "You think it's silly. I certainly don't believe in it, but that's not the point. Someone does, and I don't think you can expect much help from the police in finding him."

Lainey's lips relaxed in a rueful smile. "That was useless, wasn't it? He had enough trouble believing in a prowler. He'd probably have put me down as delusional if I started talking about witchcraft."

"At least the prowler is on the record. That's something. Anyway, I'm planning to pay a call on Doctor Mary this evening. Supposedly she's out during the day collecting herbs and so forth, but folks are welcome to come by in the evening."

"Do you think she'll talk to you?"

"Maybe not," he said. "But I suspect she'll talk to you."

"Me?" Lainey stopped, swinging to face him. "I'm not sure that's a good idea."

"Hear me out," he said, lowering his voice. "She probably knows who I am. She'll connect me with the law and clam up. But if someone seriously believes you're a practitioner, she's bound to be curious. Wouldn't you be, in her place?"

"I have trouble imagining myself in her place," Lainey said tartly. "But I guess you have a point. So you want me to go."

"I want you to go with me," he corrected. "I'm not letting you wander off into the woods looking for her cabin alone. You'd never find it. What do you say? Tonight around six?"

Lainey studied his face, frowning a little. Finally she nodded. "I don't have much choice, do I?"

"Not if you're serious about finding out who's behind what's been happening," he said. "I think—" He cut the comment off when someone grabbed his arm.

"Jake, you're just the person I need." Molly McIntyre was chairperson of the Apple Festival—at the moment a very flurried one. "Reverend Nelson was supposed to judge the children's art contest, but he was called away. You're just the person to take over. After all, everyone knows you'll be fair." Molly had an iron grip on his arm and clearly didn't intend to let go.

He glanced at Lainey, finding the expected amusement in her face.

"You'd better go," she said. "I'm sure you're needed."

If she'd said out loud she thought him a big fish in a small pond, she couldn't have made her attitude clearer.

Jake clenched his jaw, reminding himself that this was the life he'd chosen. The life he wanted. With a curt nod, he let himself be towed away.

LAINEY FOUND MEREDITH and Rachel sitting with Mandy at a picnic table set up next to the tent housing the apple dumpling stand.

"We saved you a seat." Meredith waved to the bench next to her.

"My cousin is keeping your dumpling warm," Mandy said, scrambling up. "I'll get it. Do you want ice cream? Ice cream is yummy on apple dumplings."

"Sure, why not? What are a few calories between friends?" Lainey slid onto the bench, smiling at the child's enthusiasm.

Rachel eyed her, obviously battling curiosity. "Did you settle whatever it was Jake wanted?"

Meredith jogged her elbow, laughter in her eyes. "Don't be so polite," she said. "We're old friends, remember? What did Jake want?"

Lainey hesitated for an instant, but why not? She might not have the memories of old friendship as much as the other two did, but at least they understood the situation she was in.

"Someone has been putting witch signs around the house—brooms, salt on the windowsills, chalked crosses. I know, it sounds ridiculous."

"It sounds nasty," Rachel said. "Who would do a thing like that?"

She shrugged, not wanting to speculate. "Jake found a woman he thinks can tell us something about who might have done it—a woman called Doctor Mary. Do you know anything about her?" She addressed the question primarily to Rachel. Someone who'd grown up Amish would, it seemed, be more likely to know about something like this.

Meredith looked blank, but Rachel nodded. "I

didn't realize Doctor Mary was still alive. She must be quite old."

"Don't tell me your parents actually went to a powwow doctor," Meredith said.

Rachel shrugged. "It's not as odd as it sounds. She's a *braucher*—I guess you'd say a sort of faith healer. *Brauchers* use Bible verses and herbs and so forth to heal people and animals." Rachel frowned a little. "Why does Jake think she knows something? I can't imagine her running around your house at night with a salt box. She must be ninety if she's a day."

"I don't think he suspects her," Lainey said. "But if there's someone around who seriously believes I'm a witch, he feels she would know. It seems like a stretch to me, but..."

She let that trail off, because Mandy was returning, carefully holding a plastic bowl in both hands.

"It couldn't hurt," Rachel said obliquely as Mandy set the bowl in front of Lainey. Her glance at her daughter made it clear that the subject was closed for the moment.

Aware of Mandy's gaze on her, Lainey scooped up a spoon of melting vanilla ice cream and warm dumpling. The flavors blended, spicy and sweet together, and the dumpling dough was crisp and tender. "Yummy is right." She grinned at Mandy. "This is absolutely delicious. Thanks for suggesting the ice cream."

Mandy's smile lit her small face. With her blond hair pulled back in a single braid and those blue eyes, she looked like a miniature version of her mother.

"I'll bet Jake would like some, too. He should've come with you."

Lainey blinked. Mandy was obviously a noticing child. "I think he had to go and judge some contest," she said. "So you know Jake, do you?"

"Everybody knows Jake," Mandy said. She wiped her mouth with a paper napkin and shot a glance at her mother. "Can I go see if *Grossmammi* needs help at the quilt stand? She said I could if it's all right with you."

"Sure, go ahead. But nowhere else, mind." Rachel tugged Mandy's braid lightly. "And throw away your trash first."

Mandy gathered up the debris of her snack and scurried off. Lainey found that the other two were watching her.

"What?" she asked.

"So, Jake," Meredith said. "He's certainly spending a lot of time with you."

Lainey concentrated on the dumpling. "He's just trying to do his duty to his client, that's all."

"Funny thing," Meredith said. "He's never taken me out for dinner, and I'm a client. How about you, Rachel? He ever take you out?"

Rachel smiled, shaking her head. "Don't mind her, Lainey. She's just so happy with her Zach that she sees romance everywhere she looks."

"Well, you're just as bad," Meredith retorted, not denying it. "Once you and Colin are married, you'll be even worse."

"Have you set the date yet?" Lainey made an effort to focus the conversation on Rachel's love life, not hers. The whole subject made her skittish, in fact.

"We've talked about next month, but we haven't actually set a date." Rachel had a sweet, gentle smile that seemed to declare her confidence in her love. "Colin's father suffers from dementia, and we don't want to upset him with a sudden change. But soon." Her lips twitched. "Colin claims he's loved me since he was eighteen, and he says we've wasted enough time."

"So you have," Meredith said. "You and Colin need to claim your happily ever after. Don't you think so, Lainey?"

Put on the spot, Lainey tried to find something tactful to say. "I…I'm afraid I don't know much about it." She grimaced. "As much time as my mother spent jumping into and out of matrimony, I have a jaundiced view of what forever means."

"I'm sorry," Rachel said quickly, her voice warm. "We didn't mean to embarrass you."

"It's fine. I'm not embarrassed. Just—wary."

"You and Jake make a good pair then." Meredith was apparently irrepressible on the subject. "Since his engagement ended badly, it's been rare to see him with the same woman twice. I suppose that's why we can't help noticing the amount of attention he's paying to you." She started gathering up plastic bowls and napkins. "All right, I'm done rushing in where angels fear to tread. Rachel's right—my own happiness has made me giddy."

"Don't worry about it. And as for Jake—well, he knows I won't be in Deer Run long."

That was a humiliating thought, implying that she only attracted him when he knew it couldn't lead to anything. Still, that was what she wanted, as well, so she had no reason to complain.

"What next?" Rachel said, pushing the last of the trash into the overflowing can. "More food or crafts?"

"Not more food," Meredith said quickly. "I'm stuffed already. Let's have a look at the crafts."

Lainey, not knowing where anything was, followed the other two as they headed for a row of stands that included everything from an elaborate trailer-mounted shop to a display of jewelry set out on card tables under the shade of a couple of beach umbrellas.

Lainey let herself fall behind them as they walked, ostensibly studying an assortment of earrings. What possessed her to show her prejudices so clearly at the slightest hint of matchmaking? Just because she didn't buy the idea of living happily ever after with someone didn't mean she had to share her opinion. Especially not with Rachel and Meredith, who certainly deserved whatever happiness they'd found.

Besides, love and marriage might actually work out for them. The fact that she was missing the gene that assured lasting love didn't mean that it couldn't happen for others. If she'd had any doubts about that, a string of failed romances should have convinced her, to say nothing of her entanglement with Phillip.

She lifted a necklace off the rack and studied the effect of the green jade against her skin. She'd actually made a piece like this herself once. Pity she'd let that creative outlet slip away. Designing and making jewelry was far more satisfying than designing advertisements. The pleasure she felt in designing the patches for her proposed quilting project confirmed that.

Realizing Meredith and Rachel had moved to the next stand, she put the necklace back in place with a regretful shake of her head for the craftsman. They'd invited her to spend time with them, and she really should make an effort, no matter how distracted she was.

A small group had gathered in front of a stand where a woman was demonstrating spinning. Lainey was working her way toward Meredith and Rachel when a hand closed on her arm. She swung around to find herself face to face with Laura Hammond.

Lainey's stomach gave a lurch. Instead of her usual placid, vacant look, Laura's eyes burned with intensity. Her fingers bit into Lainey's skin.

"I have to talk to you." It was more a demand than a request. She tugged at Lainey's arm. "Come."

Lainey dug her heels in, trying to manage a soothing smile. "We can talk right here," she said quietly. "I'm sure no one is paying any attention to us."

"No!" Laura's voice rose on the word. She sent an almost panicked look around and then leaned close to Lainey. "I don't want anyone to hear. We have to talk alone."

She remembered Jake's speculation about who had really killed Aaron Mast, and a shiver went through her despite the warmth of the day.

"I can't." She tried to pull her arm free, but Laura's grip was unyielding. "I'm with friends."

"Don't be stupid," Laura muttered. "You have to listen. Why won't anyone listen to me?" For a moment she looked genuinely distressed.

"Just tell me now. I'll listen." She shot a look toward Meredith and Rachel, who seemed absorbed in the demonstration. *Look at me,* she demanded silently.

"I can't, not here." Laura's eyes widened, and she released her grip. "We can't talk anymore," she whispered, backing up. "We have to meet somewhere private. I'll let you know where."

Before Lainey could answer, Laura had slipped away in the crowd.

Lainey stood where she was, rubbing the red marks on her arm, trying to reassure herself that anyone would be upset by an encounter with a person who wasn't rational. She had no glimmer of an idea what Laura wanted, but one thing was perfectly clear to her. She wasn't going to attend any private rendezvous with Laura Hammond, no matter what.

"You didn't get any idea what Laura wanted?" Jake couldn't seem to stop himself from asking the question, even though Lainey had apparently told him the entire conversation.

"I'm not sure she knew. She didn't seem as out of

it as the last time I saw her, but that doesn't mean she was making sense." Lainey leaned forward, hand on the dash, to look out the windshield. "Are you sure you know how to find this woman? It's going to be dark soon."

The truck hit a rut in the gravel road, and Lainey's grip tightened. "Have you missed any holes?"

He grinned. "That's why I brought the pickup. Dad keeps telling me to get rid of the old girl, but I can take her anywhere."

"Pickups are female?" she asked, amusement replacing the concern that had been in her voice when she talked about Laura.

"Like ships," he said promptly. "It's a compliment, not an insult."

"Right. To get back to my original question—"

"Yes, I know where I'm going. At least," honesty compelled him to add, "I'm following the directions. Whether they were accurate is another story."

He spotted the derelict barn that figured on his rough map and slowed. "There's supposed to be a lane off to the right beyond this barn."

"There it is." Lainey pointed, then grabbed for a handhold as he turned into the lane.

"Whoever called this a lane was grossly overstating the case." He hit another rut with a clang that suggested the tailpipe was in trouble. "I think we'll have to hoof it from here. Are you up for it?"

"Nothing like a little walk in the country."

Lainey sounded surprisingly cheerful. He liked

a woman who could hang on to her sense of humor when things went awry.

"Right. Let's go." He slid out, not bothering to attempt pulling the pickup over. Nothing motorized was going anywhere on this track, as far as he could tell.

He went around and caught Lainey by the elbows as she slid out. "It's a long way down," he pointed out.

"I think I can manage."

Did he imagine it, or did she sound just a little breathless as she took a step away from him?

He pulled a flashlight from his jacket pocket and trained it on what there was of a path. "The cabin should be about a half mile up the lane."

"Let's go, then." She nodded toward the flashlight. "You must have been a Boy Scout."

"Always prepared, that's me," he said lightly.

"Is that a lawyerly trait?" Lainey seemed to keep up with him without effort.

He considered. "I suppose." He slanted a glance at her and saw she was smiling. "You find that laughable?"

"No. Just…a bit different from the creative types I usually work with."

He nodded, swinging the light to show her a bramble that reached out to snag the unwary. "Advertising, isn't it? You like your job?" She didn't seem in any hurry to get back to it, he'd noticed.

"I'm looking for something else." She shrugged. "Some problems with my boss. I'll be better off elsewhere."

"Just a different job? Or a different city, as well?" He was fishing, wondering if there was a boyfriend in St. Louis who would give her a reason to return.

"I don't plan to stay in St. Louis, if that's what you're asking."

He took her hand to guide her around a fallen tree as the path entered the woods.

"Deer Run's a nice place to settle down," he said. "Always supposing you don't mind being a big fish in a little pond."

She slowed, and he realized she was studying his face. "You really like it here," she said.

He shrugged. "It's where I belong. If you find a place that makes you happy, why would you leave?"

"What about adventure? Excitement?"

He had a feeling that she really wanted to understand what made him tick. "I like travel. Experiencing new places is great, as long as you have a home to return to."

Lainey stumbled over a stone in the path. He caught her, and they were very close there in the dark, so close he could hear her breath. Her fingers tightened on his forearms for an instant, and then she pulled away.

"Not everyone is as lucky as you." She nodded to the path. "Let's get this over with."

CHAPTER TWELVE

SINCE JAKE HAD the flashlight, she had to follow him. Lainey decided that was safer anyway. They couldn't walk side by side, so there was no excuse for Jake to take her arm. His touch was altogether too disturbing to her state of mind.

Still, she was glad he was there. She wouldn't want to be wandering around in the dark woods alone. The trees seemed to crowd close, as if leaning toward them. Like her drawing, Lainey realized. Like her dreams.

"I hope this doesn't give you nightmares," Jake said, as if he'd been reading her thoughts.

"What makes you say that?" Her tone was tart. Or maybe defensive.

She saw his shoulders move in a shrug. "You mentioned something about having vivid dreams. It's probably part of having a creative personality, don't you think?"

"Maybe so. I've always dreamt in Technicolor and high definition. At least I don't sleepwalk any longer. That worried Aunt Rebecca the summer I was here."

"She'd have been afraid you'd get hurt, I suppose. It must have scared your mother, as well."

Now it was her turn to shrug. "She just locked me in my bedroom."

A stick cracked under Jake's foot with a noise like a gunshot, and she gasped.

"Sorry," he said, and she thought she heard amusement in his voice. "It's just as well to let Doctor Mary hear us coming, I think."

"She must like her privacy if she chooses to live clear out here alone." She was talking for the sake of hearing their voices.

"I suppose some mystique is useful to a pow-wow doctor." Jake paused, swinging the beam of light ahead as if searching out the path. "I don't think it's much farther." His torch focused on a row of low, leafy plants. "Looks like part of her garden."

"Peppermint, I think," she said as they passed the plants. "Smell it." Even from a few feet away, the spicy scent made itself known.

"I'll take your word for it," he said. "The cabin—"

A flap of wings, and a ghostly shape swooped over their heads, so close that Lainey ducked, gasping and grabbing Jake's jacket.

"Just an owl," he said. "It startled me, too." He aimed the torch at the branch of a tree about ten or twelve feet away. Round eyes stared back at them.

"It's white," she murmured. Ghostly was definitely the word.

"A snowy owl. Unusual to see around here, but not unheard of." He reached behind him to clasp her hand as he began moving again. "The owl is the symbol of the wisewoman, isn't it? Maybe it's a pet."

If so, Doctor Mary had developed the right props for herself. They stepped into a small clearing where yellow light glowed from the windows of a cabin constructed of rough-hewn logs. *And the right setting,* Lainey added silently.

"There's a fire burning," Jake said. "Doctor Mary must be home. Come on." Clasping her hand firmly in his, Jake led her toward the door.

The door actually stood open, but a frayed piece of fabric hung from the frame, hiding the inside. Jake rapped on the jamb.

A voice called out from inside in a language Lainey didn't understand. Jake apparently thought it was an invitation because he pulled the material back enough so that they could step inside.

Lainey stood blinking in the yellow glow of candles and the wood fire in a rough stone fireplace. The cabin was a single room, it seemed, furnished with a small bed in one corner, a couple of rocking chairs, a long wooden table, and crude cabinets and shelves along the back wall. Every available surface seemed given over to crocks and bottles and bowls of all sizes and shapes, and the drying plants hanging from the rafters practically obscured the ceiling. The mingled scents were somehow both pleasant and overwhelming.

Neither of those words properly described the woman who was bent over a mortar and pestle at the table. Not Amish, Lainey thought, somewhat surprised. Or at least, not dressed like any Amish person she'd ever seen. She was a shapeless bundle of clothes, layered over each other and covered up with a heavy black sweater that hung so loosely it must have been a man's. Her hair was entirely white, and strands had escaped her bun to hang around her face. Her long nose and heavy brows gave her an ominous look, like a witch in a fairy tale.

"Doctor Mary." Jake took a step toward the apparition. "I'm Jake Evans. We came out from Deer Run to see you."

The woman didn't speak. Nothing moved but her eyes, flicking from Jake to Lainey and back again.

"Can you help us?" Jake asked. "We can pay," he added.

"She wants something to help her sleep? Stop her from dreaming?" The apparition took a step around the table, eyes focused on Lainey's face.

Startled, Lainey shook her head. The woman couldn't have heard what they'd been talking about, could she? Or maybe she could. Wasn't that a trick fake psychics and fortune-tellers used, to find out a little about the people who came to them and use that to get them talking?

"No sleeping medicines," Jake said quickly.

"That's right," Lainey added. "I don't want to take anything to make me sleep."

"Not take," the woman said. She waddled slowly to a shelf, pulling what seemed to be a slip of paper from a bowl, then wrapping it in some sort of leaves. She came toward Lainey slowly, gaze fixed on her face, and held out the tiny bundle.

"Put under your pillow," she said. "No charge."

"Thank you." Lainey sniffed at the leaves, identifying lavender. Aromatherapy, in a way, she supposed. "But I really need help with something else." She glanced at Jake, and he gave her an encouraging nod. "Someone has been putting signs around my house."

"Signs?" The old woman took a step back. "What kind of signs?" There was something in her face—faint suspicion, maybe.

Did that mean she knew something? "A cross on the doorstep," she said. "Salt on the windowsills. A broom across the door. Witch signs."

The woman began to back away, her hands fumbling at her breast as if seeking something. "Get out." Her voice rose, cracking a little. "Get out." Moving faster than Lainey would have thought she could, she scurried behind the table, her face a mask of fury. She picked up the heavy pestle, raising it threateningly. "Go away!"

"We don't mean any harm." Lainey took a step toward her, but Jake grabbed her arm. She glanced at him, and he shook his head.

"It's no use. We'd better go."

"But she—"

The pestle flew through the air, narrowly missing Lainey's head. Shoving her behind his body, Jake propelled her out the door and pulled her into a run.

They finally slowed down when they cleared the woods and emerged into the open field.

"Looks like Doctor Mary didn't care for us," Jake said, his breath coming quickly.

"Not us." Lainey saw again the expression on the woman's face. "Just me. And only when she realized who I was."

They could walk side by side now, and the moonlight was bright enough that she could see Jake's quick glance at her face.

"When you mentioned the witch symbols," he said. "She was fine until then. That must mean she knows something about it."

"If she does, she's not going to tell us." Lainey shivered a little as a breeze swept across the field, rattling the dry grasses.

"No, I think it's safe to say she's not on our side," Jake said.

"It's not just disliking me." Lainey shivered again and zipped her jacket up to the neck. "Didn't you see it? She was afraid. Of me."

Jake's jaw tightened visibly. Lainey suspected he wanted to dismiss that idea, but he couldn't, because it was true. There had been fear in the old woman's face when she realized who Lainey was.

"Why?" The word burst out of her. "I could understand somebody like Zeb wanting to get rid of me so he could handle Aunt Rebecca's property. But I can't understand why anyone would think me a witch."

"It's nonsense." Jake clasped her hand warmly. "Some foolish rumor started by someone, that's all, and somehow Mary found out about it."

"I hope you're right," she said slowly. "But I think..." She let that trail off, frowning. "What's that by the truck?"

A shadow moved along the driver's side of the pickup. Jake froze for an instant.

"Stay here," he ordered. He took off running toward the truck.

She didn't, of course, but she couldn't overtake him. By the time Lainey reached him, Jake had someone pinned against the driver's side door. He moved as she came up to him, and she saw who it was. Thomas, Zeb's grandson.

"Thomas! What are you doing here?"

"That's obvious, isn't it?" Jake was holding the boy with a firm grip on the front of his dark jacket. "This is the person who's been playing all those tricks on you, Lainey."

"Thomas? Is that true?" Lainey leaned closer, trying to read the boy's expression.

He pressed his lips together, shaking his head.

"Come on, Thomas." Jake's grip tightened. "You've been trying to scare Lainey away. You put brooms across the door, salt on the windowsills, broke the kitchen window—"

"No!" Thomas shook his head. "I would not break the window. It belongs to Aunt Rebecca."

That sounded real enough. "But you did the other things," Lainey said. "Did Doctor Mary tell you about the witch signs?"

Thomas pressed his lips together, his eyes darting this way and that.

"You might as well be honest about it," Jake said. "Why would you be here otherwise? Did you come to ask Doctor Mary for something else to scare Lainey away?"

Thomas held out for another moment. Then he nodded, blinking rapidly as if to blink back tears.

"Why?" Jake seized the opening. "Why did you think Lainey is a witch? Who told you that? Your grandfather?"

There was no mistaking Thomas's expression now. He was frightened. He shook his head frantically, and his tears spilled over. He was trembling.

Lainey couldn't stand it any longer. "Don't, Jake."

But Jake was already letting go, obviously affected as much as she was. "Go home, Thomas," he said gruffly. "And stay away from Lainey."

The boy slid away from his hands. With a last, frightened look at them, he bolted, running down the lane.

Jake pounded his fist lightly against the truck. "It has to be Zeb, doesn't it? Who else would put Thomas up to such a thing?"

"I don't know." She felt flattened, all the tension draining out of her. "Thomas is just a boy. He wouldn't have come up with this craziness on his own, would he?"

Jake put his hand on her shoulder, his expression baffled and frustrated. "I wish I knew. Maybe I should confront Zeb myself."

"No, don't do that." Her negative response was almost automatic.

"Why?" His fingers tightened. "If Zeb is responsible—"

"Whether he is or isn't, he's still Aunt Rebecca's brother-in-law. She might not want it brought into the open."

"She's not the one who has been the target." His hand moved, cradling her face, and her heart seemed to turn over.

"Please, Jake." It was difficult to think over the pounding of her pulse. "Aunt Rebecca is doing better every day. At least hold off until she's well enough that I can talk to her about it."

"In the meantime—"

"In the meantime," she said quickly, "I think you've scared Thomas off pulling any more tricks. Let's leave it at that, all right?"

Jake hesitated, and his gaze seemed pinned to her lips. "All right," he said finally. He stepped back, his hand falling to his side. "We'll do it your way."

"So I CONVINCED Jake that we shouldn't confront Zeb about it," Lainey said, concluding telling Rachel and Meredith about their visit to Doctor Mary as they sat around Aunt Rebecca's kitchen table the next night. She'd wanted to have them over for a meal, but not being the cook that Rachel was, she'd picked up pizza and made a salad. Neither of them seemed to mind.

"I'm sure you did the right thing." Rachel's expression was troubled. "It was best not to push Thomas too far. I've seen my brother Benj afraid to keep a secret but still more afraid of telling. A boy that age is easily led, and Thomas is more naïve even than most Amish kids."

"Well, Thomas certainly didn't tell us anything. I don't think Jake should have come on so strong with the boy."

Meredith picked a slice of pepperoni from her pizza and ate it. "Jake was being protective of you, I imagine."

"I don't need a man's protection."

"No. But sometimes it's nice, anyway, isn't it?" Meredith said, smiling.

Lainey couldn't suppress a rueful laugh. "There might be something in what you say, as long as I don't get used to it." She wouldn't be here long enough for that.

"Maybe I can get Benj to talk to Thomas," Rachel suggested. "They're about the same age, and Thomas might be more likely to confide in a peer than an adult."

Meredith nodded agreement. "Thomas is so shy I can't imagine anyone else getting him to talk, but Benj might."

"That would be a relief. But I don't want to involve Benjamin if he's reluctant." Still, Rachel's suggestion was the most likely way of getting something out of Thomas.

"I'll sound him out," Rachel said. She frowned. "I can't imagine Thomas coming up with an idea like this on his own, no matter how naïve he is."

"You don't think I look like a witch?" Lainey asked laughingly.

Meredith leaned back in her chair, giving Lainey an assessing gaze. "I always thought you looked like a gypsy when we were kids. As far as I was concerned, witches were ugly, and you were never that."

"I don't think there were any witches in our fantasy world," Rachel said, her forehead crinkling. "I do remember Meredith fighting a dragon, though. Remember that, Lainey?"

To her surprise, Lainey found the memory dropping into the conscious part of her mind. "I do. She had a lance made out of a long roll of cardboard. And a good thing it wasn't anything stronger, because she speared me with it by mistake."

"Sounds like me," Meredith said. "I never was good at sports, not that dragon-fighting was considered a sport, as far as I know. I did pretty well with the sewing your aunt tried to teach us, though. Did you ever finish your doll quilt?"

"The nine-patch. Yes, I'm pretty sure I did. In fact, I started a new quilting project. It's spread out on the dining room table, if you'd like to see."

"Love to," Rachel said, and Meredith nodded, getting up.

They went through into the dining room, and Lainey switched on the battery lamp she'd moved to the table so she would have enough light to sew by.

"This is lovely," Rachel said, fingering a completed square. "You really have an eye for the colors."

"Look at those tiny stitches. You definitely take after Rebecca," Meredith said. "It must be an inherited skill."

The idea nestled into her thoughts. It would be

good to think she'd inherited a positive trait from her great-aunt.

"I still have my doll quilt," Rachel said. "Mandy loves it. Do you have yours?"

Lainey's pleasure seeped away. "I'm afraid not. When we left, my mother insisted she didn't have room for any extras in the luggage."

The quilt had been abandoned, like the rest of her childhood treasures. Her mother had liked to travel light.

"If you left it here, I'm sure Rebecca kept it," Meredith said. "She'd never get rid of something like that. You should look for it."

Somehow Lainey couldn't quite believe so easily that anyone would want to preserve a child's first sewing project. "I'll ask her about it when she's better."

"Do." Rachel reached out to squeeze her hand, as if seeing past the words to the feelings beneath. "I can't tell you how often Rebecca talks about you. You really do mean a great deal to her, you know."

Lainey tried to blink away the tears that seemed to come from nowhere. Poor Rebecca. She might have chosen a child to love who'd have been more responsive than Lainey had ever managed to be.

Now she had a chance to be the person Rebecca always seemed to believe she was, Lainey reminded herself. If she failed…well, that wasn't an option.

RACHEL WENT WITH Lainey to the hospital the next day, saying it had been too long since she'd stopped by to visit. She was carrying an armful of bronze mums, and their spicy scent seemed to fill the elevator as they rode up together.

"I hope she's having a good day," Lainey said as the elevator doors swung open. "It's still kind of up and down."

"I'm sure that's to be expected. She's improving, that's the important thing." Rachel's voice held quiet confidence.

They moved together toward Rebecca's room. Lainey pushed the door open and then froze. Aunt Rebecca was sitting up in bed, the tray table pulled into position in front of her. Zeb Stoltzfus bent over the table, seeming to push a pen into Aunt Rebecca's hand.

"What are you doing?" Lainey fairly flew across to the bed as Zeb jerked back in alarm. She snatched the paper before he could remove it.

"That's mine." He reached out. "Give it to me."

Rebecca's hand was curled on the table, and her faded blue eyes were wide with what might have been confusion or alarm. Lainey clasped Rebecca's hand reassuringly even as she scanned the papers she'd snatched.

"This is a deed for the property you farm." It took all her control to keep her voice even. She crumpled the pages. "You were trying to get her to sign it over to you."

Zeb's lips were a thin line above his beard. "I told you before. Rebecca intended to sign it over to me. It's what Isaac would want."

"You can't—" She stopped, knowing she couldn't say what she wanted in front of her aunt. "Let's go out in the hall." She glanced at Rachel.

Galvanized, Rachel hurried to the bedside. "Rebecca, I'm so happy to see you sitting up. I brought you some of those bronze mums you like so much." Chatting about the flowers, she tried to divert Rebecca's attention.

Lainey stared at Zeb. Finally he shrugged, leading the way out of the room. Lainey followed. She made sure the door was completely closed before she turned to Zeb.

"This is what Rebecca wants," he insisted. "Stop interfering."

"You don't know what Rebecca wants, and neither does anyone else. When she is better, you can ask her. Until then, stay away from her. And stop sending Thomas to spy on me. It won't do you any good."

He shook his head as if he were shaking off a pesky fly. "You have no place in our lives. I told Isaac it was a mistake to take you in the first time. He should have called the police when that woman dumped you on them. You were trouble then, and you're trouble now."

He stamped off, leaving her staring speechless after him.

"I thought you said it was a bad idea to confront Zeb."

She didn't realize until he spoke that Jake was standing by the elevator, holding a potted plant in one hand. Lainey sucked in a breath, trying to still the clamor in her mind.

"What did he mean?" She stared at Jake, willing him to have an answer. "Dump me on them. What was he talking about?"

"Here." Jake took her elbow, steering her into a small alcove across the hall that must serve as a lounge. Its chairs were empty, and sunlight streamed through the large window. "Not much privacy, but better than discussing your business in a public hallway."

Lainey felt her cheeks grow hot. "I shouldn't have said anything, but I couldn't help it." She shoved the papers at Jake, and he set the plant on the nearest table to take them. "He was trying to get Aunt Rebecca to sign those."

She stared blankly out the window at a view of the street, trying to make sense out of Zeb's words. Paper rustled.

"Do you mind if I keep these?" The hard note in Jake's voice was obviously for Zeb, not for her. "I'd like to consult my father before we consider what action should be taken."

"Yes, fine." She shoved her hand through her hair. "You heard what Zeb said. He implied that…that Aunt Rebecca and Uncle Isaac didn't want me."

Ridiculous, that it should mean so much. That she could feel as if the very foundation of her life was shaken.

"Of course they wanted you." He steered her to

a chair. "Sit down. You need a minute to compose yourself before you go back in to see Rebecca."

"I need more than that." She sat, but only because her knees were suddenly wobbly. "I need answers. Do you know anything about this?" She looked up at Jake as she spoke, and saw the movement in his green eyes. "You do, don't you?"

He grabbed a chair and pulled it over, sitting so that they were knee to knee. "I didn't, until just a day or two ago. My dad told me, but—"

"Tell me." She clenched her hands into fists. "If it's about me, don't you think I have the right to know?"

"Yes." He blew out a breath. "Apparently your mother arrived with you unexpectedly. For a visit, she said." He hesitated, and she could sense his reluctance. "She left during the night without saying anything to anyone."

"She dumped me on them." Lainey pulled her hands free. She didn't need or want comforting, not now. "Why am I not surprised?"

"Look, it doesn't mean anything. It doesn't change how they felt about you. Your aunt was delighted to have you, on any terms."

Her jaw tightened painfully. "And my uncle? Apparently he discussed it with his brother. And with an attorney. He can't have been very happy if he did that."

"I don't know about Zeb. But I do know why he went to see Dad, and it wasn't because he didn't want you. He was afraid of what might happen if and when your mother reappeared and wanted them to give you up."

Lainey studied his face carefully, searching for a sign that he was sugarcoating the truth. His gaze met hers steadily.

"You can speak to my father about it if you want." He smiled slightly. "He's normally pretty rigid about the privacy of what a client tells him, but Isaac is gone, and the truth wouldn't hurt him in any event."

No. The only person hurt by this particular truth was her, but then she'd never had many illusions about her mother.

Jake touched her hand again—lightly, as if he expected her to yank it away. "It sounds as if you didn't have a very stable childhood."

She shrugged. "Stable? We moved so often I sometimes couldn't remember my own address. But I don't think she ever actually deserted me except for that summer."

"She probably knew she could count on Rebecca and Isaac to take care of you," he said.

"I suspect it was more that she knew they wouldn't go to the police." She tried to look at what she remembered of that summer in the light of this new information, but surprisingly, it didn't seem to make any difference. She'd never felt anything but welcomed and loved with her aunt and uncle.

"If she'd asked them to take you, they'd have said yes." Jake's fingers tightened on hers. "You can count on that."

She nodded, relaxing a little. "I know. But she didn't. I suppose she didn't want to take the risk."

"Why…" Jake began, and then stopped.

"It's okay. You can ask it. Why was she so eager to get rid of me that summer?" She shrugged. "A man, I suppose. It always was. That would have been Carl, her second husband. You'd think after she'd tried so hard to get him that she'd have put more effort into keeping him."

"How long were they married?"

She suspected he was trying to keep her talking, but it didn't seem to matter. "I'm not sure. Less than a year, I think. I know I didn't finish up the next school year before we were off."

"I'm sorry."

He probably was. Jake's childhood and hers had clearly been polar opposites. No wonder he seemed so content to stay here. He was rooted here.

"It's all right." She managed a smile. "Really. You can stop trying to calm me down. I won't let any unpleasantness slip to Aunt Rebecca."

"I know that." He rose, pulling her up with him. "Let's go in and make sure she's not upset about Zeb's machinations."

"If he comes near her again—" she began.

"Don't worry. Dad and I will figure out how to keep Zeb in line." His smile warmed her. "You can count on me."

She had begun to do just that, and maybe that was

a mistake. There was no future for them, so it was better not to lean too heavily on a relationship that was sure to end.

CHAPTER THIRTEEN

THE MINUTE LAINEY walked back into the hospital room, Rebecca looked at her, anxiety plain in her face.

"It's all right," Lainey said quickly. "Zeb...he had to leave, but look at the nice plant Jake brought for you."

"I confess my mother picked it out." Jake seemed perfectly at home in the sterility of the hospital room. He set the plant on the bedside table and perched at the foot of the bed. "It's a miniature rose, and she said to tell you she'll plant it outside for you whenever you want."

Rebecca raised her hand slowly and touched the pink petals of the tiny rose. *"Denke,"* she whispered.

Lainey's heart seemed to warm at the sound. Aunt Rebecca was talking again.

Rebecca's faint smile slid into a look of concern. "Zeb?"

Lainey glanced warningly at Jake. "It's all right. We'll make sure Zeb doesn't bother you about business until you're well."

For some reason, that seemed to trouble Aunt Rebecca. She shook her head, frowning, her fingers plucking at the sheet.

Lainey glanced at Jake and saw the same question in his face that she felt.

"Rebecca, did you want to sign the papers?" Jake's voice was compelling, but the question seemed to confuse her even more.

Rebecca's lips trembled, and she shook her head in what seemed to be frustration.

"Don't worry about it now." Lainey clasped both Rebecca's hands in hers, stopping her restless movement. "All this can wait. I'm here to take care of things for you, and I'll stay as long as you need me."

It was a rash promise—one Lainey didn't think she'd ever made before.

Rebecca's gaze clung to her face. Slowly, her distress ebbed, her face relaxing.

"That's what she needed to hear," Rachel said softly.

Zeb's angry words, Jake's revelations, her aunt's dependence…they all seemed to tumble in Lainey's mind. But maybe none of it mattered. Rebecca trusted her, and she wouldn't let her down.

"Tomorrow is going to be a busy day." Lainey kept her tone light. "You're going to move over to the rehab unit, where they can help you get your strength back so you can go home. The doctor is very pleased with how well you're doing."

Rebecca smiled, clearly understanding. "Home." Just the word seemed to give her strength. She patted Lainey's hand. "You'll take care."

"That's right." A sudden uprush of emotion tightened her throat.

Rebecca struggled, frowning, as she tried to form another sentence. "Family," she said finally. "Family...together."

That obviously seemed the norm to many people, but then, most people hadn't grown up the way she had. And even with Aunt Rebecca's large and generally loving family, there were issues. Lainey had to fight back a horde of rebellious thoughts in regard to some members of Aunt Rebecca's family. But airing her grievances would only cause problems.

"That's right," she said. "Family sticks together."

"WAKE UP, JAKE." Colin dribbled around him and sank a basket easily. "You can't play one-on-one when you're half-asleep."

"Not half-asleep, just preoccupied." When he'd turned up for the noon game he'd scheduled with Colin MacDonald at the fire hall parking area on Monday, he'd still been considering how best to ensure Zeb Stoltzfus didn't pull any more tricks. The fact that Rebecca wouldn't want an outright breach made action more difficult. He'd had no doubt he could get a restraining order to keep Zeb away from Rebecca under the current circumstances, but he suspected Rebecca would be horrified at the idea.

If he was going to get any exercise, he'd have to put that aside temporarily. He put on a spurt of speed and stole the ball, sinking a layup that rattled the decrepit old backboard. The outside court at the school was better, but they couldn't play there on a school day.

"It'll be too cold for outdoor basketball soon." Colin bent, hands on his thighs, catching his breath. "I can't believe it's Halloween today."

"Feeling that time passes more quickly than it used to is a sign of aging," Jake said.

"Just remember, you're always going to be a month older than I am. Anyway, that wasn't what I meant. Halloween always seems to signal the end of mild weather."

Jake grinned. "I remember all those years when your mother made you wear a jacket over your costume when we went trick-or-treating."

"Yeah, well, I seem to recall your mother did the same if she caught you before you left the house," Colin retorted. "And we both stowed them under the porch." He made a swipe at the ball, but Jake read his intent and dribbled out of reach. "We didn't come close to the tricks kids are pulling now. Every one of my car windows was coated yesterday, and not just with soap. You have any idea how long it takes to get marker off glass?"

"Your own fault for leaving your car outside," he said heartlessly.

Colin paused, stretching a hamstring. "Has Lainey Colton had any more trouble with vandalism?"

"Not in the past day or so." He'd like to believe that meant Thomas had given up. Or that Zeb had called him off.

"We should all be in the clear tomorrow. Every kid knows that tricks pulled after Halloween lead to trouble."

"I hope so." Colin was assuming Lainey's troubles were caused by anonymous vandals taking advantage of a woman alone. Jake wasn't sure he could buy that theory.

"You're worried." Colin caught the ball, giving him an assessing look. "You really think this has been aimed at chasing Lainey away from Deer Run?"

"I think it's possible," he admitted. "Zeb Stoltzfus has—or thinks he has—reason to resent that Lainey is handling her aunt's property right now. And as for Thomas, I'm not sure what motivates him. Maybe his grandfather."

Colin's gaze didn't waver. "What aren't you telling me?"

He shrugged. "Maybe I'm making something out of nothing. But you know as well as I do the trouble that started when Meredith and Rachel got together after all those years and started talking about Aaron Mast's death."

Colin's brows drew down. "Sure, but Victor Hammond confessed. It's over now."

"Yeah, you're probably right." He seemed to be the only one who had any suspicion that the whole answer hadn't been found. "And you did okay out of that situation. You actually got Rachel to agree to marry you. So when are you two going to set a date? Or is she starting to have second thoughts about a guy like you?"

Colin shot the ball at him. "No second thoughts on either side. Rachel's just concerned about how my dad and her daughter are going to adjust."

"From what I've seen, they'll both be delighted."

Colin grinned. "That's what I keep telling her. I think I'm wearing her down. We're even going trick-or-treating tonight as a family."

"Nice." Oddly enough, he didn't have any urge to rib Colin about his sudden domesticity. "I told Lainey I'd stop by and help her give out candy."

"The Amish don't celebrate Halloween," Colin observed.

"Lainey's not Amish," he said. "Anyway, as I recall, Rebecca always managed to have a pan full of whoopee pies ready for visitors on the thirty-first of October."

Colin eyed him. "Somehow I don't think your mind's on trick-or-treaters."

He shrugged. "I figure I'd like to be on the spot tonight. If anyone comes back for some more vandalism, they're in for a surprise."

LAINEY PULLED INTO the drive Monday afternoon and spotted Rachel, in jeans and a sweatshirt, hurrying across the lawn toward her, a plastic grocery bag in her hand.

"I forgot to remind you of Halloween," she said. "Even though the Amish ignore it, your great-aunt always had something for the trick-or-treaters." She smiled. "You know Rebecca. She can't resist doing something nice for the children, even though she'd pretend she didn't know a thing about the fact that it was Halloween."

"That sounds like Aunt Rebecca." Lainey opened the back door of the car to pick up the groceries she'd put there.

"Anyway, I brought some candy for you, in case you didn't think of it." Rachel held out the bag she carried.

Lainey countered by holding up another one. "Great minds think alike." She smiled. "Although actually, Jake mentioned it to me." She hesitated, but after all, Rachel would probably notice his car. "He insists on coming over to help me, but I'm sure he's just determined to catch anyone who tries to take advantage of the night to play any tricks."

"See?" Rachel gave her a knowing smile. "We told you he was protective."

"No, you told me it was sometimes nice when a man got protective," she retorted, picking up an armload of grocery bags. "And I'm not sure I need a guard tonight."

Rachel looked as if she considered several possible responses before deciding to say none of them. Instead, she gathered up the remaining groceries. "I'll help you carry these inside."

"Shouldn't you be getting Mandy ready for her big trick-or-treating night?" she asked as they walked together to the front door.

"She's supposed to be doing her homework," Rachel said. "I'm trying to keep her calm for another hour, at least, but I think it's a losing battle."

Lainey unlocked the door, juggling the grocery bags, and pulled a couple of envelopes from the mailbox. She led the way to the kitchen, dropping her load onto the table.

"Thanks so much." She glanced down at the mail in her hand and recoiled instinctively, as if she'd picked up a snake.

"Lainey, what is it?" Rachel reached toward her. "You look as if you've seen a ghost."

That was exactly what it was—the ghost of her mistakes. She shook her head, dropping the offending envelope on the table. "I know what it is. An anonymous letter."

Rachel turned the envelope cautiously with her fingertip so that she could read the block-printed address. "You've had them before?" She seemed to see the answer in Lainey's face. "You should tell the police. If someone here is foolish enough to use the mail…" She let that trail off, and Lainey knew why. She'd seen the postmark.

"It's nothing to do with what's been happening here." Lainey pressed her lips together, torn. The urge to confide was strong, but what would Rachel think of her if she knew the truth? She sucked in a breath, steeling herself.

"I was having problems back in St. Louis. It looks as if they've followed me here."

"Do you want to talk about it?"

Rachel probably couldn't imagine having done something so bad that people would send anonymous letters. Still, the truth could hardly be worse than what she might think if Lainey refused to talk about it.

"I made a big mistake, getting involved with my boss. My married boss. He said he and his wife were getting a divorce, but…" She shook her head, hating the wobble in her voice. "That's no excuse. It was wrong. I thought I was in love, and I told myself that made it right. Now I'm paying for it." She pressed her fingers to her forehead, willing the pain away. "She tried to kill herself. His wife, I mean. Thank heaven she didn't succeed, but—" She stopped, hand dropping, and gestured to the envelope. "I deserve it."

Rachel seemed to take a moment to absorb her words, but there was no condemnation in her face. "I'm sorry," she said finally. "Are the letters abusive or threatening?"

"Both." Lainey realized she'd memorized the contents of the last one. Of the phone call. *You cant hide from me. I know where you are.* Her stomach twisted. "I don't see how anyone in St. Louis can know where I am, but still, the letters come."

"You should tell the police," Rachel said instantly. "And Jake. Have you told Jake?"

"No!" Fear shot through her. "I can't."

Rachel put her arm around Lainey's waist in a quick hug. "You could, you know. You could trust him with this, and it might have something to do with all this craziness you've been going through."

Lainey shook her head, staring at the envelope. "I can't. And anyway, I'm sure no one would have followed me from St. Louis to Deer Run just to throw a rock through the window."

Mandy's dog barked excitedly from the backyard next door, and Rachel's gaze flickered in that direction.

"You should go." Lainey pulled herself together. "I'm fine, and you have a daughter to help dress."

"To say nothing of dealing with the puppy." Rachel sounded exasperated. "She's probably going to bark every time the doorbell rings. It'll be a long night, I'm afraid. I hope she doesn't bother you."

"Not at all," Lainey said quickly. It had been a relief to unburden herself, but now she felt embarrassed to be with Rachel, to wonder what she was really thinking. "You go on. I'm fine."

Rachel nodded, heading toward the door. When she reached it she paused, glancing back at Lainey. "Tell Jake," she said. "He'll understand."

Lainey gave her a noncommittal smile, and in a moment Rachel was gone.

She rubbed her forehead wearily as the door closed. Rachel meant well, but she was wrong. Telling Jake was not just difficult. It was impossible.

Over the next hour she put the groceries away, heated up the chicken soup Cousin Katie had brought over, and tried not to think about Rachel's advice.

Tell Jake. But she couldn't. It had been a weakness to share it even with Rachel. Say what she would about their twenty-year-old friendship, it was a lot to expect Rachel to carry a burden like the truth Lainey hated to acknowledge even to herself.

Katie's soup was delicious, but she didn't seem to have an appetite. She pushed the bowl away and glanced at the window. It was beginning to get dark. Children would be setting off on their trick-or-treating soon.

And Jake would be here. She carried her bowl to the sink. Her jaw was so tight at the moment that eating anything was out of the question.

Tell Jake. But she couldn't watch his expression change when he realized who she really was.

Walking quickly toward the front of the house, she switched on one of the small battery lamps and set it in the front window. Both Rachel's and Meredith's porches held lighted jack-o'-lanterns, and Rachel's was decorated with cornstalks and mums as well. In the absence of a carved jack-o'-lantern, Lainey's lamp would have to suffice to let children know they were welcome here.

As she leaned on the window frame, she could see bobbing lights and small figures in costume down the street. Trick-or-treaters were on their way, and she hadn't opened the bags of wrapped candies yet.

There was a large pottery bowl under the sink—that would do to hold the candy. She ripped open the bags, tossing the contents into the bowl. As she did so, someone rapped at the back door.

Jake must be here. Suppressing the flutter in her stomach at the thought, she pulled the door open and stared, startled.

"You didn't tell me costumes were required for—"

The figure lunged at her and something wrapped

around her neck, pulling tighter and tighter. Her hands flew to the thing that choked off her breath. Fight back—she had to fight back, but her head was swimming, she was being forced backward into the kitchen, vision blurring. She clawed at the band around her neck, gasping for air, but she couldn't get it, it was too tight—

Her hands flailed uselessly, but her fingers touched the bowl. Forcing strength into her grip, she grabbed it and swung it toward the attacker's head.

He stumbled backward, dragging her with him through the doorway and out onto the porch. The thing binding her neck had loosened just enough to let her make a sound. She tried to scream. It came out as more of a croak. She fought to make a sound. If she didn't, no one would come, she was helpless—

A dog began barking furiously, its yelps increasing in volume. A door slammed, voices called, she was falling, she couldn't fight....

And then she was alone. The attacker had fled. The dog—Princess, it must be, still barked, the tone nearly hysterical now, and she heard Rachel calling out as she ran across the yard. Another voice, male, deep and frightened, and then Jake's arms were around her, lifting her, and Rachel was pulling away the thing that had been around her neck.

"Lainey..." Jake's voice shook.

She grasped his jacket, trying to sit up. Realizing what she was about, he helped her into a sitting position.

"I'm all right." The words came out in a whisper,

and she put her hand to her neck. Painful to touch, still more painful to speak.

"We should call…" Rachel began, but Jake already had his phone out. His voice was crisp and urgent as he spoke to the 911 dispatcher.

"Don't need an ambulance," Lainey managed to say.

"We'll just let them check you out." Rachel put a comforting arm around her. "That's all."

Jake stood, picking her up with ease, it seemed. "Let's get you comfortable and see how bad it is." He carried her through the kitchen and into the living room, where he put her down gently on the faded old sofa. She sank into its depths gratefully, feeling as if Aunt Rebecca's arms cradled her.

Rachel loosened the neck of her shirt with gentle fingers, and Lainey heard a sharp intake of breath from Jake.

"Someone tried to throttle you." His tone was incredulous.

Lainey touched her neck, fingers encountering a swollen welt. "Nearly succeeded," she murmured.

"Don't try to talk," Rachel ordered. "I'll get some ice for the swelling." She scurried off to the kitchen.

Jake clasped her hand in both of his. "I should have gotten here sooner. I never dreamed anyone would try something this early, when young kids and parents are still out. Why did you open the door?"

"Don't make her talk," Rachel ordered, coming back with an ice bag wrapped in a tea towel. She put it across Lainey's neck gently.

"Thought it was you," she whispered, and then fell silent under Rachel's frown.

"She'll have to talk when the police get here," Jake said, his voice regaining its usual practical tone. "You have any idea who it was?"

She replied with a miniscule shake of the head. "Black costume. One of those scream masks."

"And you thought it was me?" He tried for levity. "My taste isn't that bad. What scared him off?"

Lainey frowned, trying to make her mind function. "Hit him with the candy bowl. The dog…"

"Princess was tied in the backyard," Rachel said quickly. "She started barking so frantically I knew something was wrong. I came out, saw that the back door was open, and called out."

"Did you see the attacker?" Jake shot the question at her.

"Not to say see, exactly. Just something black disappearing into the shadows beyond the shed."

"Going toward the dam?"

Rachel shook her head, frowning. "I couldn't tell."

Lainey seemed to be having difficulty keeping her eyes open. Or at least, keeping them focused. "Why?" she murmured. "Why?" She could understand anonymous letters, even attempts to frighten her into leaving town.

But this had been far more serious than that. Surely nobody hated her enough for murder.

CHAPTER FOURTEEN

"DOES THIS BELONG to you?" One of Chief Burkhalter's young patrolmen marched into the crowded living room, carrying the black cat at arm's length. It promptly kicked at his wrist and lunged to the sofa, where it curled up next to Lainey and started to purr.

"Where was it?" Jake asked. He'd been wondering at the cat's absence. It had made timely appearances so often he'd begun to think it really was a substitute for a watchdog.

Lainey was stroking the cat's back, murmuring softly. The patrolman glared at the cat, nursing his scratched wrist, and then turned to Jake, who was sitting in the rocking chair pulled as close to the sofa as he could get without being too obvious.

"Shut in the woodshed. I heard it yowling when I checked the yard like the chief said."

"Never mind the cat," Chief Burkhalter interrupted, his square, ruddy face turning an even darker red. "Any sign of the intruder?"

"Uh, no, sir. I didn't see anything. Want me to look again?"

Burkhalter jerked his head toward the door, and the kid ambled out. "Look again," he grumbled.

"That kid couldn't find a black cow on a snow-covered field."

"You can have another search when it's light," Jake pointed out. He nodded toward the cat. "It seems to me shutting the cat up proves it wasn't just a prank gone awry." That had been Burkhalter's suggestion, as if the local teenagers might think throttling someone a suitable Halloween trick. "The cat might have sensed something wrong and alerted Lainey."

"Seems to me that's giving a lot of credit to a dumb animal," Burkhalter grumbled.

Lainey and the cat gave the chief such similar affronted looks that Jake could almost believe the cat understood. He saw Meredith and Rachel exchange smiles at the sight.

Meredith had come racing from her house at the sound of the police cars. Evidently she'd been on the phone in her office at the far side of the house, so she hadn't seen or heard anything useful.

Lainey turned her head on the pillow, as if trying to find a comfortable position, and Rachel was leaning over her in an instant. "Do you want me to freshen those ice bags?"

"They're all right," Lainey whispered hoarsely.

"Maybe some warm tea would help," Meredith said. "I'll fix it."

Lainey nodded, and Meredith hurried toward the kitchen.

"Now, Ms. Colton, you sure you can't give me anything more about the person you say attacked you? Size, weight?"

Lainey frowned, and Jake thought she was struggling to concentrate. The paramedics had insisted she take something for the pain, and its effects were showing.

"You said you thought at first it might be me," he prompted. "Was he or she my size?"

The frown deepened. Lainey shook her head slowly. "Not as tall as you are. I just thought, for a second, because I expected you...."

He nodded. "So someone smaller than me."

"That doesn't exactly narrow it down," Burkhalter said. "A teenager could easily be near as tall as you, I guess."

"You're not still thinking this was some kind of Halloween prank, are you?" Jake let his frustration show in his voice. Burkhalter was a decent cop, honest and dedicated, but he tended to get stuck on the first solution that popped into his head.

"Could've been," Burkhalter said, his tone stubborn. "Halloween isn't a simple matter of throwing corn and soaping windows anymore. But I was actually thinking of Thomas Stoltzfus, since Ms. Colton's had some trouble with him, it seems."

"I don't think..." Lainey began.

"I doubt he has the guts to do anything violent," Jake said.

"And how would he get here?" Rachel asked. "Most Amish parents don't let their kids go out wandering around on Halloween, and it's a long way from his dad's farm."

"Could have hitched a ride," Burkhalter said. He

blew out an annoyed breath. "Lord, I hate Halloween. If it's not the teenagers causing trouble, it's the little kids getting a belly ache from too much candy and their parents calling in to say they've been poisoned. And as for the adults…"

He sounded as if he was just getting wound up. Jake glanced at Lainey, who was drooping against the pillow, dark circles like bruises under her eyes. "You have your hands full, all right. And, I think Ms. Colton's told you all she can at the moment."

Thankfully, Burkhalter didn't argue after he took a good look at Lainey. "Guess you're right. I'll come by tomorrow." He raised an eyebrow at Jake. "Walk me out."

Jake accompanied him to the porch, where Burkhalter stopped, frowning absently at the police car that sat at the curb. He pushed his cap back, looking perplexed. "I gotta say, those three girls certainly manage to stir up trouble when they're together."

Jake suppressed a ripple of annoyance. "Not girls any longer, Chief. And without them, you'd never have caught a murderer."

"I suppose." He sounded doubtful. "That Ms. Colton…I don't know her like I do the other two. Seems like she might be the kind to overdramatize herself."

He didn't bother to suppress the irritation this time. "You can't deny the marks on her neck. Somebody did that to her."

That red, swollen line running across Lainey's slender neck sickened him.

"True, but it still might have been horseplay that got too rough. Anyway, I figure she shouldn't be alone tonight."

Anything Jake could say about Burkhalter's mention of horseplay would come out as an insult, so he swallowed his ire as best he could. "She won't be alone," he said, and went back into the house.

When he reached the living room, Meredith and Rachel were arguing that very point, each insisting that she should be the one to stay. Lainey, her fingers wrapped around a steaming mug, gave him an appealing look.

"Tell them I don't need them," she murmured.

"You heard Lainey. She doesn't need you." He went on before anyone could protest. "Because I'm going to be here."

Rachel looked troubled, and Meredith raised her eyebrows. "Willing to risk the gossip?" she said.

"Let the gossips chatter all they want," he said. "Lainey needs a bodyguard, and I'm it." He sat back down in the rocker. "Forget about arguing. Just tell me if you think this attack can be connected to Aaron Mast's death."

"You mean your idea about Laura," Meredith said. Her forehead wrinkled. "Honestly, I can't picture Laura dressing up in a costume and coming here to attack Lainey. I doubt she could keep a plan like that in her mind long enough to do it."

"Laura…" Lainey began and then stopped, frowning.

"What about Laura? Do you think she was the person who attacked you?" Jake zeroed in on her face, but Lainey was already shaking her head.

"Not that," she murmured. "But I'd nearly forgotten. She spoke to me at the festival. Insisted she had to talk to me alone."

That much speaking seemed to wear her out, and she sank back against the pillow.

"I still can't believe Laura could have killed Aaron." Rachel pleated her fingers together in distress. "She loved him. Why would she hurt him?"

"You're forgetting what Aaron told my cousin about Laura being pregnant." Meredith leaned forward, a wing of brown hair swinging against her cheek. "Suppose he wanted her to marry him right away. They might have quarreled about it. She could have seen all she stood to lose—her education, her freedom, the life she had."

"But even if she did, why attack me?" Lainey spoke with an effort, and she took a sip of the tea to punctuate her words.

"With her scrambled mind, it's hard to tell," Meredith said. "She does seem to be fascinated by you."

"You said she tried to get you to meet her alone," Jake pointed out. "Maybe when you didn't respond, she decided to come to you."

As soon as he'd spoken, he regretted it. Lainey looked upset again, her eyes darkening, and the mug shook a little. Angry at himself, he reached out to take it from her.

"Enough talk," he said. "We're not going to solve it tonight, and you need rest."

Rachel responded immediately to the warning

look he sent her. She rose, beckoning to Meredith. "You're right, of course. We can talk it over tomorrow, when we can all think more clearly."

Meredith bent to pat Lainey's hand. "Just tell Jake to call me if you need anything."

He gave her a mock frown. "What would she need that I can't get her?"

"Sometimes only another woman will do," she said loftily. "I'll see you tomorrow."

"The same goes for me," Rachel said. She dropped a light kiss on Lainey's cheek. "Try not to worry too much. Jake will keep you safe, and we'll figure it out." She held Lainey's glance for a long moment, almost as if some unspoken message was passed between them.

They left, finally, and Jake locked the door behind them, very aware of being alone in the house with Lainey.

He couldn't deny any longer the strong attraction she held for him. And he cared for her—that much was evident in his reaction to her being in danger. But Lainey Colton was still exactly the sort of woman he'd promised himself he wouldn't fall for.

She'll be leaving, a little voice in his brain reminded him. *And you're both grown-ups.*

Tucking that away to be considered later, he went back to the living room to find Lainey struggling to get up.

"Hey, what are you doing?" He rushed to steady her.

"Just thought I'd go to bed. I can make it—"

He picked her up easily in his arms. "Even if you can, you're not going to."

Ignoring her muttered protests, he carried her upstairs, the cat scampering under his feet. He pushed open the door to the bedroom she indicated, and put her gently on the bed. Predictably, the cat jumped up beside her and curled up.

Lainey relaxed against the pillow, and he suspected she had trouble keeping her eyes open.

"Pajamas? Nightgown?" he asked. "I'll bring it to you."

"Nightshirt," she murmured. "Top drawer."

He found a pale green nightshirt and brought it to her.

"I can manage," she said.

He smiled. "I don't doubt it." He bent over her, bracing himself with a hand on either side of her, and kissed her. He had a struggle to keep it light, and even so, when he drew back they were both breathing quickly.

"Jake…" she began.

"Don't worry," he said. "I have a rule. I never make love to a woman who's doped up on pain meds." He'd better get out while he could still make good on that pledge. "I'll be checking on you through the night. I'll leave this door open. If you call, I'll hear."

Not waiting for a response or an argument, he went out quickly and started down the stairs, safely away from temptation. He might as well make himself comfortable in the padded rocker.

Who could have attacked Lainey? He leaned back

in the chair. Zeb came to mind, just based on that recent quarrel over the deed to the farm. But somehow he couldn't picture Zeb in the role of attacker, not over a piece of property. He might bend the rules and exert his influence to get his own way, but outright violence was so foreign to the Amish that such an attack verged on the impossible. Still, Zeb couldn't be ignored.

He couldn't help feeling that there was more at stake here than any of them had dreamt of. Laura? Well, she was a possibility, no matter what reason she might have. And she was certainly unstable. It might pay to make some discreet inquiries as to whether someone kept an eye on her at night.

Nothing more was likely to happen, but he wasn't about to go to sleep, not with Lainey lying upstairs virtually helpless. Half the Amish in the township probably had keys to this house, and who knew how many other people might have access to those keys.

No, he'd be staying awake tonight. Anyone who attempted to get to Lainey would have to go through him.

LAINEY WAS RUNNING as fast as she could, but it wasn't fast enough. The thing behind her was coming closer. Choking back a sob, she stumbled between the trees, a branch raking her hair. It hurt, but she couldn't stop—if she stopped the thing would get her, she'd be going down, down, down in the water—

Gasping for breath, she put on a little burst of speed, free of the trees now, she could see the moon, if she could make it to the house she'd be safe. But the brambles caught at her clothes, dragged at her hair, holding her back. One slipper came off. She raced on, hearing the thing behind her crashing through the brambles. Her foot hurt, she couldn't catch her breath....

And then she was out into grass, damp and rustling as she staggered through, lightning bugs rising from the ground, only last night they'd been catching them, putting them in a jar....

A light that meant the house, a voice calling, she was almost there, but something caught at her clothing, dragging her, and she was stumbling, falling, down, down, down—

With a sharp gasp, Lainey bolted upright in the bed, scrambling for her wits. A nightmare. But someone was there, someone was touching her, trying to hold her—she fought, arms flailing, until a voice penetrated her terror.

"Lainey, it's okay. It's me, Jake. You just had a nightmare."

She stopped, blinking her eyes against the soft glow of the bedside battery lamp as he turned it on. Jake—solid, stable, looking at her with concern, his hair rumpled, his face distressed.

"Jake." She breathed the name.

Some of the worry slipped from his face. "That's right. You're safe. The attacker is long gone, and you're safe. I won't let anyone get near you."

Lainey pushed tangled hair away from her face. "Sorry. Did I..."

"You cried out," he said. "I came running from downstairs, sure someone was attacking you." His face tightened at the memory.

Lainey tried to manage a smile. "Only in my dreams."

"It's not surprising you'd relive the attack in a nightmare." He reached out for her robe, which hung over the bottom of the bed, and tucked it around her shoulders, his hands gentle.

Realizing he was carefully avoiding looking at the V of her nightshirt, she pulled the robe on.

"I suppose so." She frowned. "Funny, though," she murmured, her voice hoarse. "I didn't dream about what happened tonight. It was something else—another time." She shook her head. "The same dream I had when I first came back to this house."

Jake, sitting on the bed next to her, was very close. In the glow of the lamp she saw his face become still and watchful. "Can you tell me about it?"

Her immediate revulsion was probably obvious in her face. She didn't want to talk about it. She wanted to forget it.

"Please, Lainey," he urged. "It might be important. Tell me now, before it fades."

He was right about that, of course. Dreams, even nightmares, did fade very quickly in the light. If she was going to tell it, it had better be now.

"I was running in the woods. Lots of trees around, anyway. Running away from something terrible." Her voice shook a little, but her throat didn't hurt as much to talk now.

"Do you know what?" he asked gently.

"No." She pressed her fingers to her forehead, trying to concentrate. "Just that I'm afraid. I bump into branches, but I keep running. Then I'm out of the trees, but there are brambles tearing at me." She rubbed her arms, seeming to feel the scratches. "The thing behind is closer." She couldn't help it—her voice shook.

Jake ran his hands down her arms, their warmth taking the chill away. "You're safe."

She was caught in the dream memory. "I get out of the brambles, into the grass."

"Do you see anything else?"

"Lightning bugs. And a light ahead of me. If I can get to the light I'll be safe. But I fall—" She stopped. Took a breath. "That's all. The dream always ends when I fall." She cleared her throat. "Isn't it the height of self-absorption, telling someone your dreams?"

Jake handed her the water bottle from the bedside table, and she drank thirstily.

"I asked, remember?" Jake smiled, but she sensed that his mind was busy behind the smile.

"It was probably just my subconscious way of dealing with what happened tonight. Bringing up a childhood boogeyman."

"Why childhood?" His tone was sharp.

"I…I don't know. I guess I felt as if I were a child in the dream. What difference does it make?"

"I'm not sure," Jake said. He set the bottle back and took her hands in his, stroking them gently. Every nerve end seemed alive to his touch, and he wasn't even noticing. "Think about the details in your dream. First the woods, then the brambles, then the tall grass. That's a description of what you'd go through if you were running from the dam back toward this house. With someone chasing you."

Lainey jerked her hands away from his. "No." She didn't want to go there. She wouldn't. "You're thinking of when Aaron was killed, aren't you?"

His gaze met hers steadily. "How can I help but think of that? You were here that night. You have a recurring dream of running away with someone chasing you. You—"

"Plenty of people have nightmares about being chased in the dark. It's a classic dream, like having to take a test you're not prepared for. It doesn't mean anything."

"Answer me this, then. How do you feel when you go to the dam now?"

The question stilled the protests she wanted to make. "I haven't. I haven't gone back there." She tried to ignore the queasy feeling in her stomach at the idea—the sense of dread creeping along her skin. "That doesn't mean anything," she said quickly. "Why should I go there? I don't particularly want to see the place where Aaron died."

"Is that why you went white at the thought of it?"

She glared at him. "All right, the place scares me. And maybe the dreams do have something to do with Aaron's death. That still doesn't mean I was out that night. Why would I be?"

His eyes didn't waver. "You mentioned that you sleepwalked as a child."

"It's ridiculous." The words rasped, all the more painful because she was afraid he might be right. "Even if what you're thinking did happen, I don't remember anything useful, so what difference does it make?"

His fingers gripped her hands tightly. "Think about it, Lainey. If someone is afraid that you know, it puts you in danger. It would be a much more reasonable explanation of what happened tonight than any I've heard so far."

Lainey shook her head, feeling a longing to put her hands over her ears like a rebellious child, denying that she heard him. "I don't want to go to the dam."

"All the more reason why you should. It might help you actually remember. Dreams aren't evidence."

So much for the idea that Jake felt protective of her. He was about as protective as a bulldozer.

"I don't want to." She sounded like a stubborn child. She jerked her hands free of his and rubbed her arms. "It will be…painful."

"The truth is worth the temporary pain." His tone was uncompromising. Obviously to him, truth wasn't relative.

So where did that leave her? She ought to level with him about her past. She shouldn't try to live a lie where Jake was concerned. But if she did, he'd never look at her the same again. Either way, she lost.

Of course Jake couldn't know what was in her mind. He leaned toward her, his face softening, and touched her cheek. "I'm sorry. I shouldn't badger you about it at a time like this. Just think about it, okay?"

She nodded.

His face was very close to hers, his fingers warm against her skin. "It's going to be all right," he said, his voice soft. "Try to get some sleep. We'll talk about it in the morning."

He kissed her, his lips gentle against hers, but even that light touch sent longing surging through her. For a moment he looked at her, his eyes dark with a matching longing. Then he turned and went quickly out of the room.

She lay back against the pillows and listened to the sound of his footsteps going away from her down the stairs.

CHAPTER FIFTEEN

SITTING ACROSS FROM Lainey at the breakfast table was oddly intimate, Jake realized. At least she wasn't wearing only that thin nightshirt she'd had on last night. She'd pulled on sweatpants and a sweatshirt before coming downstairs, as if she expected to be cold. Or maybe it was a matter of longing for comfort after such a bad night.

How many people had taken note of the fact that his car had been parked there all night? Too many, he supposed. The rumors would be flying.

And they'd be true, in a way. He and Lainey had spent the night together, but not in the way that expression normally implied.

"More coffee?" Lainey gestured with the pot, and he nodded.

"I need it. Lack of sleep makes my brain foggy."

Her hand seemed steady as she poured, but the purple shadows were like bruises under her eyes. Lainey's face was closed, giving no clue to her thoughts.

His own could best be described as mixed. Logic said he shouldn't become involved with Lainey, but his feelings informed him it was too late for that solution.

He took a long gulp of hot coffee—hot enough to burn some of the fog away. They had to take action of some sort. "We have to do something."

She looked up, startled, her eyes questioning. "About what?"

"About all of it." Jake gestured, trying to include the vandalism, the witchcraft business, the attack last night. "We can't just go on waiting for the next bad thing to happen." He set the mug down with a clink on the wooden table. "But what? I don't think we can count on the local police for much help. This whole situation is too amorphous for Burkhalter to get hold of."

"I agree with you about the police." She seemed to be speaking carefully, as if an unwary word might pain her neck. "But what other options are there?"

Jake hated to say it, knowing her feelings, but he had to. "There are your nightmares."

Lainey pushed her plate away. "You want me to go back to the dam."

"I'm sorry." He reached across the top of the table to let his fingertips brush hers. "I know you don't like it. But if there's a chance you might remember something, isn't it worthwhile?"

She stared at him for a long moment, her face stony. Suddenly she seemed to wilt. "All right. I know it won't do any good, but let's go to the dam and get it over with."

"Now?" He blinked as she rose, apparently ready to walk out the door.

"I don't appreciate feeling like a coward." Her fingers tightened on the back of the chair. "We'll do it now, and then I can stop thinking about it."

Did she imagine that would end the dreams she had about the place? Well, maybe it would. He was no psychologist. "All right. You might want a jacket. It'll be chilly outside."

Lainey went to the coat closet, returning in a moment with a heavy sweater which she pulled on over the sweatshirt. Her movements were stiff, as if she were forcing her body to cooperate.

Was he doing the right thing in pushing this? He wasn't sure. He just knew that it was worth it if it led them to the truth.

Lainey hesitated at the door, so he opened it and stepped outside first. The chill air made his senses tingle. "Crisp out here," he said. He held the door, understanding when it took her a moment to come through.

Once Lainey stood on the porch she stopped, as if regrouping.

"Let me have a quick look around now that it's daylight," he said. "I might spot something the police didn't see last night."

Lainey nodded, seeming satisfied to stand gripping the porch post while he descended the couple of steps to ground level.

The soft earth around the flowers that edged the porch seemed undisturbed. He'd think the intruder must have paused somewhere nearby to reconnoiter, making sure Lainey was alone before acting.

The large shrub at the corner of the porch was the closest bit of cover. A quick look was enough to show him that someone had been there—the grass was still flattened, and several small twigs had been broken.

"Someone was here, I think," he said, and was relieved when Lainey managed to pry herself away from the porch post to join him.

"It could have been the police." She fingered a broken branch. "If it was the…the person who attacked me, why would he or she hang around here?"

He noted her careful inclusion of both pronouns. "You didn't get a sense of whether it was a man or woman?"

Lainey shook her head, frowning a little. "I don't think so. Taller than I am, certainly, but otherwise…" Her frown deepened. "It seems as if there's something I noticed, but I can't pull it out."

"A scent?" he questioned.

"I don't know." Lainey snapped the words, making him realize how near the edge she was.

"Don't try," he said quickly. "It may come back when you least expect it." And if he wanted her to get through going to the dam, he'd better not press this point.

Lainey nodded, turning to look across the mowed grass of the yard behind the house toward the band of trees that marked the dam.

"The path is behind Meredith's place." Jake touched her arm to steer her in the right direction.

"I don't think we want to go trailing through the brambles this morning."

They walked together past the shed that marked the end of the lawn and then onto Meredith's property. The path lay on the far side of the garage.

Lainey moved quickly now, as if eager to get this over with. Her arms were crossed over her chest, hands knotted into fists. The wet grass was silent under their feet.

When they reached the path, Lainey hesitated again.

"I'll go first," he said, thinking that she might find that easier. He reached out a hand to her as he started down the narrow path, and after a momentary pause, she took it. Her fingers were cold in his, and he tried to warm them with his grasp.

"You can see what I meant." He gestured toward the weeds on either side of the path. "Long grass, then a clump of berry brambles, before you reach the trees. The reverse order of what you dreamed."

Lainey nodded, making no comment.

"Not much has changed back here." He spoke as much to fill the silence between them as because he had something to say. "People didn't come here much after Aaron's death. I remember my folks threatening me with grounding for a month if they found out I'd been here without their knowledge."

"Everyone thought then that Aaron's drowning was an accident, right?" Lainey seemed to make an effort to speak, her voice still a little hoarse.

"That was the general idea, I guess. I was just a

kid, and all I remember is the grown-ups changing the subject when I came in the room." He frowned, trying to separate what he'd known at the time from what he'd learned since. "I'm sure there were rumors of suicide, but I never heard anyone say it until I was older."

"Aaron wouldn't kill himself," Lainey said abruptly, and then seemed surprised at herself. "At least…"

Jake stopped where the path entered the woods so he could turn to face her. "You sound very sure of that."

She shook her head, frowning slightly as if perplexed. "I guess I am, but I'm not sure why. Suicide just doesn't seem to fit with the Aaron I remember. Maybe the three of us didn't know him as well as we thought we did."

He studied her face, seeing the struggle there to reconcile her ten-year-old views with reality. "I don't know about that," he said finally. "Kids sometimes have a pretty good idea of what the adults around them are really like, even if they don't have the words or concepts to explain."

Lainey nodded. "Maybe so. And since we know Aaron didn't kill himself, it seems our instincts were right."

"Score one for the fearless three," he said, trying to get a smile. Lainey managed one, but it was a fairly weak effort.

He clasped her hand firmly. "Come on." The path widened out as it entered the narrow band of trees, and they could walk side by side. His imagination presented him with an image of Lainey as a child, running toward the house with someone in pursuit. The woods would have seemed dark, the trees enormous and threatening.

"Did the three of you ever actually see Aaron and Laura meeting here?"

Lainey nodded, her face pale and set. "We followed them several times. It's a wonder they didn't take a stick to us. But that was in the daytime."

"Never in the evening?"

She shook her head once and then stopped, three vertical lines forming between her eyebrows. "There was one time. Rachel was sleeping over, and the three of us were outside catching lightning bugs. I don't remember how it happened—maybe we saw Aaron and followed him."

She stopped, and he suspected she wouldn't go on unless he prompted her.

"What did you see?"

Lainey seemed to be staring into the past. "The water," she said, her voice dragging, "It was shining like a mirror. Laura and Aaron. They were holding hands. Looking at each other." She shook her head fiercely, as if to shake the image away. "That's all. We didn't want them to catch us spying. We went back to the house."

How long had that been before Aaron died? He wanted to ask the question, but she brushed past him suddenly and emerged into the clearing by the dam.

When he caught up with her, Lainey was standing. Staring. Her face was white, her hands clenched into fists at her sides.

Jake tried to see the scene through her eyes, but he couldn't. He simply saw the pool, an oval widening of the creek scoured out by the dam. And the dam itself, with the ruffle of water flowing over it.

Lainey seemed so brittle he was almost afraid to touch her.

"Do you remember the pool, now that you see it?"

She gave a jerky nod. He saw her eyes shift, so that she was looking at the three-foot-high fall of water.

"It doesn't look dangerous," she said finally.

"No. But it forms a kind of undertow where the water hits the pool." He had a vivid image of Meredith, caught in the current after Victor pushed her in. If they hadn't arrived when they did, she'd have been drowned.

"If Aaron was caught in it…" She stopped. Shook her head. "Victor confessed. Why can't you leave it at that?" She flung the question at him almost angrily.

"Because it might not be true. Because you might be in danger."

"I don't remember!" She swung on him, nearly shouting the words. "If I saw something that night, I don't remember. So how can I be a threat to anyone?"

She spun before he could answer, running toward the path. Running away, just as she had probably done the night Aaron died.

Lainey didn't remember. She'd convinced him of

that. But if someone thought she might, she was in danger, and he couldn't think of a thing to do about it.

LAINEY'S DAILY VISIT to Aunt Rebecca had been a welcome respite of relative normalcy after the terror and emotional upheavals of the past night. Her great-aunt's physical therapist had kept Lainey and Katie both busy learning how to work with her aunt when she came home, something that was beginning to seem closer to reality every day.

In the afternoon, while Aunt Rebecca napped, she and Katie had worked on their quilts. Katie had shown her a simple way of lining up the smaller pieces that hadn't occurred to her. She could understand why women enjoyed doing things like quilting in groups.

Funny. Her life and Katie's life had been so different. They only touched in this place—their devotion to Rebecca. And yet that seemed to be enough. They'd talked and laughed together, and she'd found herself sharing some of the tiny incidents of her life that had never seemed important enough to tell anyone. Maybe they weren't important, but it had still been satisfying to talk to someone who simply accepted.

Lainey made the now-familiar turn onto Main Street, realizing she didn't have to think about the route any longer. There had been only one bad moment at the rehab facility, when the neck of Lainey's shirt had slid to the side and Cousin Katie had seen the marks left by last night's attack. Katie's eyes had widened with shock, but a quick shake of the head and a glance toward Aunt Rebecca had diverted any questions.

For the moment, anyway. The Amish community was bound to hear about the police visit to Rebecca's house sometime today. Maybe she should have gotten ahead of the rumors by telling Katie what had happened, but she'd hated the idea of reliving it again. She could imagine how the rumors of the police visit would fly, adding to her already rather checkered reputation.

At least Aunt Rebecca was improving. Just seeing her attempt at a smile and then hearing the few sentences she'd managed to speak had made all Lainey's difficulties seem small in comparison.

Lainey turned into the driveway, stopped beside the front porch, and felt her nerves jolt to attention when another car pulled in behind her.

It was Jake. Not the police, not someone chasing her. Just Jake.

She slid out and waited while he came toward her. "You startled me." That sounded accusing, but she couldn't seem to help it. Her nerves were in shreds, despite all her brave thoughts.

"You must have been very intent on something not to notice me behind you." Jake's tone was light, but his steady gaze seemed to measure her stress. "Everything okay?"

"Fine." Lainey managed a smile. "Aunt Rebecca is thriving on the move to rehab. I think she sees it as proof that she's going to get back to normal."

"Good." He lifted one eyebrow. "Does the doctor agree?"

"I didn't see her today, but the physical therapist is very optimistic. They'll be starting speech therapy tomorrow, as well. Katie's excited about helping."

"That's great. I have encouraging news on another front." Jake fell into step with her when she moved toward the front porch. "We've had some interest in the mill property."

"Really?" She hadn't expected anything this soon. "Is it serious?"

"Colin seems to think so. The query came through a real estate agent in Harrisburg, so I guess it's not someone local, but the potential buyer seems to know the area."

"It would be a relief to know the money's not an issue." Lainey felt in her bag for the front door key. "With any luck, Aunt Rebecca might be well enough to make the final decision by the time it goes through."

"With your great-aunt improving and the financial end straightened out, you'll be able to think about going back to St. Louis before too long."

Was there a question contained in that statement? Lainey couldn't be sure.

"I suppose so." The idea didn't especially please her. But she didn't want him to ask her to stay, did she? And if she did, what on earth would she find to do here? "In any event, I'm not leaving until I'm sure Aunt Rebecca can do without me, no matter how long that takes."

Jake propped his hand on the door frame, watching her face as if trying to read it. "I know you said your job isn't a concern, but isn't there anything... anyone...you need to get back to?"

"Nobody." That sounded rather pitiful, and she hastened to add something more. "I have friends, of course. I mean no one who...well, would really miss me if I'm not there."

"You can't say that about Deer Run," he said. "There are plenty of people here who'd miss you if you were gone."

"And then there are the ones who'd be delighted," she pointed out.

"You can put me in the first category." The smile in his eyes seemed to draw an answering one without effort.

The mailbox was stuffed full, probably with cards wishing Rebecca well. Lainey pulled them out and began sorting through them, relieved to have something to do that didn't involve looking at Jake and wondering what he was thinking.

"If any of those are bills, you can pass them on to me to deal with," he said.

"Looks like a batch of get-well cards." She shuffled through them quickly. "I'll take them—" She stopped, staring at one long envelope.

Block printing. No return address. She'd seen similar envelopes too many times to be mistaken.

"Is something wrong?" Jake took a step closer, making a tentative gesture as if to take the envelope from her.

"No, nothing." She closed her hand around it and shoved the whole batch into her bag. "Was there anything else you wanted to discuss?" Lainey tried to smile, tried not to look as if there was something poisonous lurking in that innocent batch of mail.

"There's the little matter of your safety," he reminded her. "I still don't think you should be alone at night. I can come over—"

"No." She said it quickly, before she could give in to the longing to say yes, please. "Really, I'll be fine. And Meredith offered to stay if I need someone here."

Jake's smile seemed to stiffen at the rebuff. He gave a curt nod. "I think you should accept Meredith's offer. And I'll be available. Just give me a call if you change your mind."

She wanted to. She couldn't deny that to herself, at least. But the thought of what might happen if she and Jake were alone together again tonight deterred her. Any relationship between them was doomed to failure. The closer they got, the more difficult it would be to say goodbye.

"Thank you." Her fingers fumbled as she put the key in the lock. "I appreciate it, but no."

Jake took a step back, his face expressionless. "I'll let you know as soon as I hear anything more about the property."

Lainey nodded, giving him a meaningless smile, and escaped into the house. She waited until she heard his car drive away to pull the envelope out of her bag.

Quickly, before she could change her mind, she ripped it open.

The usual sort of thing, using all the vile language the writer had at his or her command, it seemed. Lainey glanced away from the words accusing her of being no better than a murderer to look at the envelope again.

And felt as if she were in an elevator that was suddenly falling. There was something different about this letter. It wasn't postmarked St. Louis, as all the others had been. This one had been mailed right here.

The envelope slipped from her fingers as the implication took on reality. It had been mailed here. That meant someone in Deer Run knew exactly what had happened to her in St. Louis. Her secret was out.

Wait, wait, some practical part of her mind insisted. Maybe she was reading something into the letter that wasn't there. Granted it had originated in Deer Run, but was she so sure it referred to her past? There could be—were—people who resented her assumption of control over Aunt Rebecca's property. People like Zeb, who had something to lose. Like young Thomas, who apparently thought she was a witch.

Lainey forced herself to spread the letter out and consider it carefully. Aside from the obvious obscenities and vague threats, was there anything that definitely pointed to knowledge of what had happened in St. Louis?

Well, the reference to her being a murderer certainly seemed to, but nothing about it was specific enough to be certain. If it did refer to Phillip's wife, how could someone here have found out?

Easily, given the interest and internet access, she supposed. That would seem to rule out the Amish, although some did use computers in business, and apparently it wasn't unusual for teenagers to have cell phones.

Thomas was a teenager. But he seemed too young and naïve for something as sophisticated as launching an internet search for something ugly in her background.

The Amish did write in English. She studied the block writing, but couldn't make anything from it. No misspellings, at any rate.

Aunt Rebecca's letters were always written in clear, legible cursive, and she didn't spell English words incorrectly, although she sometimes threw in a word in Pennsylvania Dutch when she apparently thought English wouldn't do.

Lainey hadn't had a glimpse of Thomas since that night at the cabin in the woods. If he was still doing yard work for Jeannette, he must be managing to do it when she was out.

Lainey went to the front window, peering across the street at the bed-and-breakfast, and discovered that her luck was in. Thomas was pruning the shrubs in front of the porch, with Jeannette standing at his shoulder and apparently directing his every move.

Even as she watched, Jeannette turned and marched to her car, parked at the curb. She slid in, and in a moment she was gone, leaving Thomas clipping away at what Lainey thought was a lilac bush.

It was a chance too good to be missed. Dropping the letter, Lainey hurried to the door.

In a couple of minutes, she was walking across the street. The afternoon sunlight slanted through the trees that lined either side, making their color blaze with fire. She crossed the lawn toward Thomas, her footsteps making no sound on the grass. Maybe that was just as well—he might run if he saw her coming.

Lainey waited until she was within a foot of him to speak. "Thomas."

The boy jerked around, his eyes widening when he saw who it was. He glanced from side to side, as if seeking a way to flee.

"Don't be afraid." She spoke as gently as if he were a frightened animal. "I'm not angry with you."

He didn't look convinced. "The lawyer—he was angry."

True, Jake had been furious when he'd caught up with Thomas that evening near the powwow doctor's cabin.

"He thought you'd been playing tricks on me. And he was right, wasn't he?"

The boy stared down at his shoes. "I didn't...I wanted..." He seemed to run out of words.

"You wanted to protect Aunt Rebecca's house, didn't you?"

He shot a quick glance at her before lowering his gaze again. *"Ja,"* he whispered.

How could she get through to him? He'd undoubtedly heard all of his grandfather's complaints about her. But why would that make him conclude that she was a witch?

"I understand." She kept her voice soft, sure she wouldn't get anywhere if she frightened him again. "I love Aunt Rebecca, too. I want to take care of her."

For a moment he looked as if he'd speak, but then he pressed his lips together.

Gently, she warned herself. "Aunt Rebecca was better today," she said. "She's going to try walking on her own soon. That's good news, isn't it?"

That seemed to disarm him, as she'd hoped it might. He nodded, smiling slightly.

The smile was a bit of a triumph, but it wasn't getting her any closer to what she wanted to know.

"Thomas, I don't mean you any harm. I just want to know something. You thought I was a witch, didn't you?"

A frozen moment. Then he gave the slightest of nods.

"Do you still think so?"

He wouldn't look at her. Instead, he shrugged— an infinitesimal movement of his bony shoulders.

That was probably better than having him convinced she was a witch, she supposed.

"I'm not," she said. "I promise you." She hesitated, but she had to risk asking the question. "Who told you I was a witch?"

Thomas wrapped his arms around himself, as if shielding himself from her. He shook his head.

"Was it your grandfather?"

There was no denying the surprise in his face at that question. He shook his head, more firmly this time.

Lainey studied the boy's face. Her instincts said he was telling the truth, but if not Zeb, then who? Who else had reason to get rid of her?

If Jake's theory was correct, Laura did, but somehow Lainey couldn't see a situation that would involve Laura Hammond telling Thomas such a story.

"Well, I wish you'd tell me. Maybe one day you will."

She couldn't miss the relief on his face that she wasn't going to press him.

"Just remember that I love Aunt Rebecca, and I'm here because she wants me. Okay?"

Thomas darted another quick glance at her face. "Okay," he said.

Maybe she'd better be content with that, because it was probably the best she could do with the boy. Unfortunately, it didn't get her much further ahead.

CHAPTER SIXTEEN

INSTEAD OF GOING home after he left Lainey, Jake detoured to the police station. Lainey had made it quite clear that she didn't want his protection tonight, but he was still concerned. Maybe she was afraid of the gossip that would result—gossip that might reach her aunt's ears.

Or maybe the point was that she didn't want to spend the night with him. She had to be as aware as he was of the attraction between them. This might be her way of saying she wasn't interested.

Fair enough. If his ego was bruised, he'd get over it. But he still didn't like the idea of leaving her alone in that house at night, and he wasn't convinced that Chief Burkhalter was taking the attack on Lainey seriously.

Parking in front of the station, he marched inside. If Burkhalter needed a little prompting to do his duty, Jake was just the person to provide it.

He found Burkhalter leaning on the desk in the outer office, apparently deep in contemplation of the computer screen. That was surprising. He usually relied on the dispatcher to handle anything computer-related. The chief looked up at the sound of the door.

"Jake. What brings you here? Looking for a client?" Burkhalter's square, ruddy face was unusually jovial.

"I want to talk to you about that attack on Lainey Colton. What have you done about it?" He suspected that the honest answer would be nothing.

Burkhalter grinned. "I've solved it, that's what I've done. Surprised you there, didn't I? You figured I'd been sitting around all day doing nothing."

Since that was just about what he'd thought, Jake could hardly deny it. Burkhalter was well-intentioned and honest, but he never went out of his way to look for trouble.

"That's fast work," he said. Diplomacy was probably the simplest way to get answers. "Who was it? How did you find him?"

"Good police work, that's how." Burkhalter puffed himself up importantly. "Fact is, we caught a guy breaking into a house over on Elm in the middle of the night. Transient, looking to support a drug habit, as near as I can tell."

Jake managed to hide his surprise. Somehow he couldn't believe in a totally random attack after everything that had been going on since Lainey came to town. "He confessed to attacking Ms. Colton?"

"Well, no. Not yet. But he will." Burkhalter swung the computer screen around so that Jake could see it. "Seems he was wanted in Williamsport for burglaries there, so they took him off our hands. Long as he gets locked up, what difference does it make who prepares a case against him?"

And it would give Burkhalter the credit for an arrest without the tedious groundwork. Jake leaned on the counter next to him to read the information on the screen.

"It looks like he's been a busy boy," Jake said. "Five break-ins in two weeks."

"The officer I spoke to in Williamsport said Goren probably thought he'd have an easier time of it in a small town. He didn't reckon on the neighbors being quite so interested in what's going on, even in the middle of the night."

James Goren, mid-thirties, six foot, two hundred pounds. A string of arrests for break-ins, several stints in rehab and in the county jail.

"Ms. Colton said the person who attacked her wasn't that much bigger than she is. Goren sounds pretty hefty."

Burkhalter shrugged. "Easy enough for the victim to be confused when something like that happens. The way I figure it, he probably thought the house was empty. An easy target."

Jake stared at him. "The lights were on," he pointed out. "And he knocked on the door."

"Checking to be sure it was empty. He could easily have heard somebody mention that the owner was in the hospital."

"Doesn't it seem needlessly violent for a burglar? Why attack Ms. Colton when she came to the door?"

Burkhalter reddened. "Look, I don't have to account for what's going on in the fried brain of a junkie. Who knows? Who cares? The point is that he was caught a few hours later breaking into a house just a couple of blocks away. You're not going to tell me that's a coincidence."

"A random break-in doesn't account for all the other odd things that have happened since Ms. Colton came to town."

"Yeah, I know, you told me. Anonymous phone calls, minor vandalism." Burkhalter waved his hands. "Easy enough to see somebody was annoyed that Rebecca left a stranger in charge. You're not going to suggest that was Zeb Stoltzfus rigged up in a Halloween costume, are you? Because I can't buy that."

"What if it has something to do with Aaron Mast's murder?" Jake knew the minute he said the words what the chief's reaction would be.

Burkhalter's face reddened to a dangerous level. "Aaron Mast? That's ridiculous! You think everything that happens in this town is connected with Aaron Mast. That case is dead and buried. Victor Hammond killed him. He confessed. We all heard him say it. That case is over and done with."

"That's what you've been saying for twenty years, but it wasn't true, was it?"

Burkhalter looked on the verge of an explosion. "I don't have to listen to this garbage. We caught the guy, and there's an end to it. I'm going to call Ms. Colton and let her know the good news. And unless you have other business with the police department, you can clear out."

Burkhalter was as stubborn as the proverbial mule. Jake had to admit he had cause. They had all heard

Victor's confession. As far as the law was concerned, that case was closed. So where did that leave Lainey?

THE CAT HAD appeared at the back door right on schedule, just as Lainey was thinking about getting something to eat. Instead, she opened a can of the cat food she'd picked up at the store and leaned against the counter, watching him eat.

"I should have mentioned you to Aunt Rebecca. She might want to know that you're eating well." Talking to the cat was better than listening to the silence, despite what she'd implied to Jake about being fine alone.

Thinking about Jake was certainly counterproductive. "You've got the right idea," she informed the cat. "Stay independent. That way you don't get hurt."

Not that she intended to allow Jake to get close enough to hurt her. She couldn't, not without telling him about Phillip, and everything in her cringed at the thought.

Enough of that fruitless longing for something that was never going to happen. Lainey went back to the table, where she'd opened the scrapbook once again. Turning to the last page, she frowned. It somehow seemed so…unfinished to her.

But she'd been through all that already. Her mother had appeared the day after the tragedy, ready to whisk her away to yet another new life.

Had her aunt and uncle realized how much Lainey wanted to stay? But even if they had, even if they'd wanted to keep her, there would have been nothing they could do. A ten-year-old wasn't allowed to make such decisions for herself, and Mom had been determined.

Heaven only knew why. The fresh start had lasted no longer than any of the others had. If…

Her cell phone rang. She picked it up and checked before answering. A local number, although not one she recognized.

"Hello?"

"Is that Lainey?" A female voice, vaguely familiar but not instantly identifiable.

"This is Lainey Colton."

"I have to talk to you." The voice dropped to a whisper. "Please, I have to talk to you."

Lainey's fingers tightened on the phone. It was Laura Hammond. How had she gotten this number?

"What can I do for you, Laura?" She wouldn't let her voice show apprehension, even though her mind was filling with Jake's suspicions of the woman.

"We have to talk. In person, not on the phone. I have to see you."

A chill seemed to work its way down Lainey's spine. The woman was unstable. Everyone said so. Still, Lainey could hardly refuse to talk to her on that basis.

"Maybe we could meet for coffee tomorrow. Say at Miller's Store?" A nice, safe, public place in the daytime—that was the only meeting site she intended to agree to.

"Not there." Laura's tone sharpened. "No one must know."

"If you want to come to the house…" She let that trail off, not especially eager to entertain the woman here, either.

"I can't do that. Someone will see." Laura sounded almost panicked at the thought.

"Does that matter?" What was so terrible about the two of them talking?

"You'll have to come to my house," Laura said rapidly. "Not now. There are still people here. Later tonight. Come around eleven."

"I can't do that." Well, she could, but she certainly wasn't going to. Jake's suspicions might be totally wrong, but she still didn't intend to be alone with a potentially dangerous woman on her own territory late at night.

"You have to. It's the only way. I have to tell you—" Laura's voice broke off, and it seemed to Lainey that she heard another voice in the background. Did Laura have a housekeeper or a nurse? It seemed doubtful that she was living alone.

"Laura?" She said questioningly, and found she was staring at the "Call ended" notification.

She clicked off, dropped the phone, and rubbed her arms. Did an encounter with someone who was not quite rational always leave you feeling chilled? Or was it that she couldn't dismiss Jake's theories about Laura from her mind?

"I need something to warm me up." Cat, cleaning himself after his dinner, looked unconcerned. "Maybe a cup of tea." She set the kettle on the stove and switched on the gas, busying herself getting out a mug and finding a tea bag.

But when she turned back to the table, she found a young Laura's face staring up at her from the scrapbook page. That Laura had been young, alive, in love. Not at all like the Laura she'd just spoken with.

Why would Aaron's death have affected Laura so badly after all these years unless she'd had something to do with it? Even if she'd been there and witnessed it, surely she'd have told someone by now. But if Laura had been the one to push him into the dam that night—

A sharp knock on the back door startled her, sending the mug clattering to the table. It couldn't be Laura, her rational mind insisted. She couldn't have gotten here that quickly, not if she'd been at her house.

Still, Lainey picked up the cell phone, holding it ready to dial. Foolish or not, if the person outside looked in the least suspicious or threatening, she was calling 911. She peered through the small pane of glass in the door.

But it was Jake, looking neither suspicious nor threatening. She opened the door quickly. "You startled me. Why did you come to the back?"

He stepped inside, lifting his brows in surprise. "I could see you were in the kitchen. What's happened?"

"Nothing happened exactly." Belatedly she realized that she'd intended to keep Jake at arm's length, and here she was turning to him the instant there was a problem. "Laura Hammond called."

Something shrieked. It took a moment for Lainey to realize it was the kettle. The cat, affronted, raced toward the living room.

Jake reached out to move the kettle off the burner and turned back to her, very close. "Suitable sound effects," he said, and his smile eased some of her tension. Or at least replaced it with another kind— that intense awareness of his presence. "Why did she call?" His smile vanished. "What did she want?"

"To talk. But not on the phone. She wanted me to come to her house tonight. Late." Lainey rubbed her arms, feeling that chill again. "She was very insistent."

Jake took her hands in his, warming them with his touch. "I trust you refused."

"I did." She tried to repress a shiver. "It was odd. But then, Laura always seems odd, just from the little I've seen of her. Doesn't she?"

He nodded. "She hasn't been what anyone would call normal for years, although she's been much worse since Rachel returned and the talk started about Aaron's death." His fingers stroked her hands. "You were smart to turn her down."

Lainey drew her hands away slowly. Reluctantly. The sad fact was that she couldn't think straight when he was doing that.

"But what if Laura knows something? Should we really pass up the opportunity to hear what she has to say?"

"Maybe not, but I still don't think you should risk talking to her alone." He frowned. "Burkhalter would have a stroke if he heard about it. He's determined that whole story was buried with Victor."

"Was that why you came back? Because of Burkhalter? He called me about the burglar, you know."

"I figured he had." Jake's frown deepened. "I tried to talk to him about the situation, but he was so pleased with himself over catching a burglar that he wouldn't listen."

"Maybe he's right." She could tell she didn't sound very convinced.

"Why would a burglar attack you when you opened the door? That's not typical behavior. The man is six foot, two hundred pounds. Does that sound like the person you encountered?"

Burkhalter hadn't mentioned that detail. "No. I might not be able to identify him, but I'm sure he wasn't nearly that big." She might have known it wouldn't turn out to be that easy.

"I told Burkhalter that, but of course he wouldn't listen. He just keeps saying we heard Victor's confession. Which we did." Frustration evident in every line of his body, Jake drove his hand through his hair. "He can't see that Victor would have done anything for Laura, including take the blame for Aaron's death."

"What started out as our fairy tale really was a tragedy." Lainey stared down at the drawing in the scrapbook.

Jake shifted position to follow her gaze. "No one found a happily ever after, that's for sure."

"If things had been different…" She touched the pictured young faces. "They really seemed to be in love, but would it have lasted?"

"First loves." He sounded nostalgic. "My first love was Amy Waller. She wore her hair in a ponytail and sat in front of me in math class. I'd stare at it, mesmerized right through long division."

Lainey smiled, as she suspected he'd intended. "That can't have helped your math grade."

"No, I can't say that it did. As I recall, the teacher moved me to the front row after the first marking period."

"And that ended your romance?" She leaned back against the table, enjoying this glimpse of Jake's early life.

"I'm afraid it did." He shook his head. "Maybe just as well. She married Seth Michaels, had five boys, and rules the roost with an iron fist."

"She probably has to, with all those males in the house."

Jake grinned. "Well, we were only nine when I fell for her ponytail, so I had plenty of time to get over it. What about you?"

She shrugged, not eager to talk about her early years. "We moved so often that I was always the new kid. By the time I made friends, my mother was ready to move on."

"Why?"

A simple question that didn't have a simple answer. "Who knows? She was restless. She's never been able to stay in one place for long. Or with one man." Might as well get that out in the open.

"Maybe she wanted something she didn't find."

"Or someone." She shrugged. "She always claims she's unlucky in love."

"What about you?" Jake's voice seemed to drop. "Are you unlucky in love?"

"You might say that." She tried for a lightness she didn't feel. "My love life has been one disaster after another. Maybe, as I'm sure my Uncle Zeb would say, the apple doesn't fall far from the tree."

"I can't buy that," he said. "Certainly Rebecca doesn't believe it about you, and I have a lot of faith in her judgment."

Somehow she thought neither he nor Aunt Rebecca would look at her the same if they knew exactly how much grief she'd caused with her last relationship.

"What about you?" she said quickly, hoping to divert him before she was forced into lying. "Don't tell me you've gotten to thirty without any serious relationships."

He raised his eyebrows. "You really want to hear my sad story?"

She nodded. "Of course."

Jake leaned back against the counter. "I met her when I was in law school. Fell head over heels, and there was no ponytail involved." He shrugged, seeming to lose the half-teasing mood he'd had when he started. "We were engaged before I realized we wanted entirely different things in life. Not much of a basis for marriage, so I broke it off."

"I'm sorry." There didn't seem anything else to say.

"My fault. I should have figured out we weren't suited before we got engaged, not afterward."

He was trying to treat it lightly, but she could see past the mask. The incident had hurt him, probably mainly because he'd been forced to hurt someone else.

"The alternative would have been worse, don't you think?" What if she'd never realized what Phillip was really like? Would she have gone on loving him?

"I hope so. I'd hate to think I acted like a jerk for no good reason." He glanced at the scrapbook. "By all accounts, Aaron and Laura were happy together for a few months. Does that make up for all the grief that came after?"

"I don't know." Her fairy-tale version of their love had certainly taken a beating since she'd come back to Deer Run.

The cat skittered back through the door from the living room, batting a crumpled ball of paper in front of him. It was one of the few times Lainey had seen him play, and she stared at him with an amused smile until she realized what the paper was. The anonymous letter—she made a dive for it, but the cat had batted it to Jake's feet, and he picked it up, smoothing it out with his hand.

"What—" He stopped, seeming to absorb the contents of the letter.

Lainey couldn't move, and her mouth went dry. How was she going to explain this? Anything she said would lead to the whole sordid story tumbling out, and…

"Here's the proof someone's trying to scare you out of town." The anger in Jake's eyes wasn't aimed at her. "Why didn't you tell me? If you're getting threatening notes, Burkhalter will have to pay attention. Have you received many of these?"

She shook her head numbly. Jake didn't seem to imagine that there might be something else in her life that would cause people to send her abusive letters. He thought it was all part of what had been going on since she'd come to Deer Run.

And maybe he was right. Maybe she'd been jumping to conclusions, thinking that someone here knew about St. Louis.

"I don't think it would make any difference to what Chief Burkhalter thinks." And the last thing she wanted was someone like him looking into her life.

"You may be right." He was frowning at the sheet of paper. Cat, deprived of his toy, wove circles around Jake's ankles. "Granted that Zeb would be glad to see the last of you, this doesn't seem like something he would do. As for Thomas—"

"I can't see Thomas writing an anonymous letter."

His gaze questioned her. "He did plant the witch signs."

"I know. But this…it just seems too sophisticated an idea for him."

"If we eliminate Zeb and Thomas, we're back to

my initial idea. Someone fears you know something about Aaron's death."

"But I don't!" She wanted to shout her protest.

Her vehemence clearly startled him. "I'm sorry. I shouldn't have said that."

Lainey shook her head, her throat tight. "It's just so frustrating." Her voice sounded strained even to herself.

Carefully, as if afraid she was breakable, Jake put his arms around her and drew her close. Half-ashamed of her weakness, she shut her eyes, focusing on the warmth of his embrace and the steady beating of his heart against her cheek.

His lips moved against her hair. "I wish I could see the way out of this mess. You don't deserve any of this."

But she did. And letting herself lean on Jake was simply compounding her wrongs. She eased herself out of the protective circle of his arms.

"I'm all right." She tried to smile. "A momentary weakness, that's all."

He studied her face. "I think I should stay tonight."

Lainey shook her head. She was afraid of what would happen if he stayed. She couldn't let this go any further without telling him the truth. And if she did tell him, he'd walk away.

"I'll be fine. I'll lock all the doors, keep the cat inside, and sleep with my cell phone in my hand. Nothing's going to happen."

She hoped.

CHAPTER SEVENTEEN

THE RAIN HAD been streaking the windows all afternoon, but inside the rehab facility everything was bright and cheerful. Obviously the designers had felt that the surroundings had an effect on the patients' recovery. Whether that was true or not Lainey didn't know, but she found it lifted her spirits despite all the worrying she'd been doing.

How could she help it? She'd effectively lied to Jake by not telling him the whole story about the abusive letters she'd received. He'd made it clear that he valued the truth at all costs. She hadn't told it. But if she did, he'd never look at her the same anyway.

She forced her attention back to the present and smiled at her aunt. The flowered curtains and colored posters were a far cry from Aunt Rebecca's usual decor, but that didn't seem to be bothering her. She leaned back onto her pillows after an excursion with the walker that Lainey suspected had tired her. It certainly had Lainey. She kept holding her breath at each halting step, ready to reach out a supporting arm but not wanting to interfere.

"Great work, Mrs. Stoltzfus." The therapist was young, cheerful and apparently untiring. She patted

Aunt Rebecca's hand. "We'll have you doing laps around the building before long."

"Go home?" Aunt Rebecca formed the question with deliberate concentration.

"It won't be too long until you're ready," the therapist said. "Rest up, now. I'll see you tomorrow." She flashed a smile at Lainey and made a quick escape before Aunt Rebecca could press the issue of going home.

Lainey had to smile at her great-aunt's expression. "You remember how you used to tell me that I had to learn patience when I pestered you about something? Well, I think maybe it's your turn to practice that."

Aunt Rebecca's smile was a little lopsided, but it was a smile, nonetheless, and it warmed Lainey's heart.

She reached for the jacket she'd hung over the bottom of the bed. "I should be going. Just hold on to the thought that we'll be taking you home soon."

Aunt Rebecca's hand closed over hers. "D-don't go."

Lainey couldn't help taking a quick glance at the clock. She'd stayed later than usual, but after all, there was no one waiting for her but the cat. She sat on the edge of the bed. "Of course I'll stay if you want."

Aunt Rebecca shook her head, her mouth working in an attempt to form the words she wanted. "No. Go home now. Supper." She frowned. "J-just don't go away again."

Understanding was like a blow to the heart. Aunt

Rebecca wasn't talking about staying at the rehab facility today. She was talking about Lainey staying in Deer Run.

I never wanted to leave. That was what she wanted to say, but it would be foolish and hurtful. Aunt Rebecca hadn't had the power to keep her, no matter how much Lainey wanted to stay. And she was a grown woman now, not a ten-year-old.

"I'll stay as long as you need me," she said, leaning over the bed. "I promise."

Her great-aunt patted Lainey's cheek. *"Gut."* She leaned back, looking tired but satisfied.

Feeling ridiculously like bursting into tears, Lainey kissed her cheek and hurried out into the hallway.

The aroma of chicken cooking wafted through the air, and from the dining room came the clink of plates as someone got the tables ready. Several patients were already moving in that direction, talking to each other as they went. There seemed to be an atmosphere of comradeship here that had been missing in the hospital, maybe because people here were all working on similar goals. Lainey skirted a pair of women using walkers with a smile and ducked out the front door, to be greeted with a chill, damp gust of air.

Out here, everything was gray, it seemed. The pole lights made a feeble effort to disperse the gloom—unsuccessfully, it seemed to Lainey. She zipped her jacket, wished she'd thought to pack a raincoat when she left St. Louis, and opened the umbrella.

She'd parked at the farthest point, apparently, in the parking lot the rehab facility shared with the hospital, but the lot had been crowded when she'd arrived. Holding the umbrella slanted against the wind-driven rain, she trudged along wet pavement.

Aunt Rebecca had taken her by surprise when she'd asked her to stay, and yet she couldn't deny that the thought had drifted through her mind several times in the last weeks. Stay in the place that had always felt like the only home she'd known—what could be wrong with that? Except that she feared she couldn't go back to being the kind of person who belonged here.

A gust of wind nearly turned her umbrella inside out. She tilted it, trying to use it as a shield against the wind that seemed to come sideways, sweeping along the lot and sending sodden leaves into her path.

Lainey groped in her bag with one hand for her keys. Nearly there now, and—

Someone darted from between two parked cars, almost colliding with her. Lainey stepped back a step, catching her breath. "What are you—" The furious question broke off when she saw who it was. "Laura."

Laura Hammond stood inches from her, rain soaking through a thin sweater and plastering her hair against her skull. If she usually looked like a carefully tended doll, now she more closely resembled one left out in a muddy yard. Her eyes were wide, staring unblinkingly at Lainey.

A jolt of apprehension went through her. If Jake were right…

Even if he was, she had no cause to be afraid. She was younger and stronger than Laura.

"I've been waiting for you forever." Laura made it sound as if they'd had an appointment here. "Where are the other two? Why aren't they with you?"

Maybe being younger and stronger had nothing to do with it. Anyone would be afraid when confronted by the irrational.

"You mean Rachel and Meredith?" Lainey tried to keep her tone calm as she mentally measured the distance to her car.

"They should be here. You're always together."

"Not always." Lainey tried to ease a step back.

Laura grabbed her wrist and the umbrella blew free, slapping against a car hood before falling, twisted, to the pavement.

"We have to end this. You understand, don't you?" Laura thrust her face toward Lainey's.

Lainey yanked at her wrist without success. Laura was stronger than she looked. "I'm sorry, but I don't understand." Lainey groped for something the woman might respond to. "You're soaking wet. Let me help you to your car. Then we can talk about anything you want."

"I don't have a car. I walked. I knew you'd be here."

Laura's single-mindedness was frightening. Her fingers tightened on Lainey's wrist, digging into the skin.

"Let me call someone for you, then." Lainey fished in her bag with her free hand and came out with her cell phone. "Do you want me to call your friend Jeannette?"

"No!" Laura swatted at the phone, and it flew from Lainey's hand to skitter across the wet pavement.

Lainey's fear ratcheted upward. She darted a quick look around. No one in sight—they were alone in a forest of parked cars, isolated by the gloom and the pelting rain.

If she offered to drive Laura home...but her mind shrank from the thought of being alone in a moving car with her.

"We'll talk all you want," she said, willing her voice to sound calm. "Let's just get in out of the rain."

Laura shook her head. "We have to talk about that night. You know what happened."

Fear scraped along her nerves. This was exactly what Jake had been worried about—that someone would assume she knew something she didn't.

"No. No, I don't." This had gone on long enough. No one was coming along to interrupt them. She'd have to wrench herself free and make a run for the car. If she could get in and lock the doors—

"You have to know." Laura's face contorted with emotion. Fear? Anger? "You have to know. You were there." Laura grabbed her, shaking her.

Lainey brought her fists up as hard as she could, knocking Laura's hands away. She didn't want to hurt an obviously sick woman, but she might not have a choice.

She pivoted, meaning to run for the car, but a vehicle shrieked to a stop beside them. In an instant Jeannette was out, grasping Laura's arms.

"Laura! Stop that this instant. What would the doctor say about this behavior? Do you want him to send you back to the hospital?"

Apparently those were the magic words. Laura subsided, sobbing now, and Lainey could breathe again.

"Help me with her," Jeannette murmured. Together, wordlessly, they bundled Laura into the back of Jeannette's car.

Jeannette closed the door and glanced at Lainey. "Sorry."

"Not your fault." Though clearly Laura needed more supervision than she was getting. "How did you find her?"

"Someone saw her walking up the hill. I thought she might have decided to try and see your aunt."

That sounded unlikely, but Lainey was too relieved to have the woman off her hands to worry about it.

"Well, I'd better get her home." Jeannette looked for a moment as if she'd say something else, but what was there to say? It had been a messy experience, and talking about it wouldn't help.

Lainey nodded, bending to rescue her cell phone. It seemed to have survived, which was more than she could say for the umbrella. Or her nerves. She was shaking, though that might be partly attributed to the fact that she was soaked.

Jeannette got into the driver's seat without another glance at Lainey. As she pulled away, Laura's face was pressed against the glass, her eyes staring at Lainey.

Shivering, Lainey ran to her car.

LAINEY FINALLY FELT warm after spending enough time in the shower to use up all the hot water. She pulled on a pair of yoga pants and a sweatshirt, thankful that the gas-powered furnace came on at the touch of a button. Cousin Katie had laughed at her when she'd expressed her fear of the monster lurking in the cellar.

Amish don't connect with the power grid, because that would make us depend on the outside world too much, and the Bible says we should live separate. We still have heat and light and food to eat. What more does anyone need?

Most people would insist they needed much more. Lainey went downstairs, to be greeted by Cat, who'd been curled up in Lainey's favorite rocker. Need was an elastic term.

She sat down, letting the cat make himself comfortable on her lap, and stared out the window at the lights in Rachel's house next door. Should she tell Rachel and Meredith about that troubling encounter with Laura Hammond? It would be a relief to talk about it with someone, but that was just shifting the burden of worry to them.

No, it was better to wait. The next time she spoke with them she could bring it up casually, without the fear of overreacting when talking about Laura's irrational behavior.

Unfortunately, one thing the woman had said couldn't really be classed as delusional and dismissed accordingly. *You have to know. You were there.*

That was what Jake feared, with his emphasis on her sleepwalking and his concerns about her nightmares. That she had been there. That she had seen what happened when Aaron died.

She hadn't. If she had, she'd remember. Lainey rubbed the back of her neck, where tension seemed to be building. Did a person's mind record the things that happened when she was sleepwalking? She had no idea. She'd never looked into the mechanics of the thing, simply relieved that it had stopped.

Jake had implied that whether she remembered or not, she could be in danger from someone who feared she might. But surely that was only an issue if his suspicions were true, and it was Laura, not Victor, who'd killed Aaron Mast.

The cat arched under her hand, demanding to be stroked. Smoothing her hand down the cat's glossy back, she frowned, reminded of the conversation with Thomas. It seemed to have taken place ages ago, not yesterday.

"Black cats," she said aloud, and Cat lifted his head in response. "No wonder Thomas thinks I'm a witch."

Still, she couldn't quite buy the idea that Thomas had come up with that on his own, no matter how many black cats were involved. Something must have prompted his belief—just the coincidence of her coming to town around Halloween, when English teens might have been talking about the occult? Her appearance? She smoothed back unruly hair, still damp from her shower. Granted she didn't look much like the Amish women Thomas was used to, but surely that wouldn't be enough to put the idea in his head.

She couldn't escape the notion that it had been done deliberately, by someone Thomas would believe. Zeb was the obvious choice for the role. Even if Jake's suspicions were correct and Laura had been involved in Aaron's death, that could have nothing to do with Thomas setting witch traps.

The wind sent a spray of rain whipping against the windows. The cat lifted his head, staring fixedly at the window, or maybe at the blackness beyond.

"It's nothing," she said, soothing him. "Just be glad you've found a comfortable berth and aren't outside."

He rose, arching in a stretch and kneading his paws against her thighs. Then he leaped to the floor and paced toward the window, tail high.

"You're making me nervous," she complained. If she had a television, she'd turn it on for the company. Maybe that was why the Amish didn't have them. It was too tempting to let the outside world into your living room at the slightest excuse.

Wind howled around the house, and she rose and went to the front window to peer out. Rain whipped down the street, making the pavement gleam in the reflected glow of the streetlights. Across the street, the windows of Jeannette's bed-and-breakfast emitted a gentle glow. Would Jeannette have taken Laura there or back to her own house? Surely she shouldn't be left alone.

Something moved on the front porch, sending her pulse into overdrive. But it was only the rocking chair, swinging back and forth as the wind hit it. Beyond the porch, the bushes moved like so many black figures, waving their branches in a wild dance.

Lainey pulled the shade down, shutting out the sight. Enough. Her imagination ran riot too easily without the prompting of such a wild night.

Turning back to the cozy room, she rubbed her arms, chilled even under the sweatshirt. "Maybe a cup of hot chocolate," she said to the cat. "It's that kind of night, isn't it?"

Cat seemed to have no opinion on the subject, but he followed her to the kitchen. Lainey was reaching for the kettle when something that might have been a strangled cry sounded in the backyard. The wind, she told herself. *It's just the wind.*

But when she turned, the cat was standing in the middle of the kitchen floor, his back ridged, his hair standing on end, his gaze fixed on the back door.

Another sound. A thud. And her heart was pounding so loudly in her ears it nearly blocked out the wind. Someone was out there.

She took a step back, grabbing for the cell phone that lay on the counter. *The door is locked. No one can get in. Go back to the living room and call for help.*

But the sound that came from beyond the back door pierced her heart. A child. Or a hurt animal. She couldn't think only of her own safety.

Cell phone in one hand. Flashlight in the other. She was as ready as she could be. She bypassed the hissing cat and approached the back door. Grasped the curtain. Pulled it aside.

Her heart jolted. Something…someone…made a dark shadow at the foot of the steps. It moved slightly, a weak cry sounding.

Lainey fumbled with the cell phone. The police? She quailed at the thought of trying to explain to a stranger. Instead she hit Jake's number.

He answered on the first ring, as if he'd been waiting for her call.

"Lainey?"

Just the sound of his voice, and she didn't feel so alone.

"Outside. Someone is lying there. At the bottom of the steps. Hurt, maybe badly."

"Stay on the line." She could hear movement at his end. "I'll call the police on my other phone. I'm on my way. Don't hang up. And don't open the door."

She nodded, as if he could see her, and stared mesmerized at the door. She didn't want to look again. But she had to. She had to know.

"Lainey? Are you still there?" He sounded afraid. For her.

"Yes," she managed to say.

"Don't open the door until I get there," he said again. "I'm in the car. The police are on their way."

A faint, mewling cry reached her ears. She had to look again. She pulled aside the curtain. A dark figure loomed over the person on the ground, stooping, raising its hand, curiously elongated, threatening—

"No!" She grabbed the knob, wrestling with the lock. She could hear Jake's voice from the cell phone, shouting at her, telling her not to open the door, but she had to, she couldn't stay inside and watch murder done—

The door gave to her frantic fingers. She swung it open, grabbing the broom that stood just outside. "Get out! Get away!"

Shouting, brandishing the broom, praying that would be enough to scare the figure away. "The police are coming!"

As if in response to her words, she heard the distant wail of a siren. The figure hesitated, hand upraised with something—a club, a bat—ready to swing.

And then it was gone, melting into the shadows.

Letting out a strangled breath, Lainey bolted to the prone figure, kneeling, shivering as the cold rain hit her. Not an animal, a person. Her fumbling fingers closed on the flashlight. Switched it on.

The figure lay facedown, ominously still. A slight figure. Dark clothing. Lainey forced her fingers to obey her brain, turning the circle of light onto the head.

Fair hair, darkened now by the rain. For an instant she thought it was Laura.

Then she realized her mistake. No. Not Laura.

It was Thomas, lying sprawled at the bottom of her porch steps, his face deadly white, his skin cold, his body motionless.

CHAPTER EIGHTEEN

IN ALL THE confusion of police, paramedics, getting Thomas to the hospital, and assuring himself that Lainey was really all right, Jake didn't have much chance to talk to her. Once things calmed down, he told himself. Then they'd talk this over calmly.

Lainey wanted to go to the hospital with Thomas, but Burkhalter insisted he had to hear her account of things first. Rachel had been a rock, promising to see that Thomas's family was notified and to go herself to the hospital to stay with him until they arrived.

Burkhalter ushered her into the kitchen, closing the door firmly on his own people, who were searching the backyard, and the cluster of neighbors who'd gathered at the sight of police and paramedics.

"I still think I should have gone with Thomas." Lainey sat down, shivering a little. "He's just a boy. He should have someone there."

"Rachel won't leave him," Meredith said, patting her hand. "I'm sure she'll call us as soon as they know anything."

Burkhalter sat down, opening a small notebook on the table. He eyed Meredith. "You might as well go home now. Excitement's over."

Meredith responded with a steady stare. "I don't have anything else to do, and Lainey can use some support after all she's been through."

Jake exchanged glances with Meredith. They were both only too aware of Burkhalter's habit of seizing the obvious answer in every situation. Meredith, having undergone the effects of his mistaken assumptions herself, was a good person to have around.

Burkhalter, apparently resigning himself to the fact that he wouldn't get rid of either of them, turned to Lainey. "Now, Ms. Colton, the way I get it is that you'd found Thomas playing some tricks on you before."

Lainey frowned slightly. "Yes, but once I…we… confronted him about it, that had stopped."

"So when you heard someone outside your back door tonight, you maybe thought it was Thomas up to his tricks again."

"No." Lainey's head came up as if she scented danger. "I didn't think that at all."

Jake moved casually around the table and put his hands on the back of Lainey's chair—not touching her, but close enough to sense her every reaction. "What Ms. Colton thought is neither here nor there, Chief. She heard someone out back, and she called me for help."

"Seems to me it'd make more sense to call 911," Burkhalter said, his square bulldog face watchful.

"I did that for her." Jake kept his tone even and casual. No point in making this confrontational unless he had to. "She told me she looked out and saw someone lying at the bottom of the steps. I cautioned her to stay inside, called you, and came right over."

"That right, Ms. Colton?"

Lainey nodded. "Yes, I think that's what he said."

"Then why did you go outside?" Burkhalter shot the question at her.

If he'd hoped to unnerve Lainey, he didn't succeed, but Jake felt her stiffen at his tone.

"I heard something that might have been a cry for help. I looked out, and I saw someone standing over the person lying on the ground. It—he or she—held something up as if about to strike. I couldn't just stay in here and watch."

"If what you say is true, the attacker might have turned on you," Burkhalter observed.

"If—" Lainey's voice rose.

Jake put his hands on her shoulders, feeling her tension. "That remark is verging on the improper, Chief Burkhalter."

Burkhalter glared at him. "Just trying to get to the truth. Seems to me Ms. Colton might have gotten a little confused, hearing someone out there, trying to defend herself—"

"Ms. Colton has told you the truth." The pressure of his hands urged Lainey to be silent, and she seemed to get the message. "She went out at considerable risk to herself to defend an unconscious boy from further attack. I'm sure an unbiased, thorough investigation will confirm her report."

Their gazes clashed for what seemed a long time. Then Burkhalter's fell. "Well, we'll see what the boy has to say once the doctors let him talk." He stood, hesitated for a moment as if he'd like to say something more, and then went out, slamming the back door.

"Every time I think Burkhalter can't possibly jump to any more wrong conclusions, he outdoes himself," Meredith said. She stood. "I'm going to spend the night, so don't even bother trying to argue about it," she said briskly. "Jake, suppose you stay here while I run next door and get what I need. Then you can take yourself off."

"Bossy, aren't you?" He grinned, relieved at her automatic defense of Lainey.

"It's the only way of dealing with stubborn people." Grabbing her jacket, she let herself out the back considerably more quietly than Burkhalter had.

"She believes me." Lainey sounded faintly surprised.

"Of course she does." He let himself squeeze her shoulder and then sat down across from her. "Now, just a couple of things before Meredith comes back and kicks me out. You have no sense of who the other person was?"

"Don't you think I'd tell you if I did?"

He smiled. "I'm glad to see your spirit is back, but save it for Burkhalter. If he should come by for any more little chats, even if he calls, you say you can't talk to him without the presence of your attorney, right?"

Lainey looked as if she'd argue, but then she nodded. "It doesn't matter. As soon as he talks to

Thomas, Burkhalter will have to acknowledge that I was telling the truth."

"About that." He hesitated, not wanting to deliver bad news, but also not wanting her unprepared. "It looked to me as if Thomas had had a solid whack to the head. It's entirely possible he won't remember what happened. And even if he does, he may not have seen who hit him."

Lainey pressed her lips together, as if to keep a protest back. "I suppose you're right. If so…is Burkhalter seriously considering charging me with a crime?"

"I doubt it." He couldn't seem to keep himself from reaching across the table to clasp her hand. "Even if he could convince the district attorney that you hit Thomas, which I doubt, there would still be a presumption that you were defending yourself."

She seemed to shiver, as if even the heavy sweater Meredith had insisted she put on wasn't enough to warm her. "It's crazy. I wonder—"

"What?" he prompted.

Her gaze met his. "I didn't have a chance to tell you. I had an encounter with Laura this afternoon."

"Laura. If we're looking for someone unbalanced, she certainly fits. Did she threaten you?"

"Not exactly." Lainey frowned. "The more I go over it in my mind, the more uncertain I am of her motives."

"Tell me." He held her hand in both of his.

"She was waiting in the parking lot when I came out of the rehab facility—soaking wet. I don't know how long she'd been there. She kept saying we had to talk, and frankly, I kept trying to get away from her. Or at least, get her someplace where there were other people around."

"I don't blame you. What did she want to talk about?"

"Aaron's death, I suppose. She wasn't exactly making sense." Lainey looked down at their clasped hands. "She kept saying that I knew what happened. Then she said I had to know, because I was there."

His fingers tightened on hers. "That's just what I was afraid of."

"But I don't remember anything. I'm not a threat to anyone." She sounded as if she didn't even convince herself.

It was his turn to stare at their hands, trying to see a path through this tangle. "She could have been the person who attacked Thomas."

"But why? He has nothing to do with her or with Aaron's death."

He shook his head, frustrated that he didn't have answers, only questions. "I don't know. Maybe she came here hoping to get at you, and somehow he was in her way." His jaw clenched, and he knew what he had to say. "Maybe the safest thing is for you to leave Deer Run."

"No." Her response was immediate. "I won't leave."

"For your own safety—" he began.

"No," she said again. Her chin set stubbornly. "I

promised Aunt Rebecca I'd stay as long as she needs me. I'm not leaving."

"If Rebecca knew all the circumstances, she'd be the first person to want you to be safe."

"She doesn't know, and you can't tell her. I won't have her recovery upset by worrying about me."

Jake studied her face. Did she even realize the contradiction between her determination to stay and her apparent conviction that she was just as lacking in commitment as her mother was? Probably not. He'd have to tell his dad that he could stop worrying about Lainey carrying her mother's genes in that respect.

"You are one very determined woman, you know that?" He stood, bending over her, and tipped her chin up, letting his fingers move along the soft, warm skin. "Okay. We'll fight it out together until we find the truth. But in the meantime, don't go wandering off by yourself."

"I'll try not to."

Her eyes seemed to grow darker as he leaned closer. He closed the distance between their lips, trying not to move too far, too fast, but she was responding, her arms going around him…

The back door sounded. With what seemed a lot of needless clatter, Meredith came in, juggling a grocery bag and a small overnight bag. Without looking at them, she put her belongings on the counter. "I had some breakfast rolls, so I brought them along in case you weren't all that prepared for company."

By the time she turned around, Jake had managed

to take a step away from Lainey. Still, it was probably very obvious what they'd been doing.

"The perfect guest, aren't you?" he said. "I'll get out of your way. Lock up behind me, okay?" He touched Lainey's cheek lightly. "I'll call you in the morning."

He went out, taking the memory of her bemused smile with him.

THE FACT THAT Meredith was still carefully not looking at her after Jake left brought Lainey's defensiveness to the fore.

"I guess you saw that." She might as well bring it out in the open. Meredith was bound to feel much closer to Jake than to her, wasn't she?

Meredith's steady brown eyes assessed her for a moment, and then she smiled. "Jake's a good guy. If things work out for the two of you, I'm glad."

"He is a good guy." Lainey's throat tightened. "But this whole situation…" She wasn't sure how to go on.

But Meredith nodded as if she understood. "I don't know if it helps, but much the same thing happened to me. When you get tangled up in a dangerous situation, emotions can run high."

"So what did you do?"

Meredith shrugged. "Tried to wait and see if the feelings lasted once life got back to normal." Her lips curved. "They have."

Good advice. Lainey just wasn't sure how well she'd do at the wait-and-see part.

"Strange, isn't it?" Meredith's thoughts seemed to

be running along a different track. "That what happened that summer should come back to cause so much grief after twenty years."

Lainey pushed her hair back wearily. "It's hard to believe. Maybe I'm really like Chief Burkhalter—looking for an easy answer."

Meredith took a pan of what seemed to be cinnamon rolls from her bag and paused, holding it in one hand. "If I'd been home that night Aaron died, maybe things would have been different."

She was probably thinking of her mother's death, Lainey realized, and she felt awkward, unsure what to say. She settled on a question.

"I don't think I knew you were away. Where were you?"

"Staying overnight with some of my Amish cousins." Meredith set the pan on the counter and smoothed the plastic wrap over it.

"Even if you'd been home, what could you have done differently that would have changed things? We were just kids, after all." It seemed wrong that Meredith should blame herself or have regrets for something she couldn't possibly have prevented.

"Nothing, I suppose," Meredith admitted. "But if I'd been awake, maybe I'd have seen or heard something that would have brought things out into the open."

"Maybe. But honestly, I wish I hadn't been here." She shook her head in immediate denial of the thought. "No, I don't really mean that. I wouldn't trade my summer here for anything."

"I'm glad. Rebecca feels the same, I know. To say nothing of Rachel and me. We wouldn't want to do without our friendship."

"Okay, don't make me get all misty." She smiled through a haze of tears. "To go back to that last day—" She paused and shook her head. "It's frustrating how little I remember. When did you find out about Aaron?"

"The first I knew of his death was when I found one of my teenage cousins crying. I'd never seen anyone I considered an adult cry before. Then my aunt told me about Aaron."

Lainey leaned back against the counter, trying to piece together her own memories of that day. All she could come up with were fragments: Aunt Rebecca looking tense and drawn, her great-uncle with a face set like stone; her mother hustling her to finish packing so they could leave.

"Did we see each other the day my mother came?"

Meredith shook her head, looking troubled. "I ran over here as soon as I got home. Rebecca stopped me on the porch. She said your mother was there to take you away. She looked…" Meredith paused, shaking her head. "I'm not sure how to describe it. Devastated, I suppose. I told her I had to see you to tell you about Aaron, but she said no."

"She didn't let you tell me?" Everything in her rebelled at the thought. "Aunt Rebecca wouldn't lie to me."

"I don't suppose she thought it was lying. She was trying to protect you. It was strange, though.

She said—" Meredith stopped, and Lainey wanted to shake the words loose.

"What did she say?"

Meredith looked troubled. "She murmured something in Pennsylvania Dutch. I didn't speak it except with my cousins, but I understood. She might not have realized I did."

A chill worked its way down Lainey's spine. "What was it?"

"She said, 'She doesn't remember. She doesn't know. It's best that way.'"

Lainey wrapped her arms around herself, trying to keep the chill at bay. "You thought she was talking about me."

Meredith nodded, eyes troubled. "Everyone was strange that day. It was as if our world had been turned upside down by what happened to Aaron. Maybe that's why I remember it so clearly. But what did she mean?"

Lainey tried to find another explanation. She couldn't. "I used to sleepwalk when I was little. Jake thinks I might have been out of the house that night. That I might have seen something."

Surprisingly, Meredith didn't seem as shocked by that as Lainey expected. "I remember the sleepwalking. You did it once when I was staying over. But why would Jake assume you were out that night?"

"Because of the dreams." Lainey said the words reluctantly. She didn't have any desire to look like some sort of nutcase in front of Meredith, but after what happened tonight, maybe it was past time to protect her image. "I've had recurring dreams about being near the water, about someone chasing me. About trying to get to the house where I'd be safe."

Meredith considered. "Dreams, not memories?"

She nodded. "That's what I keep telling Jake. If my conscious mind doesn't remember, my dreams don't mean anything."

"I don't know enough about sleepwalking to make a judgment," Meredith said. "Just all the old wives' tales about how dangerous it is to wake a person if they're sleepwalking. But I guess that's not the point, is it? If Jake's right, and Victor really didn't kill Aaron, then someone else did. And if that person thinks you saw something—"

She didn't finish. She didn't need to. Lainey already knew the rest of it. If that someone was trying to silence her, then an innocent boy might have been struck down because he got in the way.

Lainey reached the hospital early the next day, hoping to find out how Thomas was before going to see her aunt. Parking in the lot between the two buildings, she headed for the hospital entrance. The day, in sharp contrast to yesterday, was bright and sunny, with only a crisp nip in the air to remind one it was November.

The brisk air seemed to blow away the fog that had been clinging to her brain since she got up this morning. The nightmares had been worse last night, maybe because she'd been talking about the subject so much. She felt as if she'd spent the entire night running.

The sound of water in her ears, the by-now-familiar sense of being chased, terrified, trying to reach the lights of the house. Falling.

And something added that had never been there before—the sense that if only she'd looked up in that moment, she would have seen the face of her pursuer.

Shivering, Lainey shrugged it off and went to the desk to inquire as to Thomas's room. The hospital volunteer was unfamiliar today, and she consulted her computer and relayed the number with a smile but no sense of recognition.

Just as well. Lainey really wasn't up to any idle chat at this hour, not after the night she'd had. She rode up in the elevator and followed the room number signs, only to be stopped by a nurse just as she reached her destination.

"I'm sorry." The middle-aged woman was pleasant but firm. "No visitors yet for the patient. You can try again this afternoon, if you like."

Lainey glanced beyond her at the door, frustrated. "Can you at least tell me how Thomas is doing?"

The woman eyed her. "Are you a relative?" Doubt filled her voice.

"I am, as a matter of fact. Thomas is my cousin. I'm on my way to see our great-aunt in the rehab unit, and I wanted to be able to give her some news about his condition."

The nurse's expression softened. "Rebecca Stoltzfus, you mean. I hope she's doing well?"

Lainey decided she should stop being surprised that everyone in town knew Aunt Rebecca. "She's gaining strength and speaking more every day."

"Well, you tell her Rosie Sitler asked about her." The woman glanced at the door and then back at Lainey. "I really can't let you in," she said, lowering her voice. "But you can tell Rebecca it's just a concussion, the doctor feels sure. The boy should be up and about in no time."

Relief swept through Lainey. "Thanks so much. I'll tell her."

Her step felt lighter as she headed down the hallway toward the elevator. At least Thomas was recovering. She wouldn't have to carry the burden of having caused serious damage to yet another person.

The elevator doors swished open as she approached, and Zeb Stoltzfus stepped out, stopping short at the sight of her.

"What are you doing here?" He didn't bother lowering his voice.

"I came to see how Thomas is doing. I'm so sorry—"

"Sorry! You should be sorry. Hurting a poor boy who never did anything to you." His leathery face reddened.

Now was not the moment to bring up the tricks Thomas had played.

"I didn't hurt him." Surely he couldn't believe that she had attacked his grandson.

Zeb muttered something in dialect that she was

just as glad she couldn't understand. "You are to blame."

"That's not true." Wasn't it? If it hadn't been for her, Thomas wouldn't have been there. "I found him. I called for help for him." She couldn't bring herself to share that image of the dark figure over the boy, weapon upraised.

Zeb thrust his face toward hers, eyes blazing. "Stay away from that boy." He brushed past her and strode quickly down the hall.

The elevator was still waiting. Lainey escaped into it and pressed the button, hand shaking. Her heart seemed to be dropping along with the elevator.

No matter how wrong Zeb was about what had happened, he was right about one thing. Even though she hadn't wielded the weapon, Thomas's injury was her responsibility.

Lainey sucked in a breath. All right. She couldn't go back and undo what had been done. But Jake was right about one thing. Only the truth would resolve this situation once and for all. And based on what Meredith had told her, Aunt Rebecca must have a piece of the truth that she'd never revealed.

Lainey crossed the parking lot so quickly that she arrived at the rehab unit out of breath. She paused in the entrance to catch her breath and organize her thoughts.

She had to be gentle with Aunt Rebecca. She couldn't set back her recovery by upsetting her. But somehow, her great-aunt had to be persuaded to tell what she knew about Lainey's actions the night Aaron died.

Fortunately, she arrived at her aunt's room well ahead of the first physical therapy of the day. When she opened the door, Aunt Rebecca was seated in a chair by the window, fully dressed, her gray hair neatly pulled back under a snowy prayer *kapp*. She turned at the sound of the door and smiled.

"Lainey." The name came out even easier than it had the previous day. A shadow came over her expression. "Thomas?" she asked.

Lainey went to her quickly and pulled a chair up next to her aunt's. "He's doing well. I stopped at the hospital to ask. The nurse…" What was the woman's name? "Rosie Sitler, I think?"

Aunt Rebecca nodded.

"She said to tell you that Thomas has a concussion, but he's recovering and will be up and around soon. So you're not to worry about him." Lainey patted her aunt's hands, deciding there was nothing to be gained by mentioning her encounter with Zeb.

"Thank th-the *gut* Lord." Her forehead wrinkled. "You? All right?"

"I wasn't hurt," she said quickly. "I saw the person, but not to identify."

Aunt Rebecca shook her head, murmuring something in Pennsylvania Dutch. "Evil," she said distinctly.

"Yes." Lainey seized on the word. "It is evil, and it must be stopped." She paused, trying to find a way to soften what she had to say. "Aunt Rebecca, I have to know. The night Aaron died—was I out of the house?"

Rebecca's faded eyes filled with tears. *"Ja,"* she murmured. "How?"

"How do I know?"

Rebecca nodded.

Lainey held her hands firmly. "I've had nightmares for years about running away from someone or something at the dam. About trying to get to the house and someone chasing me."

Rebecca's fingers writhed in her grasp. "Ach, I...I never thought..."

"You didn't think I'd remember? Or you didn't think I'd seen anything?"

Her great-aunt's eyes closed for an instant. "D-didn't know. Bed empty. Went t-to look." She stopped, seeming exhausted by the effort.

"You found my bed empty that night, so you looked for me. Did you go outside?"

"Ja. On the g-grass. Asleep. Took you in."

Lainey could almost see it. Aunt Rebecca searching frantically, not sure where she'd gone, and finding her lying on the lawn. "You took me in and put me to bed. Did I wake up?"

Rebecca shook her head. "Crying in your sleep. I...I sat with you."

Of course she would have. The simple act would never have occurred to Lainey's mother, but would be second nature to Aunt Rebecca.

Rebecca's fingers tightened on hers. "You didn't

remember. W-we didn't ask. Maybe, in a day or two—"

"But Mom came and took me away."

"*Ja.*" Tears slid down her great-aunt's cheeks. "Should have st-stopped—"

"I know." Lainey was having trouble holding the tears back herself. "I know you wanted to keep me. But you couldn't."

"*Ja.*" Her aunt managed a crooked smile through the tears. She patted Lainey's hand. "My girl," she said clearly.

A tear dropped on their entwined hands, and Lainey wasn't sure whether it was hers or Rebecca's. She had belonged here, but fate in the shape of her mother had intervened. Still, maybe she'd always known it.

Aunt Rebecca's lips moved, as if she tried to say something more.

"It's all right," Lainey said quickly. "Don't tire yourself."

Rebecca shook her head in frustration. "Tell you. L-look in the chest." She leaned back, her eyes flickering.

"The chest," she repeated, her mind a blank. "You mean the chest where the fabric is stored?"

"*Ja.* Look. Left something for you."

"All right. I'll check it." She couldn't imagine what Aunt Rebecca meant, but the assurance seemed to satisfy her.

The door swung open just then to admit Katie, and Lainey rose to greet her with slight apprehension. What if others, besides Zeb, blamed her for what had happened to Thomas?

But Katie seemed just as usual. She gave Lainey a quick hug, pressing her cheek against Lainey's. "Does she know about Thomas?" she whispered.

Lainey nodded. "She already knew when I came in." She managed a smile. "I was just telling Aunt Rebecca that Thomas's nurse says he's going to be fine."

"Ach, that's *gut* news for sure." Katie bent to embrace Aunt Rebecca. "Don't you worry about him. Boys that age bounce back fast." She glanced at Lainey and then away. "No harm done."

Lainey's heart sank. Did that mean Katie thought she'd caused Thomas's injuries? She didn't dare ask in front of her great-aunt, and she wasn't sure she wanted to hear the answer in any event.

Coward, her conscience murmured in her ear, but she ignored it. For a little while, at least, she wanted to enjoy the sense that she'd come home, without any doubts edging in to destroy it.

CHAPTER NINETEEN

A RELATIVELY PEACEFUL day spent at the rehab center, concentrating on Rebecca's exercises and working on her quilt with Katie had done wonders for Lainey's morale by that evening. Maybe it had been the effect of the assurance she'd felt from Aunt Rebecca.

Pouring herself a second cup of tea after supper, she sat down at the familiar kitchen table. Meredith had offered to stay again tonight, but she'd declined. She couldn't let fear overpower the contentment she felt in this place.

If her mother hadn't shown up that day to snatch Lainey back into her own chaotic world, what would her life have been? Staying here, probably going to school with Meredith, having her friends at hand for all her growing up years and coming home every day to the assurance of being loved—that would have been her life. If so, maybe she'd have grown into someone who had enough confidence in herself and others to risk seizing her own happy ever after.

Was it too late for that? Could she and Jake actually let themselves love each other? Maybe, once all this trouble was cleared up, they'd be able to find out.

Lainey frowned down at the tea. There was still

plenty to be concerned about, and she shouldn't forget that. For one thing, Thomas apparently didn't remember anything about why he'd been at the house or who had hit him. According to Cousin Katie, everything after he'd helped with the milking was a blur. The doctor said he might remember, in time, or he might not.

If he didn't, Lainey had no doubts that Zeb would continue to blame her. That would make her position here difficult, but she could handle his opposition, couldn't she? As long as the people she cared about accepted her account, she was all right.

People she cared about, like Aunt Rebecca, like Jake. And that led her to another issue. She hadn't yet told Jake that Aunt Rebecca had confirmed his belief that Lainey had been out of the house on the night Aaron died.

It wasn't that she was deliberately hiding her aunt's story from him, she assured herself. She'd tell him, just not right away. Knowing Jake, the first thing he'd want to do would be to hear the story directly from Aunt Rebecca. He'd have questions, and he wouldn't be satisfied until he had answers.

Would he understand why Aunt Rebecca had kept quiet about finding Lainey outside that night? She did, but would he?

Lainey had been gone, and everyone had accepted the apparent fact that Aaron's death was an accident. No one in Deer Run so much as imagined anything else.

Aunt Rebecca's concern would always have been

for Lainey. She'd have accepted the fact that Lainey hadn't remembered her sleepwalking. She'd have told herself it was God's will, and gone on with her life.

Jake might be pleased to have his theory about Lainey's nightmares confirmed, but Rebecca's knowledge didn't change anything. Dreams weren't evidence.

She had carried the mug to the sink before she realized how the darkness outside was pressing against the glass already. She hadn't noticed how late it was getting. She should have locked up before now. With no shade on the kitchen windows, she would be clearly visible from the dark outside.

Washing the dishes could easily wait until morning. She double-checked the lock on the back door and went quickly through into the dining room, where her quilting materials were still laid out on the table, pulling down the shades on the side windows, then continuing into the living room to draw the shades there.

Once that was accomplished and she'd checked the lock on the front door, Lainey wandered back into the dining room to have another look at her project. It seemed to be habit-forming—she couldn't look at it without wanting to start working again. Some people got lost in a book, but she got lost in creating something with her hands.

She'd finished another square today in the intervals between therapy sessions. Katie had kept an unobtrusive eye on Lainey's needlecraft while working on her own quilt, and she'd seemed satisfied that Lainey knew what she was doing. She'd even mentioned that once the top was finished, she'd help Lainey spread it onto Aunt Rebecca's quilting frame and they'd have a regular quilting frolic to do the quilting.

Aunt Rebecca had smiled, obviously pleased at the idea. And Lainey, who had thought perhaps she'd be here long enough to make the patches into a place mat or table runner, found herself agreeing that a double bed quilt would be perfect.

Lainey smoothed the patch out on the table surface. Would she really be here long enough for that? Why not? There was nothing that demanded her attention anywhere else, and despite all the alarms and concerns, she was happy here.

Picking up the pieces for another patch, she began to arrange them. Working on it would keep her mind off the darkness outside the windows. The cat, already established in the chair he preferred, seemed ready for a quiet night as well.

No sooner had she picked up the materials than Lainey realized she'd forgotten about Aunt Rebecca's words. Rebecca had wanted Lainey to look in the fabric chest for something she'd left there for her.

Maybe the nine-patch doll quilt? Rachel and Meredith seemed convinced Rebecca would have saved it. If so, Lainey would love to have it.

She headed upstairs, not surprised when Cat deserted his chair and bounded up ahead of her. The cat had become so much a part of her life that she didn't know what she'd do if someone turned up and tried to claim him.

She had to smile at herself. What would any of the people she'd known over the years have said at the thought of Lainey settling down in a small town, complete with a pet? They were used to hearing from her in a different place every year.

She'd looked in the chest before, of course, when she took out the material for her quilt, but she hadn't taken everything out. Moving the battery light to a better spot so that she could see what she was doing, she opened the chest.

Aunt Rebecca had called it a dower chest, Lainey remembered. The word swam up from some long-forgotten conversation. She'd asked what a dower chest was, and Aunt Rebecca had explained that it was a sort of trunk or chest in which a girl could collect the linens she'd need when she had a home of her own. Every young Amish girl had one, in anticipation of the day she'd marry.

Lainey ran her fingers along the smooth edge of the top with its carefully crafted molding. Someone had made this chest by hand, she realized. Uncle Isaac? Or maybe even Aunt Rebecca's father, before she was married? It might easily be that old.

The top layer of fabric was familiar to her, and she lifted out piece after piece, stacking them on the floor beside her. Farther down, she came to some quilted table runners, carefully wrapped in tissue paper. Gifts, maybe, that Rebecca hadn't yet used?

Beneath that she caught a glimpse of familiar colors that stirred a faint, nostalgic memory. She drew it out with fingers that trembled a little. It was the nine-patch doll quilt, made with the fabric pieces she'd picked out that long-ago day when Aunt Rebecca had taken her fabric shopping.

Running her fingers along the stitches, Lainey could see the difference between her own uneven efforts and Aunt Rebecca's skilled, nearly invisible line of sewing. How patient Aunt Rebecca had been with her, never snatching it away to do something herself, but always gently encouraging.

Lifting the quilt, she held it against her cheek, letting a picture form in her mind. She, Meredith and Rachel had been sitting around the dining room table while Aunt Rebecca started each of them on their first steps in making the quilts. Rachel, of course, was already a sewing pro at ten, but she and Meredith were all thumbs.

Aunt Rebecca's voice, gentle and laughing, seemed to float through the years, and the scene was as clear as if it had happened yesterday.

And later, after the others had gone home and they'd cleaned up from supper, she'd snuggled beside Aunt Rebecca on the sofa. Uncle Isaac had sat in his favorite rocking chair with the newspaper, lowering it occasionally to smile at the sight of them stitching away, with Lainey mimicking her aunt's movements as best she could.

Smiling through a haze of tears, Lainey smoothed the small quilt out and folded it. This was a treasure, holding as it did such sweet memories. She wanted it in her bedroom where she could see it every day.

As she bent to return the other materials to the chest, Lainey realized she hadn't quite reached the bottom when she'd taken out the quilt. There was something else in the chest.

She pulled out a sheaf of paper, memories again flooding back. When Uncle Isaac had realized how much she loved to draw, he'd brought home a whole ream of paper for her to use. Goodness only knew how many pictures she'd done that summer, but apparently Aunt Rebecca had saved some of them.

She unfolded one after another. There were several sketches that had probably been intended to be Aunt Rebecca and Uncle Isaac, sitting in the rockers on the front porch. The proportion was off, but they were still recognizable.

Then came an image of a tree with two girls hanging from the branches—Meredith and Rachel, no doubt. She'd have to show them how she'd seen them, with Meredith dangling upside down from her knees while Rachel hung from her hands, her apron askew.

Smiling, Lainey unfolded the last one and sat staring. The smile faded from her face. This drawing was completely different from the others. Dark trees soared in the background, their jagged arms seeming to reach out with menace. An equally dark figure loomed over a small one lying on the ground, hands reaching out, grasping—

She let the paper fall to her lap. Here it was. Proof to her, if to no one else, that her nightmares were more than a fantasy. The cat, suddenly seeming to sense her feelings, pressed himself between her and the picture, rubbing against her, mewing.

Lainey patted him absently and lifted him off the paper, forcing herself to look more closely at the figure. But there was no recognizing the person in the shadow she'd drawn. If she'd ever known who it was, that knowledge was as far away as ever.

By THE NEXT morning she still wasn't sure whether she should show the image to Jake. He'd consider it confirmation of his theory, but even so, they were still no closer to identifying the person. So what was the point of opening up that can of worms?

Maybe she should take the drawing with her when she went to see Aunt Rebecca. She must have had some idea about the drawing's importance when she'd told Lainey to find it.

Lainey'd reached that point in her argument with herself when she heard a knock at the front door. Glancing at the clock, then at her sweatpants and T-shirt, she shook her head. People in Deer Run faced the day a bit too early for her.

It was Jake, and she hurried to unlock the door, self-consciously smoothing her hair as best she could. Why did he always seem to catch her when she was looking her worst?

She swung the door wide. "You always seem to arrive before I'm ready to face…" The light words faded away when she saw Jake's expression. He was

grim, the strong lines of his face tight with a suggestion of emotion held back.

He stepped inside and closed the door behind him.

"What's wrong?" Her heart did a stutter step.

"Why didn't you tell me the truth?" His tone was
hard and uncompromising.

Her mind whirled. Had he somehow found out
what her aunt had told her? But why would that make
him so angry?

"I don't know what you're talking about."

His expression didn't change. "You let me believe
that the anonymous letters had to do with what happened here. They didn't, did they?"

Everything in her froze. "No." She wouldn't be a
coward about it. Or at least, not more than she'd already been. "You know what happened in St. Louis."
It was a statement, not a question.

"Some officious busybody sent me a link to some
of the stories. I suppose I should be grateful, since I
wouldn't find out about it from you, would I?"

That stung, even through her numbness. "You're
not being fair. I can't imagine you'd go around announcing your involvement in something you're
ashamed of to someone you'd just met."

"Just met? No, not then. But we've gone a bit past
that stage, haven't we?" His eyes held hers, demanding an answer.

Lainey tried to take a deep breath, but she felt as
if her pain and guilt were strangling her.

When she didn't answer he turned away with a

brusque, dismissive gesture. "You didn't trust me with the truth."

The truth. She'd known all along that the truth mattered to Jake. She'd ignored that knowledge, and now she was going to pay the price.

She fought to keep her voice steady. "I didn't tell you because I knew that when I did, you'd look at me the way you're looking right now. As if I'm a pariah."

He took a step toward her, his expression changing to one of baffled anger. "This isn't about what happened to you. I thought we had something important between us, but the whole time you were hugging this secret to yourself. How can I trust you after that?"

Lainey's heart was shredded to ribbons, but she managed to keep her chin up and her eyes dry. "Maybe that's who I am, Jake—the kind of person who can't be trusted with anything important." Just like her mother. "I think you'd better go now."

She held her breath, not sure how long her control would last. If he tried to prolong this confrontation…

But apparently Jake had said everything he'd come to say. Without a word, he turned and walked out of the house and out of her life.

It took her great-aunt about sixty seconds to realize something was amiss. She took Lainey's hand with surprising strength.

"Was ist l-letz?"

To her surprise, Lainey found she remembered the Pennsylvania Dutch phrase. *What's wrong?*

She tried to smile. "Nothing."

Rebecca shook her hand in demand. "Not Thomas?"

"No, no, Thomas is doing fine. He's going home this afternoon, I understand." The Amish grapevine worked well, even though Lainey hadn't dared approach Thomas's hospital room again.

"What?" Aunt Rebecca might falter a bit with the words, but her tone was uncompromising. "Knew from y…your letters."

Lainey could only stare at her great-aunt. "You could tell from my letters that something was wrong? But I tried to be so careful." She'd been determined that not a hint of trouble would show in what she'd written. Obviously she'd underestimated Aunt Rebecca's insight.

"Tell me."

Lainey realized that tears were not far away, and she struggled to hold them back. Out in the hallway she could hear the clatter of trays and the sound of brisk voices, but here in Aunt Rebecca's room all was still. The sunlight streamed through the window to touch their joined hands.

"I was so ashamed. I didn't want you to know." She tried to swallow the lump in her throat. "I got involved with a man…my boss. I knew it was wrong from the start." How could she expect someone like Aunt Rebecca to understand or forgive? But she wouldn't try to whitewash it, not with the steady gaze of her aunt's soft blue eyes on her face.

"He told me that he and his wife had split up. I

believed him." She paused to examine that carefully. "At least, I wanted to believe him."

She couldn't look at her aunt now, so she stared down at their clasped hands. "His wife took an overdose of pills. She's all right…the paramedics got to her in time. But it all came out then." She couldn't stop the tears now. "I'm so ashamed. I never wanted you to know."

I never wanted you to be disappointed in me—that was what she really felt. Other people might condemn her, but Rebecca was the only one who would be disappointed. Who would have expected better from her.

Silence. Finally she looked up, trying to steel herself for whatever she might see in her aunt's face.

Tears. Aunt Rebecca was crying too, soundlessly. Her hand clasped Lainey's firmly as she struggled to speak. "God forgives a broken and contrite heart." Maybe it was only Lainey's imagination that made the words so strong and clear. "You must forgive yourself. And me."

"You?" She must have misunderstood. "There is nothing to forgive you for."

Aunt Rebecca shook her head, and a teardrop fell on the back of Lainey's hand. "I wanted to keep you. But I let y-your mother take you."

Apparently even a broken heart could twist with pain. "You couldn't have stopped her. I wanted to stay, but I knew even then that you couldn't keep me. She's my mother." She wrapped her fingers around her aunt's work-worn hand. "I'm glad to know you wanted me."

"*Ja.* Always." Rebecca leaned forward, and Lainey put her arms around her, feeling the love and comfort that flowed from her.

How different would her life have been if her mother had just gone on her way and left Lainey here? She asked herself the question she'd been pondering. Would she have been a different person, or would she have turned out the same either way?

Impossible to tell, but one thing she did know. Her summer with Rebecca had shown her a life she might never have known otherwise. Maybe that life was what she'd been looking for ever since, with her constant fresh starts.

She was here now. She could choose to stay. But how could she, after what had happened with Jake?

The text signal on her cell interrupted a painful stream of thoughts about what might have been. Wiping her face with her palms, she picked it up to check the message, noting that the number was unknown to her, and then looked up at her aunt.

"It's from someone who is interested in purchasing the old mill property from you. Jake thought it might be wise to sell in order to pay the hospital bills, but if you don't want to…" She left that open. Surely Aunt Rebecca had recovered sufficiently to make that decision herself.

Rebecca seemed to consider for a moment, her gaze fixed on something far away, or perhaps long ago. Finally she nodded.

"*Ja.* It's time. Isaac would have wanted it."

"You're sure?"

Rebecca nodded. "Time," she said again. "You do it."

She was tiring, obviously. Small wonder after the emotions they'd shared.

Lainey sent a quick response to the text and then stood. "All right. I'll run out and show this person around, and we'll go from there. We'll do exactly what you want. All right?"

Rebecca nodded. She leaned her head back against the chair. Lainey reached for her jacket and handbag, glad of some positive action that she could take. She'd help Aunt Rebecca with whatever arrangements she wanted to make, and then—

The future seemed oddly blank. She'd just have to trust that, by then, she'd know the right thing to do.

FORTUNATELY LAINEY REMEMBERED the way back to the mill from her visit to the place with Jake. It took an effort to focus on the route and not let her mind stray off in the direction of what they'd talked about or how he'd looked and smiled.

Spotting the lane, she turned into it, hoping she was right and wasn't going to end up in some farmer's field. But no, the lane looked familiar, even to the way it narrowed until the branches of the bushes on either side reached out to brush the sides of her car.

She stopped at approximately the place where Jake had parked that day and double-checked her cell phone to be sure she hadn't missed any messages.

Nothing. The prospective buyer was apparently assuming Lainey would know he or she was coming.

Lainey slid out of the car. A brisk breeze fluttered her jacket and sent a shower of yellow leaves whirling down to land on the roof of the car and catch in Lainey's hair. She detached a stray leaf from her head and buttoned her jacket. The sun had disappeared behind a cloud, for the moment at least, and it was chillier than she'd expected.

Since she didn't spot another vehicle, she must have arrived first. After a moment's mental debate, she slid her keys and cell into her jacket pockets and locked her bag in the car. No point in being burdened with anything she didn't need if she was going to be climbing around in the old mill.

Lainey's initial thought was to wait with the car, but then it occurred to her that there might be an alternate route to the mill that she didn't know about. She'd better go and check to be sure the buyer wasn't wandering around the mill wondering where she was.

The path she had taken with Jake was fairly obvious. Other people must come through here, or it would be grown over, wouldn't it? The wooded hillside seemed quieter than it had been on her previous visit. A bird chattered once and fluttered from tree to tree, but that was all. Lainey made her way along the path, avoiding the brambles that reached out to her, unpleasantly reminded of her nightmares.

Jake had held them back for her, she remembered. It seemed that as many times as she tried to banish him from her thoughts, he managed to slip back in.

The path ended suddenly at the small stream, and beyond it the mill loomed. She stood for a moment, looking at it. Why would anyone want to buy it? For the land?

Maybe the prospective buyer intended to tear down the building and put something else here. It was a rather isolated spot for a house, she'd think.

The last time, Jake had held her hand as she crossed the stream on the stepping stones. The water seemed a bit deeper than it had that day, but the flat stones were still dry. Holding her breath, Lainey stepped to the first one, relieved when it didn't wobble under her weight. Quickly, before she could start thinking about slipping into the no doubt icy water, she moved from stone to stone and reached the opposite bank.

A few more steps took her to the entrance they'd used…the only one, as far as she could tell. She hesitated. No sign of anyone, but still—

"Hello? Is anyone here?" At her call, a bird abruptly took flight from the eaves high above her. That was the only answer.

Lainey went up the rickety steps and tried the door. With a shriek like the sound effects of a horror movie, it swung reluctantly open. She stepped inside, pausing a moment to let her eyes adjust to the dim light. The sun had come out again, and it filtered through the boards of the mill. Lainey looked up, seeing dust motes swimming in the shafts of sunlight.

"Hello?" she called again.

"I've been waiting for you."

The voice, coming from behind Lainey so unexpectedly, jolted her nerves. She swung around, staring at the person who stepped out of the shadows.

"Jeannette." For an instant she could just gape at the bed-and-breakfast owner. "What are you doing here?"

"Didn't you get my message?" Jeannette came toward her, picking her way carefully across the wide planks of the floor, looking as poised and precise as if she were welcoming Lainey to her bed-and-breakfast.

"Your message?" she echoed stupidly. "You mean you're the person who's interested in buying the mill?"

Jeannette smiled, nodding her head. "We've been talking at cross-purposes, I'm afraid. Yes, I'm the person who is interested. I assumed you knew."

"Colin didn't mention it to me. Maybe he thought we'd talked about it, since we're neighbors." There'd been no opportunity, at least not recently. And she'd been fairly preoccupied with other things, as well.

Jeannette grimaced. "Careless of him, but I suppose it doesn't matter. You're here now."

"Yes, but—" Lainey's gesture was meant to including the rambling structure and its surroundings. "Why on earth are you interested in this property? I suppose that's not something a seller should say, but…"

"I know. It doesn't look like much, does it?" Jeannette glanced up at the stories above them. "Still, the place does have a certain charm. I thought something might be made of it."

"That would require a lot of rebuilding, I'd think."

"True enough, but it would be something quite unique in the end." Jeannette smiled. "You're supposed to be talking me into it, you know."

"Now we know why I'd never make a good salesperson." She paused. She hadn't seen Jeannette since that encounter with Laura in the parking lot. "I hope Laura is…all right." Not ready to be committed, she thought, but could hardly say.

Jeannette nodded. "She is doing better. I'm trying to get her interested in this project, as a matter of fact. We've talked about turning this into a bed-and-breakfast. I do feel she needs something to occupy her mind so she won't dwell so much on the past."

Lainey wouldn't have recommended restoring a dilapidated old building for a mental-health cure, but the strategy was probably sound. Apparently Laura had been released from the mental facility as being well enough to get along in the outside world.

"I hope it works." She glanced around again. "Well, what can I show you? I'm afraid I'm not an expert on grist mills. I didn't even know what they were until I came here."

"I'm really more interested in what can be made of the structure." Jeannette moved toward the steps to the second level. "Let's go up. I'd like to get a look at the view from the top so I can visualize what we might do."

Nodding, Lainey led the way, thinking just about anyone would be better at this than she was. Still, Aunt Rebecca relied on her to handle it, and that warmed what was left of her heart after the pummeling it had taken from Jake.

They reached the second level. Lainey pointed to the stone wheel, trying to remember what Jake had said about it. "That's the original stone, apparently. I suppose it might be used as a sort of decorative element."

"Excellent," Jeannette said, but she was eyeing the ladderlike steps that led up to the top level. "I'd like to see what the view is like from the top."

"Be careful," Lainey cautioned, starting up. "It's a bit rickety up here."

"I suppose it is," Jeannette said. "But I'm very sure-footed."

Her voice sounded a little odd, despite her claim. Lainey could only hope the woman wasn't afraid of heights. She wouldn't like to try getting Jeannette back down the ladder if she became dizzy.

Lainey emerged onto a platform at the top. It was nothing more than a sort of catwalk, hardly wide enough for two. Jeannette reached the top behind her, brushing against her jacket.

"Can you move a bit farther along so I can see?" she said.

Lainey nodded, taking a few more steps, only too aware of the rickety railing between her and the drop to the mill floor. "This has fallen in a good bit, as you can see." She attempted to sound as if she knew what she was talking about. "Still, I suppose you'd be gutting the inside anyway."

"I don't think I will," Jeannette said.

Lainey half turned to look at her and caught a flash of movement from the corner of her eye. Something struck her, and pain flared in her arm and shoulder. An accident, a beam breaking loose—

She was hit again, hard, knocked off balance, the boards creaking and cracking under her. She was falling, swinging out into space, scrabbling with her hands and feet for anything solid to hang on to.

And all the while Jeannette was swinging a length of board at her, trying to knock her off.

Lainey managed to drag her gaze from the board to the face of the woman who wielded it. She knew, beyond all doubt, that she was looking into the face in her nightmare.

CHAPTER TWENTY

JAKE HAD TRIED to settle in at the office after he left Lainey, but found it impossible. Her face kept coming between him and the papers on his desk.

Finally he gave up. With a muttered excuse to the receptionist, he escaped to his car, not sure where he was going, but convinced he couldn't sit there any longer, visualizing the pain Lainey had tried so hard to hide.

Hadn't she realized that he'd been hurt, too? That his anger was because she hadn't leveled with him? It didn't have anything to do with what had happened in her previous relationship. People could make stupid mistakes when they thought they were in love. He was certainly the perfect example of that.

If Lainey had only told him, so he hadn't had to find out for himself—

But he hadn't exactly found out for himself, had he? Someone had sent that link to him, and that someone had been careful not to let himself be identified.

Just a nasty-minded individual who delighted in stirring up trouble? Or the same someone who'd been going to such lengths to chase Lainey out of town?

Without his even realizing it, he'd driven to Rebecca's house. Well, maybe his subconscious mind knew what he ought to be doing. He needed to talk to Lainey calmly, without anger or pain intruding.

His good intentions seemed doomed to failure, though, when no one came in answer to his repeated knockings.

Jake was turning away from the door, when Meredith hailed him. She was coming toward him across the lawn. "Are you looking for Lainey?"

He nodded. "Did she go to see her aunt?"

"I think so." Meredith's steady gaze seemed to measure his mood. "She looked upset when she went out. That wouldn't happen to have anything to do with your earlier visit, would it?"

He raised his eyebrows, trying for a humor he didn't feel. "Spying on your neighbors, are you? What next?"

"Hey, if you live in a small town, you'd better get used to it." Her momentary smile faded. "Look, I don't know what's going on between the two of you, but I care about Lainey, and I think she could use a friend just now."

His gaze fell before hers. "Seems like she has a good one in you. Maybe I'll see if I can catch up with her."

All the way up the hill to the rehab center, he rehearsed what he was going to say. He'd have to be careful in front of Rebecca, since Lainey probably hadn't told her anything about this.

But he didn't want to wait any longer to talk to her. Quite aside from anything personal between them, if sending the link to him was another attempt to chase Lainey away, she'd better be prepared for this anonymous somebody to deliver their message to other people besides him.

But when he walked into Rebecca's room, she was alone except for an aide who was helping her to a chair.

Rebecca managed a faintly crooked smile. "Jake."

"You're looking better every time I see you." He held her hand for a moment. *Don't upset her,* he reminded himself. "Has Lainey been in? I wanted to talk to her about something."

Rebecca studied his face much as Meredith had done. Was something written there that they seemed to read? Then she nodded to the chair next to her.

He sat down, trying to suppress the little spurt of nervous energy that was insisting he should find Lainey.

"She was here." Rebecca formed the words carefully. "She left a—a few minutes ago."

"Do you know where she went?"

Rebecca frowned. "She…" She gestured with her hand. "Message. On her phone."

"She got a text from someone?"

"*Ja.* Text. To meet at the m-mill."

"Someone wanted to meet her at the old mill property?" He frowned in response to Rebecca's nod. That didn't make sense. "Do you know who?"

"Buyer."

That made even less sense. Anyone who was interested in the property should be going through Colin, not contacting Lainey directly.

Rebecca was beginning to look concerned, so he managed what he hoped was a reassuring smile.

"That's fine," he said. "I'll just go and catch up with them there." He pressed her hand and then left the room quickly, getting out his cell phone as he went.

A quick call to Colin should settle this. Skirting a cart filled with trays, he punched the number. By the time Colin answered, he had reached the parking lot and was striding toward his car.

"Listen, did you give Lainey's number to the party who was interested in the old mill property? Someone apparently asked to meet her there."

"Of course not. There's been some interest in the property, yes. I told you that. But I certainly didn't tell anyone to get in touch with Lainey. At this point, a prospective buyer wouldn't have any way of knowing who the seller is." Jake could practically see Colin's frown through the tone of his voice as he slid into the car and turned the ignition.

"I don't like this," Colin said. "I'd never give out a client's number."

"I don't like it either." Jake accelerated out of the parking lot, fear for Lainey scraping along his nerves. "I'm going out there now."

Maybe this was the result of some confusion or missed communication. He could be totally overreacting.

Or maybe it was something much more serious.

His fingers tightened on the steering wheel. Either way, he wouldn't be satisfied until he saw for himself that Lainey was all right.

LAINEY'S BREATH CAUGHT, and she tried to steady herself. Somehow, she wasn't sure how, she'd ended up clinging to some sort of brace or bracket beneath the catwalk. Hands clenching the rough wood, she felt beneath her for a foothold. There had to be something, had to be, because if there wasn't…

She glanced down, a dizzyingly long way to the floor. But just below her there was a projection in the wall—a nice sturdy bit of wood. Groping with her toes, she managed to get both feet onto it.

The strain on her arms eased instantly. The ledge was wide enough to hold her feet, no wider. But it was enough. She was clinging to the wall like a spider, but for the moment she was safe.

Lainey looked up, moving her head cautiously. Jeannette looked back at her from four or five feet above, anger and hatred twisting her face.

"Why didn't you fall? You have more lives than that stupid cat." Jeannette swung the board she held ineffectually, the angle at which she was leaning making it impossible to hit Lainey.

She couldn't count on that lasting, though. Sooner or later, Jeannette would think of some way of knocking her off her perch. It wouldn't take much.

Lainey slid her arm over the bracket, the rough wood scraping her skin through the sleeve of her jacket. That was better, wasn't it? She was facing the wall, arm securely anchored through the—

A metal pipe thrust in front of her face, grazing it. She gasped, recoiling, and nearly lost her balance. Jeannette had been quicker than she'd thought. She was poking a length of metal pipe through the slats in the catwalk. One strike from that on her head, and—

Another thrust, and she slid to her right, trying to keep the bracket between herself and the pipe.

"Jeannette, this is crazy. What are you trying to do?"

"What I should have done twenty years ago." Jeannette moved, probably trying to get a better angle. "I nearly caught up with you then."

A shudder went through her. The nightmares were true. "You were chasing me. Aunt Rebecca was calling…"

"I almost had you when you fell, but Rebecca was too close. She'd have seen me."

"You killed Aaron." She didn't remember seeing it, but she must have. "Why? What did it have to do with you?"

"Everything!" Jeannette took a wild swing with the pipe, nearly losing her own balance. "Everything. Laura was everything to me—so pretty, so popular. Nobody ever even noticed me until Laura became my friend. Then I was somebody, too."

Lainey bit back a response that teenage popularity wasn't worth someone's life. "Laura counts on you. Everyone knows that." To think she'd thought Laura was the unbalanced one. If only she could calm Jeannette, could somehow reach the rational adult that must exist within her.

"She always did. I was the one she trusted. The one she confided in. But people kept trying to spoil it." Jeannette swung again, the pipe grazing Lainey's head.

Lainey fought back a wave of dizziness. Not now, she couldn't let herself lose focus now or she'd be gone.

"You must have known she'd fall in love." Was that the right thing to say or would it push Jeannette farther? She didn't know, couldn't imagine what it was like inside Jeannette's head.

"In love, yes. Someday. With the right person, the one who could give her everything." Jeannette made a strange sound deep in her throat, and Lainey realized she was choking back a sob. "We had it all planned. We'd go to college together, have fun, get away from this god-awful place. And then she had to fall for Aaron, of all people."

There was no mistaking the hatred in her voice. "Aaron would have ruined it all, getting her pregnant, convincing her to marry him. I had to get rid of him so Laura could have the life she was meant to have. So we could both have it."

People talked about how devoted Jeannette was to her friend. They thought it was admirable. No one seemed to suspect just how twisted that devotion was.

Lainey sucked in a breath, trying to ignore the pain in her arm and shoulder. Hang on. Just hang on.

"I didn't intend to kill him. I was just going to

convince him to let her go, but he wouldn't listen. I was angry. I pushed him in. And then I heard someone and saw you, running away."

Jeannette was sitting on the catwalk now, busy doing something with the length of pipe. Probably trying to figure out a more effective way of using it.

"I'm surprised you didn't sneak into the house that night and finish me off." *Try to sound calm, but think.*

The cell phone was in her pocket. She'd have to let go with one hand to get it. Panic edged through her at the thought of releasing her grip. But she didn't have a choice.

"I should have." The venomous face thrust over the railing, and Lainey froze. "But I was young. Scared. And everyone knew about your sleepwalking. They say a sleepwalker doesn't remember. You went away the next day, and I was safe. But you came back. I knew, once I heard you were coming, that I'd have to get rid of you."

Lainey realized what she was working on, and a bolt of fear shot through her. Jeannette was tying the pipe to the length of wood to give herself a longer reach. With that, she'd knock Lainey from her perch as easily as she might swat a fly.

Clutching with the arm and hand she'd gotten over the bracket, Lainey forced herself to let go with the other hand. Her fingers were numb. She rubbed them together, trying to get some feeling back. She couldn't risk dropping the phone. She'd only have one chance. She groped in her pocket for her cell phone.

Luckily Jeannette was still talking. Maybe she

was glad to have an audience after all these years. "Laura's parents were so happy to have me to rely on. And Victor, of course. Victor was easy. All I had to do was convince him that Laura had pushed Aaron. He would do anything I said if it meant keeping her safe."

"Including killing Meredith's mother and trying to kill her." Nausea gripped her at the thought.

Aaron. Meredith's mother. Victor. How many lives was Jeannette prepared to sacrifice? At least one more, it seemed.

"I thought you'd be so easy to get rid of." Jeannette was talking again, a querulous note in her voice, as if Lainey's persistence had disappointed her. "A simple internet search told all about you. You'd already made plenty of enemies. All I had to do was post your location in one of the chat rooms. I thought they'd do the rest."

That explained the source of the anonymous letters and calls. Apparently when that hadn't worked to chase her away, Jeannette had had to take a more active role. Like attacking her. And poor Thomas.

Had Laura known? Was that what she'd wanted so desperately to tell Lainey?

The cell phone was in her hand now. She tried to feel the numbers without pulling it out where Jeannette might see, but it was hopeless. She had to get it out, punch in 911 as quickly as she could—

But Jeannette was too fast for her. The pole came down, longer this time, striking her arm, sending agonizing pain shooting through it. The phone went flying, down, down, the way Lainey would go—

No more time to think, only to react, trying to dodge out of the way of the pipe. Back and forth, inches each time, trying to gauge where it would come. Jeannette had the range now, she'd only need to connect once more, and Lainey would be gone, she was tiring, the pain in her arm, her shoulder, her feet slipping, she couldn't do this much longer—

Jake—she'd never be able to tell him how sorry she was. She was losing....

A shout from below echoed to the rafters, shocking her into hanging on. Jeannette jerked around, the heavy pole in her hands swinging outward, out of her control, throwing her off balance—

For an instant she seemed poised above Lainey like some large, ungainly bird about to take flight. And then she was falling, screaming, a scream that seemed to go on and on— A thud that shook the building. Then silence.

"Lainey!"

Jake's voice. She ought to answer, but she couldn't seem to move. She could only stand on her ledge, face pressed against the rough timbers, trying to breathe.

She could hear him scrambling up the stairs, hear his frantic voice on his cell phone calling for help. She wanted to tell him to be careful, but she couldn't seem to make any words come out of her mouth.

And then he was there, above her on the catwalk, lying down so that he could see her. "Lainey." She heard the strain in his voice. "Are you all right? Tell me where you're hurt."

"My arm." It was pressed against her side. She wasn't sure if she could move it or not, but she didn't intend to try.

"Can you reach up and take my hand?" He was leaning down precariously far. "Maybe I can pull you up."

"No." That sounded abrupt. "Sorry," she added.

"Don't be sorry." There was almost a laugh in his voice. "The police and the fire department are on their way. All you have to do is hang on until they get here with their equipment. Can you do that?"

Given that the alternative was plunging after Jeannette, there was only one answer. "Yes."

"You can. You can do anything you put your mind to, and I'm going to stay right here with you. Okay?"

"Okay." She managed to turn her head enough so that she could look up into his worried face. "I'm okay," she murmured, and turned her face back to the wall.

"I'm going to keep talking until they get here." She could hear rustling movements, as if he were changing his position. "You don't have to answer me. I just want you to stay alert and keep holding on."

She managed to nod. It might sound ridiculous that she could relax in this position, but he was right. Now that the worst danger was past, a peculiar lassitude was taking over, making her limbs heavy, her brain sluggish.

"It was Jeannette," she said.

"I know." He sounded very close. "I heard some of it. The one person we never suspected. The nice, helpful best friend."

"She made Victor think Laura killed Aaron." If she didn't make it out of here, it was important that the truth be known.

"I know. Don't worry about it. She's not going to be causing any more trouble for anyone." His voice was grim.

"She's dead?" She hadn't really doubted it.

"Yes."

The wail of a siren sounded, growing louder by the moment.

"That sounds like the township fire truck. Good. They'll be able to get you down."

Lainey could only hope they didn't expect her to climb down any ladders. With the best will in the world, she didn't think she could.

She heard the voices below, the exclamations, Jake's terse explanations. And then, almost before she had a chance to say she was sorry, but she really couldn't climb down a ladder, one had appeared next to her, and in another moment a helmeted figure was on it.

"You just take it easy, now." The man put a large hand on her back. "I don't want you to move at all. I'm going to put a harness on you, but I'll do all the work. Don't try to help yourself."

"Her arm is injured," Jake said, his voice strained. "She can't—"

"I see that." The fireman's voice was steady. "Why

don't you just climb on down now, Jake? We've got this."

"No chance," Jake said. "Lainey, I'll be right here with you. Just do as Tom says. You might not know it to look at him, but he's really a pretty smart guy."

"Same to you, buddy." The harness seemed to slip around her effortlessly. "Okay, now, Lainey, is it?"

She managed to nod.

"You don't need to hang on so tight now. The harness will hold you. Can you let go of the bracket?"

She considered. She might tell her muscles to relax, but she didn't think they'd obey. "I don't think so."

"Okay, then, I'm going to take your hand and just ease your arm back. You can hang on to me, and we'll have you down at ground level in two shakes."

Several excruciating minutes later she was free of the bracket, dangling from the harness with the fireman's hand steadying her.

"Now we're just going down together," he said. "And old Jakey's heading down, too, so he'll be at the bottom when you are. Nice and slow, now."

She wasn't sure whether that directive was intended for her or someone else, but they started slowly down. If not for his hand on her waist, she'd have probably been spinning in the air like a top.

Down and down, getting dizzy despite her efforts to focus. Surely she must be at the bottom soon—and then she felt Jake's arms go around her. She turned her face to his chest and held on, letting everything else slip away.

"THEY MIGHT AS well just reserve a room in the hospital for the Stoltzfuses and kin," Jake said as he took the chair next to her bed. "You've been giving them a lot of business lately."

"I don't see why I have to stay overnight," Lainey said, trying to prop herself up on the pillows.

Meredith came to her aid, raising the bed and adjusting the pillows. Either she or Rachel had been with Lainey constantly since the ambulance had brought her in.

"The doctor just wants to be sure you're all right," she soothed. "Be glad you're here. The reporters are buzzing around the entrance like so many bees." Meredith glanced at Jake. "I think while Jake is here, I'll run out and get a cup of coffee." She vanished before Lainey could suggest that she just go on home.

"She doesn't need to stay with me," she said, but Jake just smiled.

"I don't think you're going to convince her of that. And she's just being tactful about the coffee. She wanted to leave us alone."

Lainey wasn't sure how to respond to that. Maybe it was better if she didn't. "Is someone with Aunt Rebecca? She'll be fretting over me."

"Your cousin Katie is with her, and I stopped by and told her the whole story." He paused. "Well, I might have left out some of the bad parts, but I don't think she was fooled. Anyway, she's fine, and you can see her tomorrow and show off your cast."

Lainey glanced down at the cast that kept her forearm immobile. It was remarkably uncomfortable, but the nurses assured her she'd get used to it.

"I've never had a broken bone before," she said.

"You're lucky it wasn't your head. When I saw what Jeannette was doing—" He stopped. "I promised myself I wouldn't make you relive it again."

"I don't think I'm likely to forget very soon," she said. "Do I have to talk to Chief Burkhalter again?"

"Just to do a formal statement once you're better." Jake took control of her free hand. "I'll be with you every minute."

He'd been there earlier, when Burkhalter had insisted on questioning her. In fact, Jake had come as close to losing his temper as she'd ever seen.

"Burkhalter couldn't believe someone he'd known all her life could have done such things." Lainey could understand his feelings. Even though she'd barely known Jeannette, she'd hardly been able to take in the depth of her...what? Obsession? Evil? She didn't know.

"Jeannette managed to fool a lot of people," he said. "Fortunately, her actions at the end were fairly self-explanatory. And Thomas is finally talking."

"He is?" She'd nearly forgotten about poor Thomas. "Is he all right? Does he remember?"

"He's bounced back a lot faster than you will, probably. He's out of the hospital already, and he insisted on seeing Rebecca. He said he had to tell her the truth."

"Defying his grandfather? Thomas is braver than I thought."

"I suspect he's done some growing up over this whole situation. Much to Zeb's discomfort, Thomas confessed that Zeb had him slip in and out of the house to keep tabs on what you were doing."

That explained how the cat kept getting in. "So Aunt Rebecca knows about it." All her efforts to keep peace in the family might be slipping away.

"Oddly enough, your aunt seems to feel partially responsible for Zeb's sins. She told me she should have signed the farm over to him years ago."

"So Zeb will get what he wanted." Somehow it didn't seem fair after all he'd done. "I guess if Aunt Rebecca can forgive him, I'll have to."

"I persuaded her to let Colin negotiate a fair price with him rather than making it a gift." Jake grinned. "I didn't think Zeb should get off scot-free."

She nodded, satisfied to let it go. At least she wouldn't have to deal with Zeb. "Does Thomas know who hit him?"

Jake nodded, holding her hand in both of his. "Jeannette was behind that whole business of Thomas thinking you were a witch. I suppose she thought it might encourage you to leave town."

"She was behind the anonymous letters and calls. Apparently she kept tabs on me from the moment she heard I was coming to Deer Run."

"I'm not surprised. The longer you stayed, the greater the chance that you were going to remember what really happened the night Aaron Mast died."

Lainey moved her head restlessly on the pillow.

"I'm not sure I know even now. It's all mixed up—what Jeannette said, what I saw, what I dreamed."

"Maybe it's a good thing there's not going to be a trial." His tone was somber. "It would have been a messy case, and I'm not sure they'd have gotten a conviction. Laura may know the truth, but whether she'd talk and how much anyone would believe is up in the air."

"Poor Laura. Her only crime was to fall in love with the wrong person. I think she might have been trying to tell me, or warn me about Jeannette, these last few days. Has she had to go back to the hospital?"

"Surprisingly, having the truth come out seems to have helped her." Jake shook his head. "Strange. I don't pretend to understand the workings of her mind."

"You do understand the importance of the truth," she said. "That seems to be the bottom line."

"It's important." He held her hand between his, studying it as if it held a secret. "But I think Rebecca would say that love is even more important. I'm sorry I reacted the way I did."

He didn't need to explain what reaction he was talking about. She knew. "I'm sorry I didn't tell you myself sooner."

"We're even, then, wouldn't you say?" He smiled, and her heart seemed to turn over.

"I think so." She couldn't seem to manage more than a whisper.

He lifted her hand to his lips and kissed it, his touch sending heat along every nerve ending.

"So we can start again? You're not going to run away, are you?" He couldn't quite hide the anxiety in his eyes.

"No, I don't think I'll be doing any more running. I think I've found what I've been looking for all this time."

"In that case, I'm going to risk the wrath of any nurses that might look in and kiss you." Jake leaned across the bed, planting his hands on either side of her. "Here's to no more running," he said, and his lips found hers.

The room shrank to the small circle that was her and Jake. She had found what she'd been looking for, and she was home at last.

EPILOGUE

PEOPLE SWIRLED THROUGH the central hallway and two front rooms of Rachel's place, and it seemed to Lainey that most of Deer Run must be present. Amish and *Englisch* had all come to celebrate Rachel and Colin's marriage.

The small, private ceremony had taken place earlier at the church. Both Rachel and Colin had felt no need for a big, splashy wedding—they wanted to keep things simple for the sake of Rachel's Amish relatives.

"They have the important parts of any wedding," Meredith said from Lainey's side, as if she'd been reading her thoughts. "They love each other, and all the people they love are here to wish them well."

Across the room, Mandy was standing with Colin's father, holding his hand confidently. Even at her age, she seemed to understand that crowds bothered him, and she was quick to take on the responsibility of making him comfortable. As for Colin's dad, he had long since accepted Mandy as a cherished granddaughter. Their relationship was a lovely thing to see.

Lainey nodded. "I've never seen Rachel look so happy. Or so beautiful." Rachel had declined the idea of a gown and veil and settled instead on a simple blue dress, but her radiance easily outshone anything she might wear.

"And the same for Colin." Meredith grinned. "Well, not beautiful. But obviously very happy. He finally got Rachel to set a date, thanks to you."

"I didn't do anything," Lainey protested. "Unless you call nearly getting killed a stimulus for marrying."

"You told her to put the important things first in life. To say nothing of helping her iron out her worries over running the bed-and-breakfast."

"That was the easy part. After all, I'm right next door. I can easily help out with the bed-and-breakfast so Rachel and Mandy can move in with Colin and his dad. And it gives me something I can do while I'm taking care of Aunt Rebecca."

Meredith nodded to where Thomas was helping Rebecca to a chair near the wall. "She's making good progress, I see."

"Stronger every day, I think, but she still needs someone with her."

And that was a position Lainey was happy to fill. She'd settled into the routine of life in the old house that had sheltered her in the past, and she didn't in the least mind giving up the apartment in St. Louis. That part of her life had ended entirely. Even the nasty letters had dwindled off to nothing in recent weeks.

Zach Randal emerged from the group of men around Colin, his eyes seeking Meredith's as they always seemed to. With a murmured excuse, Meredith slipped through the crowd toward him.

"Ach, those two will be following Rachel and Colin's example in no time at all, if I'm any judge." Anna Miller was carrying a tray of small pastries, which she extended toward Lainey. "You'll have one of my sausage rolls, ain't so?"

She could hardly refuse—just the aroma had her mouth watering. "Mmm, delicious," she muttered around flaky pastry and spicy sausage and cheese. "I think you brought enough to feed the whole county, didn't you?"

"It's nothing. Rachel's Amish kin and friends wanted to do something to show our happiness. Fixing the food for the party was our pleasure."

"Rachel's parents must regret that she wasn't married in the church, don't they?"

Anna shrugged. "Maybe, but they knew it wasn't to be. And they're happy she and Colin found each other." Anna's bright, interested gaze took in Thomas, carrying a filled plate to Rebecca. "I suppose that's your doing, enlisting Thomas to help your aunt. A fine idea, that's certain sure."

"He was so eager to make up for trying to frighten me away that I thought it would make him feel better." And besides, it was probably just as well to have him out from under his grandfather's thumb once in a while.

"It's strange, all that's happened since that summer Aaron died." Anna seemed to gaze into the past. "I remember him so clearly the way he was then."

"I know," Lainey said softly. "I do, too." Aaron Mast, caught forever in the memories of those who loved him as he'd been then—forever kind, forever young, forever happy.

So much evil had filed out of that simple young love, the product of a twisted mind that turned everything it touched into sorrow. But Jeannette was gone now. The terror she'd brought into Lainey's life was already fading, replaced by the pleasures of ordinary days filled with people she loved.

An arm slipped around her waist, and she felt Jake's breath stir her hair as he pressed his cheek against hers. For an instant she let herself enjoy it.

"I don't think you should do that in public." She withdrew a few inches, smiling.

"Look at you, adopting small-town values," Jake teased. "Anna doesn't mind, do you, Anna?"

"Ach, you can squeeze your sweetie all you want as far as I'm concerned." Anna chuckled. "I must get back to passing these around, so you can be alone for your smooching." She moved away, still smiling.

"See? I have Anna's permission to do some smooching." Jake was clearly in high spirits.

"You're pretty happy about marrying off your best friend. No regrets for losing the last of the old gang to matrimony?"

"Not a one. In fact, I envy him." He drew her a little closer. "Maybe I can follow his lead before long."

"Maybe." Her heart gave a little leap at the thought.

"I'm not pushing," he said, his eyes growing more

serious. "I promise. As long as I know you're not going wandering again, I can wait for the woman I love."

Lainey turned to him, knowing it was important to both of them to voice what she believed so strongly now. "I found a home here in Deer Run once, and I never forgot how it felt to be loved and accepted unconditionally. All the roaming I've done since then—well, I think now I was always looking for what I'd lost, even though I didn't know it. Now…" She looked into Jake's face, seeing the love shining in his eyes. "Now I've found it again. I love you, and I'm home to stay."

* * * * *

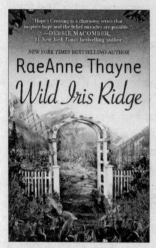

REQUEST YOUR
FREE BOOKS!

2 FREE NOVELS
FROM THE SUSPENSE COLLECTION
PLUS 2 FREE GIFTS!

YES! Please send me 2 FREE novels from the Suspense Collection and my 2 FREE gifts (gifts are worth about $10). After receiving them, if I don't wish to receive any more books, I can return the shipping statement marked "cancel." If I don't cancel, I will receive 4 brand-new novels every month and be billed just $6.24 per book in the U.S. or $6.74 per book in Canada. That's a savings of at least 22% off the cover price. It's quite a bargain! Shipping and handling is just 50¢ per book in the U.S. and 75¢ per book in Canada.* I understand that accepting the 2 free books and gifts places me under no obligation to buy anything. I can always return a shipment and cancel at any time. Even if I never buy another book, the two free books and gifts are mine to keep forever.

191/391 MDN F4XN

Name _____ (PLEASE PRINT)

Address _____ Apt. #

City _____ State/Prov. _____ Zip/Postal Code

Signature (if under 18, a parent or guardian must sign)

Mail to the **Harlequin® Reader Service:**
IN U.S.A.: P.O. Box 1867, Buffalo, NY 14240-1867
IN CANADA: P.O. Box 609, Fort Erie, Ontario L2A 5X3

Want to try two free books from another line?
Call 1-800-873-8635 or visit www.ReaderService.com.

* Terms and prices subject to change without notice. Prices do not include applicable taxes. Sales tax applicable in N.Y. Canadian residents will be charged applicable taxes. Offer not valid in Quebec. This offer is limited to one order per household. Not valid for current subscribers to the Suspense Collection or the Romance/Suspense Collection. All orders subject to credit approval. Credit or debit balances in a customer's account(s) may be offset by any other outstanding balance owed by or to the customer. Please allow 4 to 6 weeks for delivery. Offer available while quantities last.

Your Privacy—The Harlequin® Reader Service is committed to protecting your privacy. Our Privacy Policy is available online at www.ReaderService.com or upon request from the Harlequin Reader Service.

We make a portion of our mailing list available to reputable third parties that offer products we believe may interest you. If you prefer that we not exchange your name with third parties, or if you wish to clarify or modify your communication preferences, please visit us at www.ReaderService.com/consumerschoice or write to us at Harlequin Reader Service Preference Service, P.O. Box 9062, Buffalo, NY 14269. Include your complete name and address.

SUS13R